I0685853

LONDON CALLING

A BETA FORCE THRILLER

ERNEST DEMPSEY

138 PUBLISHING

1

LONDON

The target exited the building and paused on the sidewalk, taking a moment to look both ways to make sure he wasn't being followed. Satisfied, he slipped on his wire-frame sunglasses and took off to the left. He pulled the gray hoodie over his head, tugging on it to make it snug.

"What's with the sunglasses?" Zeke asked as he watched the man from a sedan parked along the sidewalk. He was positioned a hundred yards from the building the target had just left and had been watching the entrance for the last four hours. Empty fish-and-chips trays, napkins, and a half-empty bottle of water littered the vehicle's interior, evidence of the passage of time.

"Maybe he wants to look cool," Phoenix answered. "Why are you worried about it? We're supposed to be following him, not wondering about the guy's fashion choices."

"I'm just saying it's a cloudy day."

"Most days are cloudy in London this time of year."

"That's my point. Don't you think the sunglasses might make him stand out more than he would without them?"

"Are you wearing sunglasses?" Phoenix asked into the radio.

Zeke sighed and thumbed the left temple of his Oakley Turbines. "No."

"You are, aren't you? I knew it."

"First of all, you don't know me."

"I do."

"Second, I have very sensitive eyes. The slightest brightness hurts."

"You know you're really judgmental? Judging a guy wearing sunglasses on a cloudy day when you're wearing a pair, too? How do you know he doesn't have sensitive eyes?"

"Are you done?" Zeke asked.

"Yeah. Are you done?"

"Yes because our guy is on the move, and I just lost visual."

"What?"

"He's rolling to you."

"Oh great. Thank you for that."

"Hey, you know what? Look for a guy with a hoodie and wearing sunglasses on a cloudy day, Agent Underwood," Zeke said, his tone lathered in cynicism.

"Thanks for the tip, Agent Marshall."

Zeke turned on the engine, checked the rearview mirror, and accelerated out into traffic.

"You have him yet?"

Three blocks away, Phoenix stood outside a pub pretending to read a newspaper. He was so preoccupied with keeping an eye out for their suspect that he didn't even realize the paper in his hands was upside down.

"No, not yet. I should any...oh never mind. Target acquired. I repeat, I have visual."

"Good. Keep an eye on him. We can't let this guy get away."

"Oh really? Because I was thinking maybe no one would notice if we let one of the biggest cyberterrorists in the world slip through our fingers."

"There's no need to get snippy, Agent Underwood."

"Actually, this is the perfect time to get snippy!" He spoke louder than he intended, drawing the attention of a few passersby who clearly thought he was the local crazy person. The upside-down newspaper wasn't helping.

The target continued toward him with the hoodie pulled down so low over his forehead that it touched the top of the man's sunglasses. The suspect kept his head down, his eyes focused on the ground as he walked. White wires dangled from his ears and merged into one, trailing down into his pocket.

"He's listening to something," Phoenix said. "And clearly, he hasn't heard of wireless technology."

Zeke turned the car into the street where he'd seen the target go and merged into a parking spot. He saw his partner across the street holding a newspaper and looking incredibly conspicuous in his effort to look inconspicuous.

"Some people prefer the wires. That wireless stuff gets choppy sometimes, especially when the batteries are running low. You know, like when you forget to charge them!"

"Oh, so you're going to blame me for that, too?"

"No, but your newspaper is upside down."

Phoenix looked up and saw his partner sitting across the street in the black Jaguar sedan. He shook his head and corrected the paper as the target passed by.

"Nice sunglasses," Phoenix muttered into the radio at a volume only Zeke could hear. Then he tucked the paper under his arm and fell in behind the target.

"I...have...sensitive...eyes," Zeke answered in a sharp staccato.

"Yeah, okay. I have the target."

Phoenix followed the gray hoodie another block until they came to an intersection and a crosswalk. The light was red going their direction, and a cluster of people had already gathered to wait for the change.

Phoenix stood there nervously, letting his eyes wander over the crowd and across the street to make it look like he was just an ordinary pedestrian on his way to an appointment.

The target's casual façade crumbled as he leaped away from the group on the sidewalk and into the moving traffic.

Car horns blared, and tires screeched as the man nimbly jumped over one car, sliding across the hood to safety on the other side. Another skidded to a stop just before it hit him. The target spun around, planted his hand on the hood for balance, and took off at a full sprint.

"You gotta be kidding me."

"What?" Zeke demanded. "What's going on? What was that noise? I can't see."

"Target is on the move. I think we've been made."

"I knew you should have worn sunglasses."

Phoenix took off after the man, weaving between the cars, confusing drivers and passengers alike. He held up his hands, shouting, "It's okay, I'm a cop...or something!"

"Smooth," Zeke said as he joined the flow of traffic. Unfortunately, the light was still red, and the vehicles were bumper to bumper. "Perfect."

"What?" Phoenix asked, already panting for breath as he flew past the walking signal and dashed ahead after the suspect.

"Stuck here for the moment. You're on your own until I can catch up."

"Of course I am."

"Oh, don't start with—" He cut off his sentence as he nudged the car in front of another vehicle with only inches to spare. He waved his mocking gratitude at the other driver, who'd given him almost no space. "Thanks for letting me out," Zeke said as the angry driver flashed a number of hand signals. Zeke didn't have to be an expert lip reader to understand the slew of obscenities the man was throwing his way. "Jerk," he muttered.

Phoenix pumped his legs harder in pursuit of the target. He twisted his body sideways to slip through a couple of forty- to fiftysomethings casually walking along with their coffees in hand. He bumped one of them in the shoulder as he passed through the narrow gap. The black man, his hair sticking up all over the place, looked back through dark sunglasses, irritated that he'd almost spilled his coffee.

"Hey, watch it, Bro," the guy said in an American accent.

"What was that?" Zeke asked into the radio.

Phoenix slowed long enough to swivel around and offer a quick "I'm sorry." Then he pinched his eyebrows together and continued the chase. "I'm not sure, but I think I just bumped into Lenny Kravitz."

"What?"

"Like, literally bumped into him. He still looks great. I wonder how he does it."

"Whatever, man. Do you still have eyes on the target?"

"Yeah," Phoenix said between breaths. "I got him." His lungs were working overtime now despite the considerable increase in training he'd been doing in the last few months. After the events in Afghanistan, the new head of the Global Intelligence Commission, Jessica Benson, had ordered Phoenix and his partner to perform more rigorous training and exercise, much more than they'd ever endured before.

The man in the hoodie didn't appear to be wearing down, though, and Phoenix didn't feel like keeping up the pace for much longer. He could do it—he just didn't want to. The sooner they could wrangle this guy in, the better.

The target ran into a young couple, barreling over the man and knocking the guy onto his back. The woman screamed at him about watching where he was going, but the mark kept running with barely a break in his step.

Phoenix watched his quarry abruptly turn right, and another right a few seconds later.

"He's heading onto Brewer," Phoenix said. "Any time you feel like getting in on this, that would be great."

"Yeah, I'm working it."

Zeke spun the wheel suddenly and cut through a narrow opening between two other vehicles. The action drew more angry honking, but Zeke soon left the ire behind as he sped down the alley toward Brewer Street.

Phoenix's lungs ached. The muscles in his legs burned. He knew he could go for miles at a slower pace, but this was a near sprint.

"Stop...running!" he shouted at the target. "We just want to ask you some questions!"

The man didn't even look back. He kept his nose down and picked up his pace even more, adding to the gap between himself and his pursuer with every step.

"Come on, man!" Phoenix pleaded. "I just want to talk!"

This time, the target twisted his head slightly. Phoenix knew the guy wasn't going to stop, but anything he could do to get him to slow down or get distracted was a positive—while Zeke dallied around doing whatever he was doing.

Suddenly, a black Jaguar XE shot out of a side street and into the empty crosswalk directly in front of their target. His head swiveled back just in time to see the sedan, but not in time to avoid slamming into its side.

The guy crumpled to the ground for a moment then began to scramble to his feet. It was all Phoenix needed to catch up.

Phoenix skidded to a stop and slammed his hand down on the guy's back, just below the neck. He clutched the collar hard as the man continued to struggle.

"I told you we just want to talk," Phoenix said. "Now you will have to get that bump looked at."

The man finally turned and looked up into his captor's eyes. Curiosity got the better of him. "What bump?"

"This one." Phoenix shoved the man's head into the hood.

The guy wobbled, dazed from the blow but not knocked unconscious.

"You run pretty well for a hacker," Phoenix commented. "Not well enough, but still, I'm impressed."

Zeke climbed out of the car and grabbed the man, slipping a pair of zip ties around his wrists and tightening them in an instant. Then he opened the back door of the car, and the two Americans shoved the guy in.

They slammed the door shut as the guy writhed in the back, still dazed from the head injury.

Pedestrians stared at the two men as they strolled by, faces aghast at what they'd just witnessed. Some were on their cell phones, clearly calling the police.

"Don't be alarmed, citizens," Zeke said, "we have the situation under control." He held out his badge for some of the concerned people to see, and they peered at the identification with curiosity.

He turned to Phoenix, who looked like he was about to vomit. He was bent over at the hips and clutching his waist as he caught his breath.

"Why are you so out of breath, Bro?" Zeke asked.

Phoenix looked up and fired daggers from his eyes. "Shut...up. What were you doing anyway?"

"Traffic. I already told you."

"Glad you managed to get through it."

"Yeah," Zeke agreed with a look in the back seat. "Guess it was lucky I got here."

More daggers flung from Phoenix's eyes, but he was too fatigued to say anything else.

"Nothing to see here, folks," Zeke continued pandering to the pedestrians as they passed. "Official GI...." He caught himself nearly giving away the agency's secrecy. "Um...official, GI Joe business. We'll be out of the way shortly."

A moment later, the two men got into the sedan and sped away, disappearing into the mayhem of London traffic, leaving no trace of what happened just moments before.

"GI Joe?" Phoenix asked, incredulous. "Smooth."

"Yeah, well, I didn't hear you chiming in with any gems."

As Zeke whipped the car around the next corner, Phoenix looked back through the rear window. "The best part is no one will know we were even there."

2

LONDON

"I can't believe how many people knew we were there!" Zeke muttered.

They stared at the video footage obtained from surveillance cameras in the area that provided three different angles of the abduction. Some passersby witnessed the incident and some even took videos, then posted them online. That wasn't helpful, especially when Zeke sounded like he was bragging about their mission so that people wouldn't freak out. That cleanup took more than a little effort from the GIC's cyber division. There were accounts to disable, shares to wipe, and all told, the elimination of any trace of the two men's presence in London cost the agency more money than Zeke and Phoenix would make in a year—combined.

"Yeah, you know you were supposed to be keeping a low profile, right?" Jessica Benson, director of the GIC, glared at the two agents with lava oozing from her eyes. She spoke so loudly that the speakers on the wall-mounted television sounded as if they would burst.

Agents Underwood and Marshall cringed, shrinking visibly to shoulder level. They were glad she was only on the monitor and not actually in the room with them.

The two men sat in a makeshift conference room that was housed in the back of an old printing company. The company had gone out of business years ago, and the GIC took the opportunity to place one of their safe houses there due to its proximity to the center of London. It gave agents the perfect hub to retreat to for safety, rendezvous with other operatives, and—in this case—bring a subject in for questioning.

At the moment, Phoenix and Zeke weren't thinking about the interrogation. Their minds, ears, and eyes were focused on one thing: the lashing being dished out by Director Benson.

"Do you two idiots have any idea how many cameras caught your little abduction?" she asked, her voice still raised to the level of severe agitation.

"First of all, idiots is a strong word, and not a very nice one at that," Zeke offered.

The woman on the screen seethed at the comment, her arms folded loosely across her chest.

"It might be the right word," he admitted. "Still, it's mean."

"From the looks of it, there were three cameras," Phoenix said.

She directed her searing gaze at him.

"Not counting the cell phone videos," he added quickly.

"Director Benson," Zeke cut in, "I know this looks bad. And I know that you went through a ton of resources to clean this up for us, but we got the guy. That was the primary objective."

"The primary objective was to get the guy *and* do it without being spotted or causing a scene. Now every terrorist, cybercriminal, and anyone else that fits in the bad guy mold knows who you are and what you do."

"We're sorry," Phoenix said.

"I'm sure you are, but that doesn't cut it. And it certainly doesn't make this go away. The only thing that will cause people to forget is time."

"Yeah, the moment another video comes out and goes viral with some cute cat video or a couple fighting it out while cussing up a storm on an airline, no one will remember this." Zeke sounded more hopeful than confident.

"Maybe," Benson conceded. There was merit to his comment. Still, they'd screwed up. Big time.

"Director," Phoenix pleaded, "we didn't have a choice. The target ran. What were we supposed to do?"

"Not get spotted. He ran because he made you."

Phoenix and Zeke weren't so sure about that.

"I don't think so," Zeke said.

"What was that?" Benson arched one eyebrow and fired another warning glare at him. If he overstepped, she would come down hard on him.

"I said I don't think so, Jessica." He said her name as if it annoyed him.

The truth was she had more experience in the agency and more time in leadership roles, but they'd all been at GIC a comparable length of time, and Zeke didn't appreciate the attitude she suddenly displayed. "There's no way he saw us. I was in the car, blending in, minding my own. Phoenix was a block away, also incognito."

"He's right," Phoenix agreed, not that it helped.

"I was tailing the guy, and he got spooked, but it wasn't by us. Something or someone else caused him to run."

For a moment, it looked as though she might consider what he was saying, that his explanation possibly held some merit. Then the moment was gone, and her face blended back into a mix of anger and skepticism.

"I can't put you two back in the field right now. It's too hot, and you would probably just screw it up anyway."

"That's hurtful."

"Shut...up...Zeke." She drew an exasperated breath and shook her head. "You just never know when to shut up, do you?"

"Got me through high school. Not shutting up, I mean. Well, that and Marcy Dorcester. She was really good at math tests. My scores were through the roof. All it took was a little baseball cap on test day, and I could copy my way to..." His voice trailed off as he realized Director Benson was neither amused nor entertained by the story.

"Typical," she said. "You two are suspended for one month."

"What?" Phoenix blurted. "You can't be serious."

"With pay."

Zeke cocked his head to the side. "That softens the blow a bit."

"You keep making those smart aleck comments, and it will be without pay, for good. You understand?"

"Termination? Sure. I get it."

She rolled her eyes. "Stay out of trouble, and lie low for the next four weeks, and we will see what happens. I've got people to answer to, gentlemen, and they are not happy about what went down in London. They wanted you gone, eliminated, fired, whatever you want to call it. I went to bat for you because of what you did in Afghanistan. I think you're good agents. But you cocked this one up."

"Four weeks?" Phoenix said in a daze.

"Get some rest, do some research or training or whatever you do. Go play golf. I don't care. Just stay out of the public eye for the next month until this blows over. You understand?"

The two men nodded, albeit with heavy reluctance.

"Yes, ma'am," Zeke said sardonically.

"Good. I'll be in touch."

The screen blinked to black and then returned to the main menu. Neither of the guys said anything. Seconds ticked by in silence. Zeke stared at the screen while Phoenix gazed down at the floor with vapid eyes.

"Suspended," Phoenix said in disbelief. "We're suspended."

"Yeah, but with pay, buddy. I say we hit the beach, maybe some casinos; lots of things to do here in Europe. Maybe we head down to Croatia and check out the beaches there. I hear they're nice."

"Everything is a joke to you, isn't it?"

"It's a coping mechanism. Probably because I wasn't hugged enough as a child. Or maybe I was hugged too much by my creepy Aunt Mae. Always thought there was something off about her. But yes, pretty much everything is a joke to me—or it should be."

"You just don't get it, do you?" Phoenix boomed. "This was our chance, our first chance to do something important, something better than the crap we were doing before. Remember that? Remember how boring our jobs were, how much we hated them, how badly we wanted to do field work?"

It was a sobering question, and Zeke felt his heart sink a little. "Yeah. I do."

"Well, we just screwed it up."

"True, but not for good. You heard her. Give it a month; we'll be back in the rotation. They can't keep us down forever."

"That's just it, Zeke," Phoenix argued. "They *can*. She said a month, but that's no guarantee they'll reinstate us in four weeks. They may decide to send us back to the desk jobs we had before."

"You're right. I know you're right, I'm just...I'm trying to stay positive, that's all." Dejection filled his voice, and he lowered his head. "I always wanted to be in the field, to do the dangerous stuff that could save lives or help people or whatever. I don't want to blow this, either."

"Well, congratulations because that very well might be what happened." Phoenix stood and paced to the back of the room. He ran his fingers through his hair and stopped on the back of his skull, then turned and looked toward his partner. "Ugh, this sucks."

Zeke fell silent, contemplating his forced vacation. He didn't like it any more than Phoenix, but what could they do? They were off the job, off the grid, temporarily burned—so to speak. They were powerless to do anything until the agency reinstated them.

Or were they?

"You're sure the target didn't see us, right?" he asked, the question sprinkled with a dusting of hope.

Phoenix shrugged. "I know he didn't see me, though he did start running right after he went by. I noticed you left out that little tidbit with Jessica."

"We have to have each other's backs."

"I appreciate that."

"Still, though, you weren't made, and I know for sure I wasn't. He never even looked my way."

Phoenix walked back across the room and slumped into the chair he'd been using before. "What are you getting at, Zeke?"

"If he wasn't running from us, then who was he running from?" Zeke's eyebrows lifted as he waited for the lightbulb in his partner's head to switch on.

It didn't take more than a few seconds.

Phoenix's eyes widened. "He wasn't running from us."

"Bingo."

"Then who? What spooked him?"

"That's what we need to find out."

"Yeah, but..." Phoenix let his voice trail off for a moment. "We don't have access to any of our stuff, and we have zero clearance right now. How are we supposed to do any kind of investigation without that, not to mention we're on zero authority at the moment."

"You're good with computers," Zeke said, cocking his head to one side. "Maybe we need to do a little hacking of our own."

Zeke's lips creased slightly, curling at one end.

"No. Oh no. You don't mean what I think you mean. Do you?"

"That depends."

"On?"

"Whether or not you think I mean that we should hack into the city's surveillance footage."

Phoenix's eyes shot wide. He laughed after staring at his partner for a moment. "Yeah. Okay, buddy. Seriously, what's your plan?"

Zeke rolled his shoulders and tilted his head to the side. "I mean, it's that, or we kidnap our guy, take him somewhere else, and make him talk."

"Wait. What? You mean re-abduct the guy we abducted yesterday?"

"I just said; it's that or the other thing. Personally, I don't think kidnapping a prisoner the GIC plans on interrogating is a good idea. Not to mention I have no clue how we'd pull it off."

Phoenix pressed his thumb to his lips and gnawed on the nail as he thought. "You might be right about hacking the surveillance footage. If we can get into the system and see what or who he was running from, maybe we can get a positive ID and track them down."

"So, you like the idea?"

"I didn't say that," Phoenix countered. "But the first thing we should do—if we're going to do this—is ask the prisoner."

"Hold on," Zeke said, raising a hand and furrowing his brow. "Did you say ask the prisoner? You know we can't get to him, right? Jessica just told us she's revoking our clearance. We have zero resources right now. If we're going to do this, we'll be on our own."

"Not necessarily. Jessica is back in the States. It could take a few hours before our orders are sent here. And she didn't say anything about our suspension being effective immediately. If we get in trouble, we could just say that we thought we would work the rest of the day and then it would start tomorrow."

Zeke's face curled into an appreciative grin. "I have to hand it to you, partner. Usually, I'm the one who tries to find the loopholes or gray areas." He stepped over to Phoenix and clapped his hand on Phoenix's shoulder. "I'm proud of you."

"Yeah, well, don't get excited just yet. We still have to figure out how to get into the holding area to see the prisoner."

A mischievous twinkle escaped Zeke's eyes. "Leave that to me. What about the hacking into the system?"

"That might be difficult, but luckily I think we know someone who can help us."

"Freeman?"

"Freeman."

3

LONDON

"Seriously? This is what you meant when you said leave it to you?" Phoenix groused as the two men stood outside the interrogation room waiting to be granted access. "I thought maybe you had some kind of slick plan to sneak into the holding area or the guy's cell or something. I didn't know you meant we were just going to try to go in through the front door like everything was fine."

"Sorry," Zeke said with a snicker. "But it's like you said: Our clearance should work until the end of the day. Maybe even into tomorrow. I'd say there's a small chance Jessica won't even remember to send out the memo or whatever she does for something like this."

"Okay, you're pushing it. You know that's not how that works, right?"

"Maybe. My point is we're going to be fine, and I am putting all of my faith in your idea."

"My idea?" Phoenix hissed, trying not to draw the attention of the guards at the end of the corridor.

They were standing in a hallway lined with brick and crumbling mortar. Three single bulbs dangled from the ceiling to provide light, but other than that it was dark and musty—evidence of the building's age and the heavy use it had endured during its lifetime.

"I still don't think this is a good idea. Not really what I had in mind," Phoenix said.

"It'll be fine," Zeke offered. "We'll be in and out in a jiff. We just need to find out what that guy saw that spooked him so much. It had to be some kind of threat; otherwise, he wouldn't have run."

"Yes, that's true, but at this point it feels more like we're going against orders, which is something I don't want to do. I've heard horror stories about assets like us who disobey directors. It doesn't end well, almost ever."

"I know. It's a big risk, but if we don't do it, then who will? Jessica doesn't understand what's going on here. Someone else was after this guy. That means this whole thing could be way bigger than we first thought."

"Right, but going in through the—" He cut himself off as one of the guards approached. The man had light brown skin with hair cropped short on the top and pointed sideburns that came down below his earlobes. He wore a scowl, and neither Zeke nor Phoenix was sure he was going allow them in.

"You're clear," the man said. His badge claimed his name was Roger Dickens. "You'll have half an hour with the suspect. Then we have to move him to another facility."

"You're moving him?" Phoenix asked.

"Standard procedure. Of course, guys with your level of clearance probably see this sort of thing all the time. This is just a temp holding facility. He'll be going to a more secure place."

"Oh yeah. Just making sure you guys were doing it by the book."

Phoenix clearly had no clue, but Roger didn't seem to care. The tired look in his eyes told them that the man had probably had a long week, or at the very least, a long day.

He scanned his card and entered some numbers into a keypad. The metal door buzzed then clicked as the lock released.

The door swung free, and Zeke led the way in. "We won't be long," he said to Roger. "Could you get us a couple of cups of coffee? Two creams, two sugars in each?"

Roger raised an eyebrow. "No. You have thirty minutes."

The door closed with a thud, and Zeke and Phoenix were left facing the man they'd apprehended on the street.

There were two metal chairs on their side and a matching steel table. The suspect was shackled to the table with cuffs, his head bowed low so the visitors couldn't see his eyes.

They knew his name, or at least the moniker he chose to use. Philipe Gaston was a well-known hacktivist in the hacker community, though beyond the borders of the shadowy underworld, few probably knew much about the man. He was a registered citizen of France, paid his taxes, and on the surface appeared to be just an ordinary guy. Except he was anything but ordinary.

Philipe had engineered hacking jobs on computer systems in every industrialized nation on the planet, including the United States and the UK. In those instances, his targets were primarily large corporations, though he'd once managed to thrust one of the smaller social media companies into an abyss for over eight hours before the company's security team was able to lock down the threat.

Most of the time, the viruses he planted or the jobs he pulled were innocuous, doing little damage to users or to the companies themselves. Most of his critics in the hacking world thought he didn't take things far enough. Others considered him an amateur, an egomaniac who simply hacked high-security systems for the fun of it, or to get attention, even though he never showed his face. Whenever and whatever he did, there was always the same calling card: a symbol of a lightning bolt in a triangle—and he went by the hacker name of Zeus.

Some of the more conspiratorially minded theorists thought that perhaps he was a member of the elusive Illuminati, that he was running their digital crime division—if such a thing existed.

That kind of speculation, however, was probably extreme. Zeke and Phoenix suspected the man did it as a hobby. While that might have sounded ridiculous to most, considering Zeus's—or rather, Philipe's—profile, it kind of made sense. The guy was a law-abiding citizen who spent much of his time in London on a work visa. He had no criminal record save for a few speeding tickets he'd received while racing around on his motorcycle. Other than that, the guy was an angel, which made the allegations of this most recent hacking attempt all the more difficult to piece together.

Interpol both received tips that a high-profile hacker was targeting one of the largest social media startups in the world to scrape the databases for passwords, emails, and any other information he could pull. Up to that point, Philipe Gaston had never, to anyone's knowledge, done something so egregious. Then again, criminals had to start somewhere, and usually it was with simple crimes. You don't rob a bank on your first job. You steal chewing gum from the supermarket, or maybe a candy bar. Then you work your way up to pickpocketing tourists or aloof commuters on the sidewalk. Criminals usually worked up to the big jobs, and the one Zeke and Phoenix apprehended Philipe for was most certainly a big one.

The data he might have collected would have been worth millions, maybe tens of millions if there were accounts connected to electronic payment systems, store checkouts, and user profiles. Larger companies could usually detect such activity, but sometimes the timeframe of detection could be between hours and days. By the time news outlets released the story, personal information from millions of accounts was already obtained and the damage done. All of that, however, was a mere cover for the hacker's real intentions, the true target. He never intended to use an ordinary person's information for profit. This hacker, it seemed, had a code of ethics.

The social media job was nothing more than a cover up, a decoy to distract from the real target. He set his sights on NATO's proprietary payment system for Western defense contractors. But before he could pull it off, he'd gone off the grid—as much as a hacker was able.

Most people would never see any damage because it would be covered up, written off. Security measures would be revamped. But he'd been caught before he could pull it off. Such a heist would have set him up for life as well as his great grandchildren. Instead, he'd attempted to screw with the international banking system with a powerful virus.

Zeke sauntered around behind the man and stopped, crossing his arms. Phoenix stepped up to the table and pulled out a chair, slid into it, and folded his hands on the table. A cup of water sat next to the prisoner, nearly out of his reach.

"Hello, Zeus," Zeke said, spitting the nickname with venom. "How's the head?" He motioned to the purple bump on the man's forehead but only got a seething glare in return. "Do you know who we are?"

The man kept his clean-shaven head down as he stared at the table's surface. His shoulders jarred as he laughed. "You're the two imbeciles that arrested me earlier today." He inclined his head, revealing gray eyes beneath dark lashes. Philipe wasn't huge, but it was clear he worked out.

Zeke glowered at the back of the man's bald head. He pursed his lips and nodded. "First of all, our boss prefers to call us idiots. Not imbeciles."

"That's true," Phoenix agreed.

"Secondly, it's one thing if you think it, but saying it out loud—that's not very nice."

"I don't care," Philipe said with a few other choice nouns thrown in regarding his opinion of his two inquisitors.

"I'm Agent Phoenix Underwood, and this is Agent Zeke Marshall," Phoenix said, ignoring the man's jab. He did not intend to let a guy who was no older than twenty-three cause him to lose his temper, even though he and Zeke were both still in their twenties.

"We know you weren't running from us, Philipe," Zeke chimed in and then walked around to the side of the table. He leaned down and pressed his palms onto the surface as he'd seen on television shows where someone was being questioned.

That caught the man's attention.

"We know you go by the hacker name of Zeus," Phoenix continued. "We know that you do more mischief than harm on the internet."

"You don't know anything about me," Philipe countered. He tilted his head at an angle and glanced up at the blinking red light on the camera in the corner.

Phoenix twisted his head around and looked at the camera then back to the prisoner. "We have that under control," he said. "The agency, Interpol, no one will know what we say in this room. Understand?"

"How?"

"You're a tech guy," Zeke said. "We may not be as good at the hacking stuff as you, but we have some resources, and Phoenix there isn't too bad with that stuff, either."

The prisoner snorted derisively.

"We need to know who you were running from," Phoenix pressed. "It wasn't us."

"How do you know?"

"Because you didn't see us. We're trained to be invisible while still being in plain sight." Zeke embellished the truth, but he hoped it would pay off.

Philipe clenched his jaw for a moment and tightened the muscles around his eyes as he considered the question. "I'm not telling you two anything. I need some ibuprofen and a lawyer."

"That's fine," Phoenix said, standing up. "Sorry about your head, by the way. We couldn't risk you getting away."

"You can shove your apology."

"Fair enough," Zeke said. He made his way toward the door. "But you know as well as I do that there is nowhere you'll be safe. If you really were that afraid of someone, you'll be on the run no matter where you go. Prison, another country...it won't matter. You're a high-profile target for multiple agencies around the globe. That means you're probably important to some high-level crime lords, too."

That jab struck home. Zeke and Phoenix both noticed the man's face ripple with worry.

"I'm sure you'll be fine, though," Zeke continued. "You look like a strong guy, capable of handling himself in a fight."

Phoenix stood up and started for the door, but Philipe stopped him. "I want a guarantee."

The two agents froze and looked back at the prisoner. "What kind of guarantee?" Zeke asked.

Philipe stared down at his hands for a moment, pensive as he considered his next words. "I need you to guarantee that my daughter will be safe."

4

LONDON

The weary mobs shuffled along the packed London sidewalks as commuters made their way back home or to the pubs after a long day of work.

The waning sun in the distant sky cast streaks of orange and pink hues across the atmosphere, pushing away the gray clouds to the east. It was a gorgeous sight to behold this time of the year, usually appearing more frequently during the late spring early fall.

Jordan Bradley stepped out of the fading sunlight and into a dimly lit pub called the Dancing Fern, identified by an old iron sign depicting a fern leaf that hung over the sidewalk.

He'd always thought it interesting how pubs could take even the brightest of days and make it feel like it was deep into the night simply by stepping through the doors.

No one seemed to notice him as he passed the bar full of patrons washing their worries away with pints of ale and lager. Some were munching on the obligatory fish and chips, though others were dining on a more elaborate fare of meat pies, corned beef, cabbage, potatoes, and roast chicken.

Standing at six feet four inches, Jordan towered over many of the pub's occupants. He was easy to spot, though his cold, calculating gaze unnerved anyone who accidentally locked eyes with him. His dark brown hair was cut high above the right ear and swept to the left, locked in place by pomade or perhaps some cheap hairspray.

His gray trench coat was probably a bit much for the warm summer's day. While London rarely reached intolerably high temperatures, it was certainly a day for shorts and a short-sleeved shirt.

Jordan only wore summer dress when he was at the beach, and those were rare times. He was a man closed off from the world, living on his own island in a rented apartment a short walk away.

Such was the life of a man like him: a killer, a hunter, a mercenary.

He had no friends, and likewise no enemies save for those he was hired to abduct, kill, or question. Even they weren't technically his enemies. They were merely his means to an end, pawns in the high-stakes game he played. It wasn't personal. Ever. He simply did his job with ruthless and cold efficiency.

Jordan scanned the room with an almost imperceptible flick of the eyes. Taking inventory of any space was second nature to him, a habit forged in the fires of both his training and his experiential mistakes from the past. One such error had nearly cost him his life in the early days of his new career, but he'd learned from that experience, telling himself that what didn't kill him had to make him stronger and better at the job.

From the looks of it, the people in the pub presented no real threat. There were a few grunts at the bar. One guy had a dark brown beer that nearly matched the color of his hair. He was portly, and from the fleshy jiggle of his flabby chin, it was clear he spent much of his free time in that very seat.

A thick golden chain dangled from the man's neck and stretched down to a chest that was covered with thick, curly black hair. Jordan imagined the man was probably a local lowlife, a criminal who'd made a success of himself despite an obvious lack of intellect, intelligence, or physical prowess.

Jordan caught a whiff of stale cigarette smoke combined with perspiration and high-end cologne. It was an odd mixture and one that caused Jordan's nose to twitch.

Just as Jordan passed by the man's left shoulder on his way to the back of the room, the guy turned to him.

"Looks like we got a pretty one here, Merl," the man said into Jordan's back.

The guy next to him was hunched over a pint of amber liquid, his graying curly hair dangled halfway down his ears. His long, reddish nose loomed over the glass.

"Oy?" Merl said and twisted to look at Jordan as he continued to glide toward the back.

"I guess he doesn't want to chat," the first guy said.

Merl shrugged and went back to his glass, taking a long swig. He set the pint down on the counter and went back to staring at it.

When it was clear Jordan was going to give no attention to the instigator, the man snarled, waved a hand, and then went back to his drink.

Jordan found his appointment sitting in a booth in the rear corner to the left.

The man extended a hand toward Jordan, inviting the newcomer to have a seat across from him.

Leopold Bannister was an older man, but Jordan couldn't guess his age. In his eyes, Jordan could see the decades of experience. The hair on Bannister's head was thin and white, revealing a few spots from being in the sun too long, probably on his fifty-million-dollar yacht. He wore a navy-blue suit with white pinstripes and a gray tie over top of a white shirt. The exposed cufflinks on the man's wrists were pure gold and embellished with large diamonds. Jordan assessed the gems to be worth at least ten to fifteen thousand dollars each.

The moment Jordan eased into the seat across from Bannister, a server shuffled to the table and asked what the newcomer wanted to drink.

"Water. Thank you," Jordan said.

The waiter looked surprised. His black mop of hair jiggled as he turned to Bannister. "Would you like another MacAllan, sir?"

Bannister lifted the glass, eyed the last bit of scotch swirling around in the bottom, and nodded. "Sure, Timmy. I'll have another. And bring my friend one, please."

Timmy nodded and rushed away toward the bar.

"I don't drink on the job," Jordan commented. "But I do appreciate the offer. I assume you're drinking an 18?"

The right eyebrow on Bannister's head rose slightly. Long wrinkles stretched across his forehead, and his ears pricked back. "Eighteen? Why not 25?"

Jordan cocked his head to the side and then let it roll back to center as he shrugged. "You can afford it, obviously. But it's not always about the best and biggest for you, Mr. Bannister. Despite those rocks on your sleeves"—he nodded and pointed at the cuff links—"the Breitling on your wrist, and what I have to assume is a fairly expensive tailored suit, you don't waste money merely for the sake of being able to spend it. You appreciate the best. In my opinion, the MacAllan 25 is a little overdone, especially for the price. And while it's certainly a tremendous scotch, I would assume a man of your taste and cunning prefers the 18."

Bannister inclined his head, sizing up the man across from him as Timmy delivered the two drinks. He set one in front of Bannister and the other near Jordan. "MacAllan 18, sir."

Timmy bowed as he stepped away, and Jordan smirked as he eyed the drink.

"That's why you're one of my best," Bannister said. He finished the first glass and raised the second.

It was Jordan's turn to arch an eyebrow, though he said nothing, letting his expression do the talking.

"Fine. *The* best." He motioned to the glass in front of Jordan. "Cheers."

"I don't drink when I'm working, sir," Jordan reiterated. "I need to stay sharp. And while I appreciate you choosing a seat in the back with a direct line of sight to the front door, I need to keep my wits about me."

Bannister's head bobbed in several directions, and then he relented. "Fine." He pulled Jordan's drink to his side of the table and left it next to the empty one.

"When are you not working, Jordan?"

"Never."

"Ah."

"Men like me are always on alert. Even when not on assignment, we're still acting as though we were. It never switches off."

Bannister sighed. "Sounds exhausting."

Jordan shrugged.

"Well, I have an assignment for you, speaking of."

"Oh?" Jordan leaned forward.

"Yes. One of my men failed to...apprehend a particularly important asset earlier today."

"How important?" He already knew the job. That answer was given away in the statement. Get the guy who got away. Now the question was who.

"He's a hacker. Pretty good one, actually. He's been responsible for quite a few troublesome jobs in the past. The authorities could never keep up with him, though. They never had enough to pin him for anything." Bannister's voice switched to a lower volume, though still maintaining the same gravelly sound. "I need him."

"Looking to do a little hacking yourself? I wouldn't think a man in your position would need someone like that."

Leopold Bannister was a mystery wrapped in a scotch-infused enigma. The man's history was scrubbed to the point that it read like a blank page, and finding any real details about his past was an episode in tedious futility. There simply wasn't much to unravel about the man, which meant he was hiding plenty.

Jordan had dealt with men like Bannister in the past, or so he first thought. He made it a routine part of his job to investigate the person paying him every bit as much as he delved into a mark or a location.

Never, though, had he been so thwarted at every turn to uncover intel on an employer—and that was unnerving.

In Jordan's experience, the sketchier the backstory, the more dangerous the employer. No backstory at all, though? It took an immense amount of effort and resources for someone to be completely off Jordan's extensive radar. That meant Bannister wasn't just wealthy; he was extremely powerful.

"We all have our hobbies," Bannister offered coyly.

Jordan replied with a snort, his head rocking back for a moment.

"I need him," Bannister continued.

"Who is he?"

The older man reached down to the bench at his side, and for a moment Jordan tensed reflexively, anticipating a weapon being drawn. He had to consciously push that aside, knowing that Bannister would not kill him for asking a question.

Bannister's hand reappeared with a black file folder. He set it on the table and shoved it toward his companion.

Jordan eyed the file suspiciously but drew it to the edge of the table with two fingers. He flipped it open.

"Philipe Gaston," Bannister whispered, his tone nearly drowned out by the tumult in the pub.

Jordan scanned the document and the images provided. He ran through the list of confirmed jobs the man had done, pausing to consider several before he sifted through the remaining two pages of the dossier.

"If you wanted a new hobby, this is your guy," he said and closed the folder. "Doesn't look like the type to do something big, like a heist or a data scrape. Just some punk getting their kicks."

"Yes, I'm aware of his qualifications and his résumé."

"Then why do you want him? Someone of your means could get a real pro, not some hobbyist do-gooder or prankster. Those guys are out there, not too hard to find them, either." His English accent turned almost twangy at the last sentence.

Bannister's lips twitched, and Jordan knew he'd struck a nerve, and that was something he wanted to avoid. Still, he needed to know why someone powerful enough to be as invisible as Bannister was would be so desperate for a two-bit hacktivist.

"Perhaps, if you succeed, I will fill you in on all the details." Bannister's steady tone unnerved Jordan, and no one unnerved him. This was a man that was accustomed to pulling strings, lots of them, and it was clear that no one ever told him how. Who was he? More importantly, *what* was he? Jordan had the feeling that if he wanted to know, it was going to cost him, perhaps more than he was willing to pay.

For now, he needed to get paid. Jordan was close to his goal. Thirty million, and he was out of the game. If he figured this man correctly, the job he had on offer might be the one that put Jordan over the top.

"I don't care what you do with this guy," Jordan said. It was only a half lie. "He's important to you, and you want him. My only question is—"

"Two million. In your account the minute you drop him off with my men."

Jordan's heart nearly stopped. He'd tuned his reactions over the years to the point that no one could tell what he was thinking or feeling. If he played poker, he'd have been stellar at it. In this moment, however, he caught himself blinking rapidly, his breath caught in his chest.

"That...will suffice," he managed.

"Excellent. Take that file," Bannister said as he downed the remaining scotch with disturbing ease. He slid out of the booth and straightened his suit, smoothing out any wrinkles that had made their way into the fabric. "I'll send you the rest of the details soon."

"Thank you, sir," Jordan said.

Bannister took a step toward the front of the pub and paused when he was next to his guest. He placed a palm on Jordan's shoulder and looked down at him with cool, calculating blue eyes. "Oh, and Jordan...take out the two agents who intervened earlier. No loose ends."

With that, Bannister strode to the entrance and walked out onto the sidewalk, disappearing a second later into the streaming mass of people.

Jordan took a deep breath and looked down at the folder again. Two million dollars? That would put him well beyond his goal of thirty. This was it. This would be his last job. After that, he could go anywhere, do whatever he wanted. Beaches, golf courses, mountains, whatever.

All he had to do was bring in this Philipe Gaston, a lowly hacker. That would be easy enough. People couldn't hide from Jordan forever. He always found his man. That reputation was why Bannister had hired him.

Jordan caught himself nearly salivating at the thought of the big payday. He scooped the file off the table and started to get up when he sensed someone behind him.

He sighed. Getting into a bar brawl wasn't on his to-do list for the day, but he knew there was no way around it.

He looked over his shoulder at the fat man from the bar.

"Hey, again," Jordan said with his best fake smile. "I'm fine, thank you. Timmy took our order earlier."

"Get up," the man growled.

"Actually, I think it's rather comfortable here. I may stay a bit longer if it's all the same to you."

The hairy-chested man turned to his associate, who stood behind Jordan's chair. He motioned with a flick of the head, and the man clapped his hands onto Jordan's shoulders in an attempt to pry him from the seat.

One second, the henchman's hands were firmly gripping Jordan's shoulders; the next, Jordan grabbed both of the man's wrists and jerked him forward. Jordan blindly drove the top of his skull into the man's nose, using momentum and a quick jolt from his legs to shatter the bone within the appendage.

Blood gushed from the henchman's nostrils, and he screamed a sound that was more like a young schoolgirl who'd fallen off the monkey bars. He grabbed at the wound as Jordan spun from his seat and grabbed the man by the back of the head. Then Jordan smashed the man's face against the table, and the assailant went limp, all while his employer watched in horrified amazement.

That stunned look on the guy's face swiftly turned to fear the second Jordan put his gaze to him. It didn't, however, keep the man from putting on some false bravado.

"You shouldn't have done that," the guy said, whipping out a switchblade from his pocket.

The metal gleamed in the dim pub light as he tossed the weapon back and forth, letting it dance between his hands in a show of what the man must have thought was skill.

Jordan didn't have to look around to know that most of the patrons had eyes fixed in a perpetually curious gaze, unable to tear them away from the two men. It was clear no one in the room intended to intervene.

"What's your name?" Jordan asked nonchalantly, as if meeting a new friend for the first time.

"What?" The man looked perplexed.

"The other guy, the one who's knocked out on the floor, he said your name was Merl or something. That right?"

"That's none of your concern, boy."

"Actually," Jordan said, "it is. I like to know the names of people I intend to humiliate. Adds to the enjoyment."

"Oh, that's it. You're a cheeky one, aren't you?"

Merl lunged forward, leading with the tip of the blade.

His attack was sloppy, which is precisely what Jordan expected. The man stumbled as he surged toward his target, the knife wiggling back and forth clumsily.

The man's intent was to kill. Jordan knew that if the guy had the skill, he would have spilled Jordan's blood right there and then hired some goons to come in and take care of the issue, including what he figured would be bribes to all the witnesses.

A simple sidestep allowed Jordan to dodge the first attack. The man clomped by, holding on to the knife as he would have the reins of a wild horse, and barely managed to stop himself before running headfirst into the wall.

"Seriously, if it's Merl, I'll just go with that," Jordan said.

The man spun around, renewed anger brewing in his eyes.

"I'm gonna gut you now, boy!" he roared as he lunged toward his target.

Jordan rolled his eyes and took one short step toward the attacker. As the man stabbed straight ahead with his knife, Jordan easily twisted his torso to the right, grabbed the man's wrist and forearm, then pressed the back of Merl's elbow to the base of his own.

When Jordan pulled back quickly on the wrist, an audible snapping sound echoed sickeningly through the pub. More than a few patrons lost their desire to keep watching, suddenly overcome by nausea.

Merl howled in agony, unleashing a string of obscenities unlike Jordan had ever heard.

"My arm!" he screamed, followed by more expletives.

Jordan spun the man around, kicked his legs out from under him, and dropped him to his knees as he deftly wrapped his left arm around the man's neck. He bent down as he squeezed, crushing the assailant's windpipe.

"I'm not going to kill you, Merl. Too many witnesses. And I may have use of you in the future. So, the next time I come in here, try to be a little nicer. Okay?"

The man could only protest with spittle bubbling out from between his lips as he desperately gasped for air.

"You're going to take a nap now, Merl. Just let the darkness come. You'll wake in a bit."

Jordan could feel the man relaxing in his arms, not because of his words but because he knew Merl's brain was demanding oxygen that wasn't coming. When the body went limp and became a dead weight, Jordan let him collapse to the floor in a heap.

He stood and dusted off his jacket, concerned he may have gotten something on it. Happy to see it was clean, he immediately made for the front door.

Jordan Bradley paid no attention to the gawking patrons as they stared after him, this man who dared to take on one of the local crime bosses.

Once he was out on the sidewalk again, he turned to the right and disappeared into the crowd—a ghost leaving nothing but a legendary story behind.

He had a job to do. Bring in this Philipe Gaston before he left the country—if he hadn't already. He wished he knew more about why his employer wanted this low-level hacker, but he figured the only chance he'd have of getting that information was to bring the guy in.

And that's exactly what Jordan would do.

5

LONDON

"Daughter?" Zeke asked. He cast a wayward glance at his partner, who returned the baffled expression.

Philipe looked up from the table. "I need to know my daughter will be kept safe. If they get their hands on her..." His voice faded, still leaving the interrogators with more questions than answers.

"Who will get their hands on her, Philipe?"

His eyes flitted to the camera in the corner. The red light blinked monotonously.

Phoenix saw the look. "You don't have to worry about them," he reassured. "We're controlling the feed."

A sudden look of panic flashed across the prisoner's face. "What? Are you with them?"

"With who?" Zeke pressed.

Philipe offered a sardonic grin in reply. "You know who. You *are* with them. I knew it. I knew they'd track me down."

"Listen, Bro," Zeke snapped, "we don't know what you're talking about. Okay? But we only have a few more minutes before we have to switch the cameras back on. You need to start talking, and fast. Who was chasing you? Why were you running in the first place?"

Philipe searched Zeke's eyes for the truth, or maybe he was searching for a lie. If he was, there wasn't one to be found. He looked at Phoenix for a moment. The other American gave a sympathetic nod.

"Look, Philipe, we don't know much about you. From what we can tell, you seem like a pretty nice guy. Mischievous but not evil. If you want us to help you, you need to level with us. Give us something."

The prisoner's eyes darted back and forth between the two men. Something in their expressions softened his paranoid look.

"My daughter," he said again. "I need to know she'll be kept safe."

Zeke let out a sigh. A look from Phoenix told him his partner didn't know if that was something they could do or not.

"Where is she?" Zeke asked.

Philipe stared into his eyes as if searching Zeke's soul to ensure he wasn't prying him for the information for devious reasons.

"Look, man. We don't have much time," Phoenix said, exasperated. "We can only keep the cameras down another few minutes. We'll do what we can to protect your daughter. But we can't help you or her if you don't help us. Who was chasing you? What did they want?"

"Why were you following me?" Philipe asked.

The two agents looked at each other. Zeke answered first. "We had a tip you were the one who sent out a virus that locked down every major bank's computer systems in the UK for twenty minutes last week. Took us a while to track you down."

"I like to keep a low profile."

"I'm sure, but that virus could have wrecked international economies all over the world, including this one. And for what, some laughs?"

Philipe giggled, recalling what he'd seen when the virus essentially shut down hundreds of millions in transactions within just a few short minutes. "It is pretty funny when you think about it."

Phoenix's face flushed. It wasn't a reaction his partner was accustomed to seeing. Typically, Phoenix was calm and slow to anger. Apparently, the hacker's nonchalant attitude about the financial upheaval that occurred, and could have been much worse, was unacceptable.

"It's not funny, Philipe. It affected millions of people. This is more than just some kind of Robin Hood hack job where someone takes money from the rich and gives it to the poor. And even that isn't right. Most wealthy people I know got there by taking risks, working long hours. So, if that's why you did it—to punish the wealthy—then you're wrong. And that doesn't even bring into account the ordinary people you screwed over."

Philipe's face turned somber and he nodded. "I guess I never really thought about it like that before. I was just thinking about the screen image that appeared on infected devices and machines. You know, the one with the safe with a crack through it?"

"Yes, we both know about the virus," Zeke said. "That doesn't help your daughter, and it doesn't tell us why you did it or why someone was after you."

Philipe nodded and slumped a little into his chair. His eyes passed from one inquisitor to the other. "I didn't create the bank virus. That was someone else. I was actually one of those ordinary people," he raised his hands and used air quotes for the last two words, "who were affected by it. Luckily, I have several accounts, and usually my money bounces around in a sequence that only I know."

"Bounces around?"

"I shift it from one country to another, keep it on the move at all times. It only freezes when I tell it to, like when I need to make a transaction."

"I guess it must be annoying to keep changing your Netflix password," Zeke quipped. He chuckled at his own joke, but the other two simply looked over at him with disdain. He cleared his throat and nodded. "Right. Sorry. Continue."

"I don't know who created the bank virus," Philipe said, "but I have a few theories. As to the man who was chasing me, I don't know who he is, but I know what he wants, or rather, what his employer wants."

"Employer?"

"Before you ask, I don't know who he is, either. I don't even know *what* he is."

The two agents exchanged a befuddled glance.

"Oh, that has your attention?" Philipe asked incredulously. "Well, whoever or whatever he is, he's bad. Very bad."

"What do you mean?" Phoenix asked.

Philipe leaned back and took in a deep breath then exhaled slowly. "What would you think of someone with no past, no family, no friends, no attachments, and no name?"

Phoenix considered the question for a moment and tried to apply the context of their current situation. "I'd say that person was either a ghost, doesn't exist, or is trying really hard to hide something...or everything."

"Precisely," Philipe concurred.

"And the person who was after you?"

"I received a message a few weeks ago from a man calling himself Perses."

Zeke couldn't help the snort that escaped through his nose. "What? Did you just say Perses?"

"Yes. To be honest, I thought it was pretty funny, too...until I saw what he wanted."

"What did he want?"

"My daughter."

"He wanted your daughter? Why?"

"No," the prisoner rubbed his face. "I need to make sure she's safe. Promise me you'll keep her safe."

"Okay, you're jumping around just a tad here," Zeke countered. "Yes. We'll help your daughter."

"Not help. Secure. I need to make certain she's in a safe place. Do that, and I will tell you everything you need to know."

Zeke and Phoenix both knew that was a guarantee they couldn't make. But they had little choice.

"We will do everything, and I mean everything, in our power to protect her, Philipe. But you have to give us something. They're going to pin the bank virus on you. And we are running out of time."

Philipe seemed to ponder the answer before he responded. "I didn't make the bank virus. I already told you that. But I may be able to help you figure out who did."

Another glance passed between the two partners.

"Who?"

"The same man who tried to hire me." Philipe leaned closer, folding his hands on the table. When he spoke, his voice remained but a whisper. "Perses was the one behind the bank virus. He wanted me to create a virus that would disrupt commerce, finance, all of that stuff. Said he only needed things to be down for an hour. I guess whoever he got to handle it could only pull off a few minutes." He let out a scoffing guffaw.

"It was enough to do some serious damage," Phoenix said, his tone still stern.

"I'm sure it was."

"Who was the hacker?"

"I don't know, but I can find out. You'll have to get me out of here, though, and I have the feeling that you two don't have that kind of pull."

Zeke lowered his eyebrows. "What makes you say that?"

"If you did, you wouldn't be blocking the video feed. And you wouldn't be concerned about a time limit in here. I'd say you're probably using someone, a connection, a friend maybe, to hold off the feed before anyone gets suspicious. I wonder, do you two even have clearance to be here? Are you real cops?"

"We're not cops," Zeke said. "We're with the GIC."

Concern cascaded down the prisoner's face. "GIC? I...thought that organization was just an urban legend, a fiction."

"No. We're real. And we're really out of time. Give us a name. We can't get you out of here yet, but we will do what we can to bring the real hacker in. You'll be safe here. And we'll take care of your daughter..." He let his words linger.

"Theresa," Philipe said. "Her name is Theresa. And I won't be safe here. This man who calls himself Perses won't stop until I'm dead. I know too much. He tried to get me before, but you two stepped in.

I'm sure the man he had following me is already dead. You won't have to wait long to hear about that, unless the body is somewhere out in the Atlantic. The only way I survive is if you get me out of here."

"We'll do what we can, but we need the name of any of your contacts who can help us track down the man you say did the bank job."

Philipe bit his lower lip as he considered the request. He knew the only chance he had to keep his daughter safe was to trust these two, though the vibe he was getting from them didn't seem exactly...competent.

"The hacker's alias was Katros. He doesn't exactly keep a low profile in the hacker community. You dig around a little; you should be able to find him."

"What about Perses? Is there anything else you can tell us about him?" Phoenix pushed.

"I've told you all I know," Philipe said frankly. "The guy is a ghost. No one knows who he is. I even asked a few people, though to be fair I tend not to associate with others. I prefer to keep to myself."

"So, this virus, Katros couldn't make it do what this Perses fellow wanted it to do. Sounds like that could be bad for Katros, based on what you've told us."

"That's not all," Philipe said. He paused for effect and to make sure his interrogators were paying close attention. "After Perses contacted me, I started snooping around. When I didn't find anything on him, I watched and waited. The virus struck and disrupted financial transactions for exactly four minutes. I can't track all of them, but from what I heard, not a single bank account was missing any money."

"Wait a second," Phoenix interrupted, holding up a hand. "Are you telling us that no one stole a single cent from any accounts? Why else would someone want to cause that kind of chaos if it wasn't a heist?"

"I get the impression this man doesn't need money," Philipe answered. "Though I have no idea why he would want to break the banking system. Perhaps he is an anarchist or one of those activists who wants to reset everything."

"In my experience, wealthy and powerful people don't desire such things," Zeke said.

"Then I'm sorry; I don't have an answer for you on his motives."

Phoenix fell into a deep, pensive silence as he ran through the scenarios of what the prisoner had discussed and what it could all mean. No answers emerged from the fog in his brain, but another question bubbled to the top.

"You said this guy—Perses—wanted you to fix the virus that the other hacker—Katros—couldn't make work like he wanted."

"Correct."

"So, could you do it?"

Philipe lowered his gaze at Phoenix, peering at him from behind the tops of his eyelids. "I did it."

Phoenix's eyebrows lowered in disbelief. "What do you mean, you did it?"

"I created the code that would enable the shutdown to last longer."

"Like, what," Zeke chimed in, "an hour?"

"Indefinitely." A dramatic silence filled the room for a moment. "I designed it so it could be switched off whenever the user decided to. That's why Perses approached me. He knew I could do it."

"But you turned him down."

"I'm not a terrorist," Philipe said in a candid tone. "I don't want to cause global chaos or even local problems. This man, Perses, I believe that's what he's trying to do."

"Why? Why would someone, especially someone with money and power, want to break down a system he seems to be thriving in?"

"I can't answer that. Believe me; I've wondered the same thing many times. Clearly, this man has some sort of vendetta against someone, maybe the world, I don't know, but it would be suicide for his own finances if he were to use that code."

"I'm sorry," Phoenix said. "If you did not intend to use the virus the way he intended, why did you adjust it in the first place? If he were to get hold of your corrected one, that could be catastrophic."

"Why do people climb Mount Everest? Hmm? Because it's there."

His matter-of-fact answer did little to satisfy Phoenix's query, but he could see the man was satisfied with the response he'd given.

"Where is it now?"

"In a file on my computer. It's protected by a highly encrypted passcode. Two wrong attempts, and the virus will destroy itself."

"But why keep it?" Zeke asked. "In the wrong hands, like Phoenix said, it could be devastating."

Before the prisoner could answer, the lights flickered overhead, and darkness consumed the room.

"Phoenix?" Zeke said.

"Yeah?"

"What's going on?"

"Blackout? Emergency backup generators should kick in soon."

"There won't be any generators," Philipe said, his voice cutting eerily through the darkness. "He's here."

6

LONDON

Panicked voices echoed from the hallway outside. Zeke and Phoenix hurriedly retrieved the phones from their pockets and turned on the flashlights. The miniature LEDs provided more than enough light in the room, but they didn't help the overall situation.

"Who's here?" Zeke asked.

"Could be anyone. Might be someone working for Interpol, a cop, or some other hit man. You won't have to wait long to find out."

Phoenix looked to his partner. "We have to get him out of here."

Zeke nodded and shifted to the door. He banged on it twice. There was no answer. He hit the metal again, harder this time. The latch turned, and he saw a familiar face standing in the corridor with a phone in his hand, light shining brightly into the doorway.

"What's going on?" Zeke asked.

"No clue," the guard said. "Power is down and so are the generators."

"We need to get him out of here," Zeke said. "My partner and I will get him to a secure location."

The man standing in the hallway narrowed his eyes at the request, but Zeke could see he was considering it.

"You've seen my credentials," Zeke pressed. "He's not getting away from us. We're experts."

Roger looked skeptical but finally relented as two more people rushed by. His radio sparked to life with the sounds of loud pops and screaming voices.

Zeke didn't catch all of it, but he understood enough: shots fired, guards down, send backup.

The guard swore under his breath and handed the keys to Zeke. "Get him out of here. Don't lose those keys."

"I won't."

The cop took off down the corridor and disappeared around the corner into the darkness.

Zeke spun around and tossed the keys across the room to his friend. "Get him out of those things," he ordered.

Phoenix snatched the keys out of the air and went to work on the cuffs.

"You don't understand," Philipe said, a sadness in his voice. "I'm already dead."

"Not yet, you're not. How about a little positivity," Phoenix insisted.

"He's actually probably right, though," Zeke chirped. "I mean, we had to check our weapons at the front desk. We're unarmed, so not sure how we will manage in a gunfight."

"We skip the gunfight," Phoenix answered.

"Yeah, okay. You know another way out of this place?"

"There's always another way." Phoenix finished unlocking the cuffs, and the prisoner wrung his hands for a moment to get the circulation going again.

"This hall goes in two directions," Zeke said. The comment was frosted in snark.

"Yeah, so we head away from the sounds of gunfire and screaming."

"Are you two sure you're GIC agents?" Philipe asked, panic evident on his face.

"Shut up," Zeke snapped. "We can't go headlong into a firefight without weapons. Unless you have a death wish."

"To the right, then," Phoenix stated and stepped into the doorway, holding his phone out in front of him to light the way. He checked both directions and then looked over his shoulder into the interrogation room. "Clear. Let's move."

The three men stepped into the dark hallway. Sounds of chaos reverberated through the corridor. The gunfire grew louder as the telltale pops increased in frequency and decibels.

"Need to hurry," Phoenix said.

The three rushed down the hall and then turned to the right. The hallway went straight for another forty feet before it turned to the left. More guards rushed past the three men. Two more in suits ran by, as well, just as the three escapees reached the next turn. Three pops abruptly rang out, and Zeke spun around to find each of the guards had been dropped. Two of them writhed on the floor with blood leaking from their torsos. One had a bullet wound to the shoulder, the thick claret soaking his black suit jacket.

Zeke sighed then grunted. "We have to get him out of here. Now."

"Getting you a weapon might help too." Phoenix added.

Zeke didn't listen. He dove toward the nearest guard and ripped the pistol from the dying man's hand. The gunman at the other end of the hall had stepped back to reload his weapon. The second he appeared again, Zeke raised the guard's pistol and fired wildly.

His aim was terrible, unsteady at best. Bullets thumped into the wall while others ricocheted off painted cinder blocks, flashing the darkened area with bright white and orange sparks. The gunman seemed unfazed and stalked out of his cover with his pistol extended.

Just as he was about to fire, Zeke shot the last round of the guard's magazine. The bullet was far to the right of the attacker, but it managed to find its way through a glass door protecting a fire extinguisher.

The slug pierced the cylinder, and a cloud of white instantly spewed out of the alcove.

The man screamed as the powdery smoke overwhelmed him, causing him to unintentionally inhale the dangerous vapor.

Zeke grabbed two fresh magazines from the dead guard's belt before shifting over to one of the other men and taking his gun and two more magazines. He raised the second weapon and fired another three shots, spraying bullets across the hall, hoping to hit the unseen target.

An abrupt yelp signaled he'd hit the gunman, and a thud confirmed the guy was down. There was no way to know if he was dead, but as long as it slowed him, that was all that mattered at the moment.

Zeke spun around and made his way to the corner where Phoenix and the prisoner were waiting. He handed the spare pistol and two magazines to his partner. "Now we have guns."

"Should we go back and help the others?" Phoenix asked.

Zeke thought about it for a moment. "No, we have to get him out of here. The cavalry will be here to help them, but if we don't go, we could be pinned down in here. We have to get him to safety."

Philipe almost looked guilty for being a burden, but he said nothing.

"You're right," Phoenix said. "Let's keep moving. There should be another exit somewhere."

Phoenix led the way down the corridor and through another door. There were more doors on the left and right, but they weren't marked as exits. The three men kept moving forward as the sounds of fighting faded and they were plunged into the eerie silence flooding the dark passageways.

Finally, they saw a sign with an arrow marking the way to the nearest exit.

New sounds erupted from the end of the hallway—men were shouting amid a cacophony of violent blasts of bone on metal, metal on metal, and thunderous gunfire.

"Oh no," Phoenix said as he raised his weapon and aimed it at the reinforced window set in the steel door to the right. "The prisoners are escaping."

"Whoever took down the power must have unlocked the doors remotely," Philipe realized out loud.

"What should we do?" Phoenix asked.

Through the window, they could see angry men approaching. Zeke thought fast. He looked up at the exit sign and knew that if the prisoners found their way outside, it would be difficult—nearly impossible—for police to round all of them up before a few slipped out of the country, or worse, stayed hidden in the city.

With only seconds to spare, Zeke jumped up and smacked the end of the exit sign with the heel of his gun's grip. The sign already looked in disrepair, and it broke free easily, now dangling from a collection of wires. Zeke jumped again, grabbed the corner of the sign, and used gravity to pull it free from the ceiling. He threw it in the direction it had been pointing and then took up a position in front of the other two men just as the door to the cells burst open and men flooded the corridor.

Angry faces stared back at the three companions. Two of the men in front were carrying weapons, black shotguns that had clearly been the source of the earlier gunfire. Two others held pistols. All four raised the weapons.

"Don't shoot!" Zeke said. "We're with you guys! Hurry up! This way to freedom!"

He shouted the words as if leading some kind of revolution, waving his arm back in the direction they'd just come and pointing the pistol in the same direction.

The prisoners didn't think twice. Grateful for the guidance, they hurried toward the three men and then turned in the prescribed direction. The men shouted and hollered, full of hope that they would avoid justice.

There were dozens of them, all wearing the same uniforms. Within seconds, the prisoners were gone, disappearing through the next door as they continued their raucous shouts in celebration of their successful escape.

They had no idea they were rushing head on into a gunfight in the belly of the facility.

"That was...risky," Phoenix said, unsure if he should praise his friend's quick thinking or berate him for nearly getting them killed.

"They could have killed us," Philipe said, mirroring Phoenix's thoughts.

"Well, I've learned that if you act like you know what you're doing, and like you're one of the gang, that goes a long way." He turned back toward the door leading to the exit. "Since it seems most of these doors are unlocked, we should still have time to get out of here. Once we're gone, we'll find a place to lie low."

"I know a place," Philipe offered, sounding confident for the first time since the three met. "Follow me."

They rushed through the corridor and around the next corner. They slowed as they neared the exit, Philipe suddenly spooked by something. He raised his hand to slow the others and pressed an index finger to his lips.

"What?" Zeke asked. He looked twenty feet ahead to an open barred gate leading into a holding chamber where another gate hung wide open, leading to an exit. "Let's go," Zeke hissed, uncertain why he needed to be quiet.

"Something isn't right," Philipe said. He looked to the left and saw a metal door leading into a control room. Through the reinforced glass, he noticed several security monitors, empty chairs, computers, buttons, and switches. The room was curiously unoccupied. "Quickly. In here," he insisted.

Philipe turned the knob and found the door to be unlocked. He ducked inside, and the two agents followed begrudgingly, still unsure about the prisoner's sudden paranoia. Philipe twisted the knob so the door wouldn't click as it closed.

Mere seconds later, Phoenix noticed movement on one of the monitors. Two men dressed in tight black T-shirts and matching cargo pants appeared on the screen. They were carrying submachine guns and wearing some kind of masks that stretched from the base of their necks up to their noses. They also wore matching black baseball caps turned around backward. The combination revealed only their eyes.

Both of the agents knew immediately—based on how the gunmen were moving and their weaponry—that they were professionals, most likely hit men.

"Get down," Zeke hissed. "Against the wall."

He ducked low and pressed his back against the wall next to the door. The other two did the same with no time to spare as the two gunmen neared the room. Phoenix kept his eyes locked on the monitor showing the view of the corridor.

Zeke came to a sickening realization. The door was still unlocked. He bit his lower lip and reached up with his left hand as he crouched on the floor, still pressing his shoulders against the cinder block wall. He pinched the lock cautiously, fully aware that if he twisted it too hard, it would click and signal to the gunmen that someone was inside.

Gently, he turned the mechanism until it clicked into place.

The sound was subtle, almost unnoticeable, but one of the passing gunmen *did* notice. He held up a fist to his partner, and the man stopped. Then the first man turned his head and looked in through the window set in the door.

The room's occupants pressed harder against the wall, pulling their legs up under their tails to keep out of sight.

Outside, the man narrowed his eyes and peered through the glass. He was about to reach down and grab the doorknob when a shout from around the corner drew his attention.

He and his partner hurried down the hall with weapons ready, and as they spun around the corner, muffled gunshots echoed through the corridor. On the monitors, the three men in the room could see the gunmen mowing through another gaggle of three prisoners who'd tried to find another way out.

"Now's our chance," Zeke said.

He received no protest from the others, and they stood as one. Zeke opened the door, ushered the other two out, and followed them through the two open gates and out into the fresh air.

As they rushed toward a sedan parked across the street, Zeke realized he'd never gotten his answer to the question about why Philipe hadn't destroyed the virus to begin with.

"The virus," Zeke said as they hurried to the parked vehicle. "You never told me why you didn't destroy it."

They reached the vehicle, and Phoenix hit the unlock button on the fob.

Philipe looked over the roof at Zeke, his eyes piercing Zeke's like spears. "Leverage."

7

LONDON

Jordan listened to the mayhem through the radios his men were wearing. He'd brought in a team of the best mercenaries he could buy, and since he had plenty of money, these guys were extremely good.

Breaking into an Interpol black site, however, was a challenge he'd never considered taking on. He'd known about the ultra secret locations for years, accidentally stumbling on one while doing a little recon on the web. He started seeing strange, encoded messages coming from a location that was supposedly abandoned.

Naturally curious, he decided to visit the place.

Sure enough, there was nothing there, nothing visible, anyway. It appeared to be a condemned fishing warehouse with no signs of life save for the digital codes coming in and going out.

So he sat and waited. Hours passed, and he was about to give up, ready to attribute the messages to some kind of screwup in the fiber optics network. Then the huge metal doors on the side of the building slid open. Two men in black suits stepped out, each holding submachine guns. Once they were done with their routine check, they gave an all-clear to someone inside, and a black luxury sedan exited and drove off the property.

With his quarry in play, Jordan followed the sedan at a safe distance until it pulled into one of the Interpol offices in London, right next to the mayor's office.

Jordan had known about CIA black sites for years, places where the American spy agency interrogated and even tortured prisoners— usually terrorists with information on key targets. Of course, the American government covered up rumors such as those, but eventually the truth came out. And what a staggering truth it was—the American government admitting to having hundreds of sites throughout the world.

It was easy enough to connect the dots with Interpol operating similar sites, most likely with other European defense agencies such as MI6.

With the knowledge of one site, Jordan spent months tracking down other such locations to create a detailed map of the western part of Europe, along with a couple of places in the former Eastern Bloc.

Once he had the maps, he set up ways to track people who were going in and out of the facilities. Despite the clandestine nature of the sites, and their high level of web security, it was no match for Jordan's team. The viruses he had created were veritable masterpieces, works of art in a world full of journeymen hackers. No one could touch him.

Cracking security systems had been one way Jordan had accumulated so much wealth in such a short time.

There was a time when a hacker in Michigan had noticed Jordan's activity on the deep web and tried to pry into his files. That hacker ended up receiving a twenty-five-year sentence in Leavenworth for trying to hack into the Pentagon and alter missile codes. Of course, the man had done no such thing, but the defenses Jordan had in place for such intrusions were not for the faint of heart, and if someone was going to try to mess with him, they were going to pay a heavy price.

Such defenses were worth the high payments he made to his team of experts.

Thirty minutes after leaving the quarrel in the bar, Jordan had arrived at his apartment and begun searching for anything that looked suspicious, particularly new arrivals in the black sites in and around London, the coast of France, and Scotland. Fortunately, those kinds of facilities only brought in the worst offenders, usually extremists set on terrorism. His query only produced two results, and since one was in Paris, he knew his guy had to be at the other place, less than three miles away.

Once he narrowed down the target's location, he sent his team in. When they were in position, Jordan gave the order to knock out the power and remove any connection to the emergency generators, all of which were controlled by the same system. Of course, there was a failsafe in place, but Jordan's men made quick work of that with a few lines of code. Once the lights were out, Jordan's assault team stormed the black site.

He listened intently to the firefight as his unit penetrated the Interpol black site and pushed through the building in search of the prisoner. Information on the man he was supposed to bring in was easy enough to find. Philipe Gaston was hardly a difficult target to acquire. The man had been involved in several hacking incidents, but nothing had ever been malicious. If anything, the guy was a prankster who enjoyed adding a little chaos to people's lives. From what Jordan could find, the man had never stolen so much as a single pound. That need to cause chaos had made him a kind of terrorist, but people were never hurt by his actions, merely inconvenienced.

Jordan had seen people like that before, hackers who wanted to make a statement. They were little more than street artists who painted graffiti on walls. He had no regard for such a waste of talent or time. They were anarchists, nothing more. While some of their antics provided a laugh or two, they hardly carried any real purpose.

A voice in his earpiece broke his concentration. "Sir, there's no sign of the target," a man said. The voice was gruff, belonging to the unit's second-in-command. His name was Ben Stubbs—Stubby to his team. He'd been a ranger in the United States Army when he was honorably discharged as the result of a minor injury. Unhappy with the way things went down with the military, and desperate to make some real money, Stubbs sold his skills to the highest bidders around the world, an action that led to him also selling his morals, what little he had left. Money paid the bills and bought the drinks. Righteousness had never picked up a tab.

The gunfire had ceased, which meant Jordan's team had pacified the facility, as far as he could tell.

"The prisoners escaped from their cells," Stubbs went on. "We... had to take them down. Some of them were armed."

"That's of no concern. What does concern me is your first statement."

Jordan stood from his seat in the back of the van and flung open the rear doors. The dim light of evening barely registered to him as he stalked across the street and down one block to the entrance of the underground Interpol facility.

"Have you swept the entire building?" Jordan pressed.

"Yes, sir. There's no sign of him. If he was here, we would have found him."

"You're certain there is no other way out?"

"Yes, sir." Stubbs sounded irritated that his employer would doubt him. He understood why Jordan had to ask, but still, it made Stubbs feel incompetent. And he was far from that.

Jordan rounded the corner of the chain-link fence his men had rolled open after infiltrating the building. Two of them stood guard with their weapons hanging at their waists. To a novice observer, the men might have appeared casual. They were anything but. Within a fraction of a second, both could have their weapons shouldered and firing with deadly speed and precision.

"Sir," one of them said with a nod.

Jordan returned the nod, but his irritated expression betrayed his real thoughts. He was clearly not happy.

He stepped into the building and discovered a vastly different world to the rough and rusty exterior. Inside, concrete walls climbed to the ceiling forty feet above. It was lower than the tin roof, providing a buffer between the two barriers. Bright white lights provided illumination from above.

Three black sedans and one matching SUV were parked along the right-hand wall. To the left, an elevator with brushed steel doors was fixed into the wall next to a door that Jordan assumed led to the stairwell. One of his men stood by the elevator and touched the down button to call the lift.

So, the underground Interpol site is literally underground. Interesting, Jordan thought.

The elevator arrived quickly, and within two minutes Jordan was down below on the main floor of the facility.

He stepped out of the elevator and over the body of one of the guards. More bodies littered the hallway, some in uniform, most in suits and ties. These were highly trained agents his men had taken down, though he was hardly surprised by that fact.

He knew what they would be up against and had been rightly confident in his unit's abilities.

Jordan recognized a few of the motionless figures as part of his team. The visual barely registered a thought, save that he would have to recruit their replacements. That was easy enough to do, and for those who'd survived, the money for the job would be evenly divided from the share of the deceased.

He stepped over another body, this one a pale, bald man in a black windbreaker. Jordan may as well have been walking over a dead squirrel, so careless was his demeanor as he stalked deeper into the facility.

He didn't have to go far before he met his second.

Stubbs was six feet tall with broad shoulders and thick arms. His hair was cut short, spiked on one side and swept toward the ridge from the opposite ear. His beard was buzzed short against his face, giving the appearance he'd not shaven for a few days, though from the clean lines under his neck it was clear that look was intentional.

He was a contrast in appearance to Jordan, whose lean, muscular figure stretched over a slightly taller frame. One looked like a warrior, the other, an Olympian.

"How did they escape?" Jordan asked without greeting.

"We're analyzing that now, sir."

"I don't need analyzing, Stubbs. I need answers."

"Yes, sir."

"Sir?" A new voice came through Jordan's radio. It was his point man on tech. "Go ahead, Rollins."

"We detected a slight anomaly during the breach."

"Anomaly?"

"Yes, sir. We didn't think it was anything at first, but it appears someone was tampering with the facility's video feeds."

Jordan turned his head and pressed his hand to the earpiece to make sure he'd heard correctly. "What did you just say? Did you say someone was tampering with the video feeds?"

"Affirmative."

"How was someone tampering with the video if we killed the power?" His face scrunched as he tried to figure out the answer for himself.

"It was just before the power shut down. The signal was fairly innocuous, so we continued as planned."

"Fairly innocuous?" Jordan's nostrils flared. The insinuation was that this video feed thing had no impact on the mission.

"It didn't affect what we were doing, sir. With the power down, the video feeds went with it. We did manage to trace the signal, though."

Finally, someone was providing him with something useful. "Where did it come from?"

"Pulling up the address now, sir."

Within ten seconds, they had the location.

"You can't hide from me," Jordan muttered to himself. "No one can hide from me."

8

LONDON

"Where are we going?" Philipe demanded. "I told you, I have a place we can hide out. My friend, you can trust him. I swear."

"Yeah, that's great, Zeus, or Philipe, whatever you want to be called," Zeke said sardonically, "but we have to get back to the rest of our team first. They're coming with us."

"Rest of your team?"

"Specifcially, Gary our communications and tech guy. We knew something was up when you ran," Phoenix said as he steered the vehicle around a turn on the left. "Like we said when we came to interrogate you, we weren't the ones you were afraid of. Not until we started chasing you, anyway."

Philipe sighed and contemplated the scenario again. "I thought you were with him."

"Who?"

"I don't know who he was," Philipe said honestly. "But I have a feeling I know who he works for."

"The ghost you told us about?"

"Yes. Perses. In Greek mythology, Perses was a god, a Titan, actually. He was the god of destruction, a force for change. I'm not sure why this man has chosen that moniker, but it's certainly imposing."

"And maybe a touch egotistical," Phoenix added.

"You said this Perses guy, he approached you about a job?" Zeke asked.

"Something like that. I didn't tell you everything."

"There's a shocker," Zeke chirped.

"He found out about something I'd been working on, something big."

Silence permeated the car's cabin for a moment as the two Americans waited for their ward to continue.

Phoenix let his curiosity get the better of him. "What was it?"

"That's the thing," Philipe said. "It wasn't my virus. It was something I stumbled on when I was skimming around through the web. I found a conversation between this Perses and another hacker. They were working on a piece of code that could burrow into systems and cause total disruption."

"Systems such as what, exactly?" Zeke asked, glancing across the back seat at the hacker.

Philipe's shoulders lifted then dropped. "Anything. You could hack major financial institutions, education systems, power companies, cable companies, even the military."

"No way," Phoenix argued. "Most of the world's top militaries use encryption that's virtually uncrackable."

"Virtually," Philipe reiterated.

Phoenix narrowed his eyes as he glanced in the mirror at Philipe.

"If someone were to understand how the encryption works, they could slip the virus into the code where it wouldn't be noticed. Describing it is much easier than the actual task, but yes, it's doable."

"How did Perses know about it, your modifications? Or did he just assume you were capable?"

"That, I don't know. The only thing I can figure is someone else might have been watching my computer, but I have measures in place to prevent that. Still, to be safe, I copied the code onto my hard drive."

Dead silence soaked the car's interior once more.

"Wait. You did what?" Phoenix had enough knowledge about computers and technology to know that doing such a thing was dangerous. It could be tracked, or at the very least, could destroy anything on the receiving computer's hard drive.

"I took precautions," Philipe said. His gaze remained on the passing pubs, restaurants, and other buildings outside the vehicle.

"Not good enough ones, apparently," Zeke said. "They found you. Didn't they?"

"Yes. They did. I believe my mistake was opening the file and tweaking it, though I always use a VPN when I'm doing anything online, from shopping to...well, you know. When I looked at it, the thing was incomplete, but it was clear to me what the designer of it was trying to accomplish."

"Which was what?"

"Chaos on a massive scale," Philipe answered. "A virus like that could topple nations, not just one. If a nation was big enough, say the United States or China, the domino effect on the rest of the world would be catastrophic. Money would be useless. Riots, looting, murder, theft—all of it would happen within a day or two of the collapse."

Phoenix listened as he steered the vehicle to the right and down another street toward the flat where Freeman was waiting to be picked up.

"And you just thought it was a good idea to store that kind of virus on your computer?"

"I took precautions."

"Again, not enough."

"No. In the end, they tracked me down. I must have triggered something when I was looking through their systems. My daughter was staying with my mother at the time, so she was safe. Now, I'm not so sure."

"You're right to be uncertain about that," Zeke said. "If these guys are as bad as you say, the next place they'll check is any relatives living nearby."

"My mother is in Cambridge, in a little farmhouse. It's in the country, quiet and safe."

That was good to hear, though it hardly solved their problems in London.

"Is that cabin traceable to you?" Phoenix asked.

"I purchased it through an umbrella corporation I created a few years ago. I have several such entities, so it makes tracking movement of funds far more difficult for authorities." Philipe spoke about illegal, or at least potentially illegal, activities as though they were as easy as opening a can of Coke.

"You know, I'm not going to say anything about that," Phoenix quipped, "even though everything you just said is super shady. Still, if you downloaded the virus and someone tracked you down, why didn't they just kill you on sight?"

Philipe turned his head away from the window and locked eyes in the rearview mirror with the driver. "Because...I figured out how to make the thing work."

Phoenix stepped on the brakes and slipped the car into an empty parking spot along the sidewalk. They were in a part of town that was less busy with tourists and commuters. There were more hipsters there than anything, as evidenced by the clichés of long beards, knit caps, and drab clothing.

The buildings were mostly four stories tall, with shops, cafés, pubs, and other small businesses occupying the ground floors along the street.

"Where are we?" Philipe asked.

"Just picking up a friend," Zeke said as he opened the door. "Come on."

"You...want me to get out of the car?" The former prisoner seemed dubious at the request.

"You're not our captive," Zeke informed him. "Right now, you're a fugitive, though I'm not sure who knows about your...our escape. I doubt anyone knows we were there, although we had to sign in, so there's that."

"I hope everyone survived the attack," Phoenix said as he closed the door to the car. There was a hint of regret in his voice. "It sounded bad."

"The cops always win those fights," Zeke said. "They probably called in a bunch of backup, and they're likely swarming the entire facility right now, rounding up the troublemakers."

"Yeah," Phoenix said. "I guess you're right."

"If anyone in that building was left alive," Philipe pointed out in a subdued tone. The other two doubted if the man cared about the lives of the agents in the facility, and certainly not the criminals, despite the tone of his voice.

Philipe led the way up a short flight of stairs and then entered a four-digit code on a keypad. The lock on the door buzzed and then clicked. The men entered and stepped into a dimly lit hall with a black-and-white checkerboard floor.

The group continued on, passing several red doors on either side. Heavy bass thumped behind one. The sounds of gunfire and explosions seeped through another, signaling the occupant was playing a video game or watching an action movie. It was pointless to determine which.

They reached the end of the hallway and stopped at a door painted a bright, royal blue.

Philipe turned to the other two men with a serious look on his face. "Just let me do the talking, okay? He gets a little...jumpy when he feels threatened."

"What do you mean by that?" Zeke asked.

"You'll see. Oh, and don't stare. Vincent has...eccentric tastes."

"What?" Phoenix wondered. "What's that supposed to mean?"

"Again, you'll see. But please, don't stare. And for the love of all things decent, don't bring it up. Okay?"

"Sure," the two said with a shrug and a few nods of their heads.

"No problem," Zeke said.

He didn't understand why Philipe was looking at him so strangely but blew it off as paranoia.

"Can we mention the oddly colored doors in this place?" Zeke asked with a smirk. "Did this place used to be a daycare or something?"

Philipe raised one finger, signaling his wardens to be on their best behavior.

Zeke merely raised both hands in surrender.

The Frenchman rapped on the door three times, then two more times, then once, all in a precise staccato.

"Hold on," a man's voice said from the inside in a sharp English accent.

A moment later, locks started sliding through their housings, and chains rattled, accompanied by several clicks. Then the door swung open, and the group was greeted by a short, skinny man in a black pinstripe zoot suit. The brimmed hat matched the suit jacket, while a white ribbon tied in perfectly with the pinstripes and the bright white, wing tips. On the walls at the very back of the apartment hung pictures displaying various performing artists from the 1930s, '40s, and '50s.

"Well, well, well. If it isn't my old friend, Zeus," the man said. "The prodigal son has returned."

"Vincent," Philipe said. "Good to see you again."

The two embraced in a firm hug while the two Americans continued staring at the indescribable leap in time they'd made from the modern era of technology to post World War II...Europe? America? It was difficult to tell.

"What have you been up to, mate?" Vincent asked. "I heard you got nabbed. Guess I heard wrong."

"No, you heard right," Philipe corrected. "These two were the ones who nabbed me."

A sudden look of concern swept over the host's face. Fear replaced it almost immediately as he followed the jerked thumb of his friend and stared at the two men behind Philipe.

"Are you off your rocker, mate? You brought two cops here to my place? What's wrong with you?" He included a few choice expletives that would have made the saltiest sailor in the world need a new pair of drawers.

"They helped me escape," Philipe said. "And we need a place to lie low for a while."

"Escape? You're on the run?" He almost sounded proud. "And why would the two men who arrested you help you escape? Is that bump on your head making you a tad loopy?"

"I'm fine," Philipe said, though he touched the bump on his skull again; it was still tender. "But can we come in? I'll tell you everything."

"Were you followed?"

"No."

"You're sure? I can't have any fuzz coming down on me right now."

"Trust me, I know you can't. We wouldn't have come here if we thought we would bring you trouble."

Zeke and Phoenix glanced at each other, curious about the man's terminology, but they held back...for the moment.

Vincent's eyes narrowed as he glowered at the two Americans. The indication of mistrust couldn't be ignored. "That right? You two didn't bring me trouble, did you? Because I'll tell you what, if this is some kind of setup to bring me in, it will not go well for you."

Zeke and Phoenix could barely hear the man's words, so intense was their focus on the man's outfit and behavior.

"No, we understand," Phoenix said. "We won't cause any problems."

"Right," Zeke added. "Just trying to reel in this big fish, is all."

"What did you just say?" Vincent asked.

Phoenix slapped his friend on the shoulder and grinned broadly. "He said we aren't here to arrest anyone. We're GIC, but we're working on another case, a cyberterrorism deal. Would be a riot if we don't stop them."

Zeke pouted his lips and nodded at his friend. "Okay, yeah, I see that one. Subtle, maybe a reach, but I'll allow it."

"What, did you bring me a couple of wise guys, Zeus?" The short man stepped forward, edging past his acquaintance toward the two agents. He was a good six inches shorter than both of them, but the menace in his eyes told them he wasn't one to back down from a fight. In fact, the nearly healed shiner under his eye told them both that he'd been in a brawl recently, probably at a local pub or night-club. And there was something weird about one of the guy's ears. It looked like someone had long ago tried to rip it off his head.

"No, no. They're cool. Please, can we just come in for a minute?"

The host continued glaring at the two Americans. "Are you two insulting me?"

"No, sir," Zeke said, flattening his shirt and putting on his best sincere face. "I have no idea what you're talking about. I do love this hallway and the doors, though. And from the looks of it, your apartment is really cool."

Vincent eyed the two suspiciously, unsure whether he should trust them.

"Sorry," Phoenix said. "It's just that...well, we need a safe place for Philipe...Zeus to hide for an hour or two so we can go pick up our communications guy. In fact, we need to get going soon. He's probably freaking out right now if he heard about the attack on the Interpol facility."

"Attack?" Vincent's tone changed to one of intense concern. "What attack?"

"Can we talk inside...please?" Philipe insisted.

Vincent narrowed his eyelids at the two men again. The suspicion oozed out of his eyes, but he finally relented. "Fine. Come in. But if you two keep it up, I'll feed you to the pigs."

Phoenix furrowed his brow as they followed the other two into the apartment. "Pigs?" he muttered to his partner, but Zeke simply shook his head silently and stepped into the foyer.

The host shut the door hard behind them and reset all the locks, seven in total. There were deadbolts, chains, and a knob lock to keep out intruders.

Once inside, the Americans took a quick look around, inspecting their surroundings with quick eyes. They were astounded at how clean the place was. After all, most of the hackers they'd met lived in sloppy, sometimes derelict, conditions. They'd expected to find empty pizza boxes and burger wrappers on the floor next to soda cans and paper cups. What they found, instead, was a pristine apartment.

The kitchen to their right looked newly furnished, adorned with modern black cabinetry and steel appliances. A wide ventilation fan loomed over the stove, much like Zeke and Phoenix had seen in famous chefs' kitchens. A bamboo cutting board rested on the counter with a fresh cucumber splayed out on it next to a cutting knife. Next to that sat a loaf of freshly baked bread.

Beyond the kitchen, the living room opened into a wide space with a flatscreen hanging in the corner. A gray-upholstered sofa and matching chairs wrapped around in a U shape to provide all visitors with an equally good view of the television. A balcony extended beyond a pair of double doors. It was furnished with a small bistro table and matching teak chairs. To the left, a short hallway led to opposing bedrooms, a single hallway bathroom, and an alcove with stacked, front-loading washer and dryer.

The dark, hardwood floor looked almost black and created a beautiful contrast with the white countertops around the kitchen's island sink.

Of course, those were the modern furnishings. The walls were covered in art, posters, and even some vinyl records from the swing era of the 1930s and '40s. There were images of men and women in speakeasies, raising glasses of liquid that may or may not have been potable alcohol, depending on who'd made it.

"This is...a really nice place," Phoenix commented.

"Not what you expected, eh? Thought I was one of them fellas that lives in trash?"

"Well, I mean, Big Bad Voodoo Daddy would love it," Zeke cut himself off when he saw the chastising look from Philipe.

"Thank you for your help," Philipe said before Zeke could make a bigger spectacle of himself. "I truly appreciate it, my friend."

"Not a problem," Vincent said as he rounded the counter and picked up the knife. He held it menacingly toward the two Americans for a moment and then began slicing the cucumber into thin discs. "So, what's the story with the two yanks from the GIC? Why are they helping you? You said they arrested you?"

"They did, sort of. It's lucky they caught me, though."

"Lucky? Doesn't sound lucky?"

"Someone else was after me. If they hadn't caught me, that man might have."

Vincent looked up from his cucumber long enough to offer a quizzical look at his friend. "Who was this other man?"

"I'm not sure, but I think he works—or worked—for someone who calls himself Perses."

Vincent scowled at the moniker. "Perses? That's an odd name. Never heard of him."

"I hadn't either until he approached me about a job. Wanted some code I'd been working on. I honestly don't know how he knew about it, but I think I know why he wants it."

"What kind of code?" Vincent asked as he finished the cucumber and placed all the slices in a bowl. Then he picked up a serrated knife and went to work on slicing the loaf of bread.

"Are you making cucumber sandwiches?" Zeke asked with a hint of confusion in his voice.

"Yeah," Vincent said, holding the knife menacingly toward the inquisitive guest. "You got a problem with that?"

"No. No, sir, I don't. I just—"

"Think it's weird that a criminal like me is making cucumber sandwiches?"

"I wasn't going to say that."

"I like cucumber sandwiches. My mum used to make 'em for me when I was a kid."

"And I don't judge that at all." Zeke couldn't help but glance at the man's strangely huge ear again.

"Are you looking at my ear again?" Vincent asked.

"No. Not at all. In fact, there's no sense in us dangling...hanging around here. We need to get to Freeman and bring him back here."

Vincent narrowed his eyes, certain he'd just heard another reference to his overgrown appendage.

"Yes," Phoenix added. "Our comms guy is still in place, and we need to extract him." He turned to Philipe. "You stay put. You're safer here than out on the street."

"You're going to trust me not to run?" Philipe looked surprised.

"Like I just said, out on the street, you're a dead man. Zeke and I, and your friend here, are your only hope for survival. So don't be stupid. Lie low. Enjoy a sandwich. Have some tea, or whatever goes with that, and we'll be back in two shakes."

Philipe bit his lower lip. "All right. I'll stay here. I appreciate your help, even though you did put this bump on my head."

Vincent chuckled as he spread cream cheese on a slice of bread. "Yeah, I noticed that. You say these guys did it?"

"He was running from us," Zeke defended.

"Tell you what, mate. You put a bump like that on my head, I cut your hands off." He brandished the knife again to back up the threat.

"Fine. Whatever, Benny Goodman. You mind locking up after we leave? I hear Al Capone is still on the lam."

Once the blue apartment door was closed behind them, Zeke and Phoenix hurried down the hallway toward the exit. They glanced back when they reached the door, then pushed through onto the steps outside.

"You think we can trust that guy with our prisoner?" Phoenix asked.

They turned and made their way toward the sedan parked along the sidewalk.

"No," Zeke said frankly. "But right now we can't even trust our own people. They took away our clearance. Remember?"

"Good point. I guess we don't have a choice but to trust Squirrel Nut Zipper in there."

The two shared a cackle and then started down the hall.

"I would have accepted Brian Setzer."

"He's sort of in between, isn't he? More like a bridge between swing and 1950s rock 'n' roll?"

Zeke shrugged. "Okay, we're done."

"Let's just hope Gary is okay. I have a bad feeling for some reason."

9

LONDON

Gary Freeman watched through a window of the rented apartment as a man, probably in his late twenties, opened the back door of a black SUV and stepped out onto the sidewalk. A cool breeze washed over the man and rolled down the street, curling around the corner a few hundred feet away.

The guy peered at the building from behind darkly tinted aviator sunglasses. It was the same look a hawk might give its prey moments before descending to earth and scooping up its next meal with deadly precision.

Freeman noticed two more SUVs—one parked behind the leader, the other across the street. A support team of seven men exited the vehicles and joined the man who was still staring up at the apartment building. Their weapons were concealed beneath black windbreakers, but Freeman knew they were armed. This was a hit squad; an easy assessment even for a non-field operative like himself.

He was in the field for the second time, so maybe he was incorrect in assuming he wasn't a field asset. He'd been through some training, though this mission was strictly off the books. There would be no backup if things went wrong, and from the looks of it, that's exactly the direction this mission was headed.

He stepped back away from the window when he thought the man in the sunglasses was looking directly at him. Panic seeped into Freeman's blood, and he quickly turned and began scooping his equipment into a gear bag. He'd traveled light for this one, partly by design and partly because he couldn't get most of his gear out of the head office without raising suspicion. While he hadn't been suspended like Zeke and Phoenix, the connection to the two was obvious to anyone at the top of the GIC, especially Director Benson.

So, he'd brought along his personal laptop, signal boosters, and a few other choice items he'd picked up from his home. Fortunately, he'd not always been on the right side of the law, and he'd collected a few handy tools along the way, like the one he'd used to hack into the video feed of the Interpol hideout.

It took Freeman less than a minute to stuff his gear bag with all his belongings. A quick look outside told him the men had already begun their assault on the building. He didn't have to stick around to know that they'd probably already pinned his location.

But how?

The only two people who knew he was there were Zeke and Phoenix. Whoever this hit squad was, they must have tracked him somehow. Doing that would have required sophisticated equipment, a signal tracker, perhaps? He shrugged off the avalanche of theories crashing through his mind and stepped out of the apartment and into the hallway.

If these men had tracked his location, they would have also assessed the layout of the building and covered the rear exits— assuming the eight men he saw out front weren't the only ones there. They would also have the two stairwells and the lone elevator covered.

The only way out for Freeman was to go up to the roof.

He twisted to the left and ran to the nearest door into a stairwell about thirty feet away. He crushed the bar with his hip and burst through, immediately regretting the noise he'd made as it echoed through the shaft.

Freeman paused to listen and, sure enough, heard footsteps pounding the stairs as the men rushed toward his floor.

He let the door close quietly behind him and then took off, padding quietly on the edge of each step as he ascended the remaining couple of floors to the rooftop.

The men below made no attempt to stay silent as they hurried toward the floor where Freeman had been just moments ago.

When he reached the top floor, Freeman waited for a moment. It was a risky move. Conventional wisdom would suggest that he not stop, that he keep moving until he reached the relative safety of the roof. Going through the door, though, would have made a noise and alerted the gunmen below to his location.

If he was wrong, and they'd seen or heard him going up to the top of the building, his head start would be much shorter, and he would have almost no time to get away.

He waited, holding his breath, until the two hit men arrived at his floor. As he'd hoped, they barged through the door and disappeared into the corridor. Freeman knew the men would go straight to his apartment. They'd known the exact floor where he'd been hiding, so it was an easy conclusion to figure they'd know the apartment number, as well.

The second the door shut behind the gunmen, Freeman pushed through the access door to the rooftop and stepped outside. The setting sun blinded him for moment and he shielded his eyes with a raised arm. Then he took off to the left, heading for the edge of the roof.

His plan, for the moment, was to jump to the next rooftop, but on arriving at the knee-high brick wall, he realized that would not be an option—the gap was over ten feet, a narrow alley four stories below.

He cursed under his breath and sprinted toward the other wall. It was over two hundred feet away, and he knew the clock was ticking. By now, the gunmen would have entered the apartment and realized their quarry had escaped. They would check the rest of the building, and the roof would be near the top of that list.

Freeman skidded to a stop at the other wall, bracing himself with his palms against the warm brick surface. Instantly, his heart sank into his stomach, and a lump caught in his throat. This gap was wider —there was no way out.

He knew the men were probably on their way up. His only option was to chance the leap on the other side—if he could get there before the gunmen reached the rooftop.

As he spun around to head that way, he caught sight of another option.

The lift motor room was nothing more than an oversized shed built out of cinder blocks and a metal, corrugated roof. Freeman stepped to the nearby door and twisted the knob.

It was locked.

"Come on," he said, frustrated. He twisted the knob harder, but it wouldn't move. "I'm dead," he muttered.

The men would be on the roof in seconds, and he knew what would happen when they found him. He hung his head, ready to accept his fate despite the disbelief that his life was about to end at such a young age. There were so many things he had left to do, places he wanted to visit, accomplishments to achieve. Now, he was going to die on a rooftop.

As he stared at the surface beneath his feet, his eyes caught sight of something on the side of the shed. It was a vent cover. He glanced back at the door to the stairwell and then hurried around to the side of the shed.

He was relieved to find that the vent cover was fixed to the wall with two hinges at the top and a clasp on the bottom for easy access. A rusty padlock lay on the ground; evidence that whoever serviced the elevator didn't pay attention to detail—a fact that was unnerving in its own right.

Freeman flipped the clasp and lifted the cover, shoved his bag onto a ledge just inside, and then climbed in. He grabbed the padlock and looped it through the clasp to give the appearance it was locked, and then gently lowered the panel.

Inside the lift motor room, Freeman quickly looked around to get his bearings. An ill-advised move would cause him to plummet to his death at the bottom of the elevator shaft.

The little light the vent cover provided was all he needed to assess his surroundings. The door to his left remained closed. In the center, the square shaft held a large motor in place with multiple steel cables looped through a series of pulleys. A narrow walkway wrapped around the opening to allow easy access for maintenance workers. There was also a series of metal support beams attached to the ceiling by even more metal beams to give extra strength to the motor mount. Freeman figured the lift could probably hold several thousand pounds at a minimum.

The motor whined abruptly, and his attention locked on the pulleys winding the steel cable. The elevator was on the way up.

Freeman leaned over the open shaft and looked down. It was hard to see much in the dim light, but he noted the lift was ascending at a rapid rate. Light seeped through the cracks in the elevator doors, acting as a countdown as it passed each floor.

The lift slowed to a stop at the top floor, right below Freeman. He heard the doors open and knew that while some of the men would take the stairs to the top floor, their leader was probably on board the lift. Shadows passed through the slender beams of light radiating up from the shaft; they were getting off.

Freeman didn't waste time overthinking his next move in case he missed his one chance at escape.

He grabbed his bag and hefted it over his shoulder, then with his free hand, he reached out over the lift and grabbed one of the two cables attached to the center. The elevator doors below closed, and the lift shuddered as he stepped onto the roof. Nothing happened for a moment, and he wondered if one of the men was holding the elevator for the others.

Then he heard the voices. Men shouted over the sounds of machinery and the ventilation van blowing gently overhead. Someone was outside issuing orders. He bent down, still holding on to the cable, and looked through the gap at the bottom of the door. He recognized the black boots the men were wearing. Shadows were running in various directions, covering every corner of the roof.

One pair of shoes was different; they were shinier, far more luxurious than the tactical boots the rest of the men had donned. Freeman had been right in assuming the leader would come up on the elevator. Now, the man was stalking toward the lift motor room. Even though Freeman couldn't see the man's face, he knew he had to be wearing a smug expression. The shoes paused at the door with a pair of boots stopping next to them, probably belonging to the leader's second-in-command.

Freeman watched in fear as the doorknob twitched, but it didn't budge. Would they shoot the lock and open it that way? Would they walk around to the side and see the vent cover, and would the dummy lock he left in place deceive them?

No way was Freeman going to be that lucky. He knew his time was up. He glanced back at the rear wall, thinking he could make his final stand there, somehow. Then he remembered the pistol in his backpack. It was his personal weapon, a subcompact 9 mm with twelve rounds in the magazine.

He reached into his bag as the shoes shifted and moved around to the side of the shed where the vent cover was located. Freeman's fingers wrapped around the pistol, and he drew it out of the rucksack, angry he hadn't thought about it before. But in his own defense, escape was the only thing then flooding his mind.

With his left hand, he eased the slide back to make sure there was a round in the chamber, and then he gently allowed it to move back into place.

Shadows stopped in front of the vent cover, but the men didn't seem to notice anything peculiar about it.

One of the men spoke up. "Round up the others. Tell them to search the area: streets, sidewalks, coffee shops, pubs, everywhere. If there's a candy shop nearby, I want it turned upside down. Whoever was behind that signal will lead us to the others. Find him. Now."

"Yes, sir," another British voice said. The second took off at a trot while the boss remained near the vent cover.

The odds had evened, at least for the moment, and Freeman felt a twinge of confidence course through him as he aimed the weapon toward the inside of the ventilation cover. He didn't want to shoot if he didn't have to, but he would defend himself as best he could. He knew that if he fired, it would signal the rest of the hit squad to his position. Outnumbered and outgunned, he'd be torn to shreds within seconds. The best Freeman could hope for was taking a few of them with him.

The gunfight never happened.

The man in charge pivoted on his heels and strode away, out of sight. Freeman waited until he could see the man's fancy shoes appear once more in the gap at the bottom of the door. The guy was walking back to the access stairwell.

Relief flooded Freeman, and his grip on the cable loosened for a second. Then he heard voices below. The second-in-command was issuing orders, and a flurry of action followed. The elevator shuddered as people stepped onto the lift, then the motor whined, and the lift dropped abruptly.

Freeman's loose grip nearly gave him away as he felt his body rise as the roof he was crouched on plummeted through the shaft. His fingers tensed, and he managed to keep his balance enough so that he didn't fall and bang against the elevator's top side. He wavered but stayed rigid enough to ride it out until the lift reached the bottom.

The machine's sudden halt at the bottom put pressure on his knees and feet, but he held firm. The doors opened, and the hit men on board exited the elevator. Freeman couldn't see them, but based on the orders they'd been given, the men would be rushing out onto the streets to set up a wide perimeter, hoping to catch their quarry.

The elevator doors closed, and the lift began to ascend again. Freeman became acutely aware that he might be stuck on the thing indefinitely, only able to climb off when someone took a ride to the top.

He didn't have that kind of time to wait. He retrieved the phone from his pocket and looked up Zeke's number, then proceeded to text his location.

Once the text message was sent, Freeman sat down on the roof of the lift and clutched the cable to brace himself. He hoped he wouldn't be there long. He also hoped his fellow agents found a way out of the Interpol facility, unharmed.

10

"What is that?" Phoenix asked as he stared through the windshield of the sedan, watching in horror as the men in black outfits poured out of the building and filed back into their SUVs.

A few of them jogged across the street to a vehicle parked two spaces ahead of where Phoenix and Zeke were sitting. Apparently, the men weren't aware of who they were, which may well have been their only salvation.

The SUVs sped away after the men scoured the area for several minutes. The vehicles disappeared around the next corner, and then the area fell relatively silent. Zeke was still holding his breath, mouth agape, when the last of the vehicles vanished.

He let out a sigh of relief and started breathing normally again. "That, my friend, was a death squad."

"A death squad?"

"Hit squad. Assassins. You know, contract killers? Mercenaries?"

"Yes, I know what a death squad is, moron. I mean, what are they doing here?"

"I guess they were looking for us."

"Or Freeman," Phoenix realized. Then another epiphany struck. "You don't think?"

"Crap."

The partners jumped out of their ride and hurried across the street, careful not to get hit by the sparse oncoming traffic. Darkness had nearly taken the day, and the sun's top edge was all that remained as daylight waned in the sky.

They rushed into the building and skidded to a stop in front of the only elevator in the lobby. Phoenix tried texting the third member of their team hoping to get a response, any response that would signal Freeman was still alive.

As he sent the message, he felt like the chances of them finding Freeman still breathing were almost nil, but they had to try. Fear shrouded the men as they stood there waiting for the lift to arrive. The signal dinged as the elevator came to a stop, and a moment later, the brass doors opened. The men stepped inside as Phoenix felt his phone vibrate.

He looked down at it and saw a reply from Freeman's phone.

"He's alive," Phoenix said, showing the screen to his partner.

"That's good to know."

The elevator climbed to the floor where their rented apartment was located, and the two started to get off when the device vibrated again.

The second text read, "I'm on the roof of the lift. Get me out of here."

Phoenix frowned and looked up at the ceiling. Zeke was about to exit the lift when his partner stopped him.

"He's up there," Phoenix said, pointing at the ceiling.

"What?"

Phoenix showed the screen to Zeke.

"Oh. Wow. Okay. Um, Freeman? Are you up there? It's Zeke." He sounded like an idiot talking to the ceiling, but it was the only way he could think of to confirm their friend was alive and where the text claimed he was.

"Yeah! I'm here!" Freeman shouted back.

"What are you doing up there?"

"Long story. Get me out of here!"

Zeke and Phoenix scanned the confined space for an access panel, anything they could pry open to get their friend down, but the ceiling appeared to be seamless, a single steel tile with a long, slender lightbulbs running through the center.

Phoenix held the doors open with his hand as they searched, but they found nothing.

"Um, Freeman?" Zeke shouted up. "Is there like a trapdoor or something you can drop through?"

"No. You'll have to ride the lift to the top, and then one of you will need to hold the elevator there. I can get off at the rooftop and come down. Just make sure when you reach the top floor that you don't let the doors close, or else the lift will descend if someone calls it."

"Sounds easy enough."

"Okay, Freeman," Phoenix said loudly. "I'm pressing the button for the top floor."

The doors closed a second later, and the two men rode the remaining floors to the top. When they reached their destination, the doors opened again and Zeke stepped into the corridor with his pistol in hand, just in case anyone from the hit squad was still around.

An older woman with curly white hair stepped out from her apartment holding a thick gray cat. She was dressed in a pink night-gown and wore lipstick that matched. The sight was something to behold, as was the sight of a man in the hallway with a gun hanging at his waist.

Her eyes shot wide with fear.

"Sorry," Zeke said in his best British accent. "I'm with MI6. Every-thing's fine. Just looking for one of our agents. You haven't seen a guy with a laptop running around here, have you?"

The woman scowled at him and then slunk back into her apart-ment with the speed of a drunken snail.

"Might want to hurry," Zeke said to his partner.

"Me? I can't do anything. Freeman's the one who needs to hurry."

"I...I know, I was just saying that in case he was still up there and could hear us."

"Freeman?" Phoenix asked, making his voice louder without shouting. "Did you hear that? Probably need to hurry. Seems Zeke just made a new friend that might not be a friend."

"She's an old lady with a cat," Zeke rebuffed.

"And a phone. If she thinks you're a bad guy with a gun, the cops will be here before we can get out."

"You know you're really not helping," Zeke said, wagging his gun around at his side.

The metal door at the end of the hall burst open. Zeke spun around and aimed his weapon but saw it was Freeman and immediately lowered his pistol.

"Oh good. It's you." Zeke shook his head as the third member of the team hurried down the stairs with his backpack bouncing behind him.

"We need to get out of here," Freeman announced on his approach.

"Yeah, no kidding. Apparently, there's a cat lady on this floor with a phone and a license to use it."

"What?"

"Never mind. Get on the elevator."

Freeman stepped onto the lift, and Zeke followed.

"Good to see you're not dead," Phoenix quipped.

"Same to you," Freeman returned. "There was a squad of guys that just left. They were all in black outfits and carrying submachine guns. Some had pistols. I think they were here to kill me."

The elevator doors closed, and Zeke eyed Freeman curiously. "Why would they be here to kill you? We saw the men leave the building, by the way."

"You saw them?"

"Yeah. Like, eight of them. Couple of 'em went right by us, got in an SUV two spots up, and drove off."

"So they're gone?"

"Looks like it."

"That's good," Freeman said and took a few deep breaths.

"You said they were here to kill you," Phoenix said. "Why?"

"Not sure. And I have no idea how they knew where I was. I thought I heard one of them say something about the signal, but I can't know for certain."

Phoenix thought hard for a moment as the lift reached the third floor and came to a stop.

"Oh come on. Really?" Zeke complained.

The doors eased open, and an older man with a fluffy white dog entered. He was wearing a long, drab trench coat that was way too warm for that time of year. His thin gray hair was combed over his scalp, and his glasses were so thick they would have made Harry Caray jealous. The man inched his way onto the lift, moving at a dreadfully slow pace, then deliberately turned around and pressed the button for the first floor, despite the fact it was clearly already illuminated.

The agents stood in awkward silence as the lift descended the final two floors.

The elevator dinged mercifully, but the three agents weren't free yet. The older man shuffled his feet, inching his way toward the door. He paused to look back at the other occupants, who were doing their best to be patient as the guy nodded his gratitude on his way out.

It was all Zeke could do not to throw the guy aside and rush past him, but he resisted the urge.

Finally, after what seemed like the longest elevator exit of all time, the three Americans leaped out of the lift and sprinted by the older gentleman. They burst through the doors and out onto the street, immediately checking for signs of a lingering hit squad.

The area was clear as far as they could tell, but to a man they knew that could change at any second.

They ran to the sedan and didn't say a word until all three were safely inside and speeding away from the building.

"What was that?" Freeman boomed between breaths.

"What was what?" Zeke asked, looking back from the front passenger seat.

Phoenix kept both hands on the wheel and his eyes locked on the road.

"The team of assassins that came to kill me just now?" Freeman motioned to the rear window, indicating the place they had just left. "Those guys were there to kill me."

"Or abduct you," Zeke said irreverently.

"Not...helping."

"Relax. We got you out. It's all good. You're safe. Zeus...or Philipe, the hacker, is in a secure location."

"I wouldn't call it secure," Phoenix argued. "He's in a location. That's about it."

Zeke's head bobbed as though he were debating the issue in his mind. "Meh, secure enough. I doubt anyone knows where he is."

"Wait. Where did you take the hacker?" Freeman asked. "Why isn't he with you?"

"We dropped him off with one of his associates," Zeke answered. "He trusts the guy. His name is Vincent."

Freeman eyed Zeke suspiciously but said no more.

"We'll be at Vincent's place in a few minutes."

"Then what?" Freeman wondered. "Is this Vincent character someone *we* can trust? Doesn't sound like it. I mean, you guys apprehended a known hacker. Then you busted him out of an Interpol holding facility. Are you sure you two know what you're doing?"

Phoenix and Zeke passed a glance between each other, then simultaneously said, "No."

Freeman slumped back in his seat and threw his hands up. "Well, that's just perfect."

"Gary?" Phoenix said, using his first name—a rare occurrence —"when do we ever know what we're doing? Seriously. Sometimes I feel like we just lucked into these jobs with the GIC. You know? Like we weren't really meant to be agents or something."

"Seriously?" Freeman asked. "Even after your heroics in Afghanistan?"

"I know. I know. Obviously, we're good at what we do, but I

wonder if other special agents out there like us have the same self-doubts, the same insecurities. You know what I mean?"

"I know what you mean," Zeke agreed. "I still feel like everyone looks at us funny when we walk through the head office."

"Exactly," Phoenix agreed. "Sometimes it really feels like everyone is laughing behind our backs."

"I think you two are just paranoid," Freeman said. He leaned forward and planted his palms on the seatbacks to brace himself. "You guys are the best. That's why you've been given this assignment. I was just thinking out loud, I guess. It's just...this particular mission feels a little strange to me, going to a hacker's safe house and all."

"It wasn't our first choice. Believe me," Phoenix reiterated. "I thought it was sketchy at first, too."

"Yeah," Zeke added as he turned around to look at Freeman. "But I was pleasantly surprised by the way Vincent's place looked. It's really modern. Looks like he got most of his stuff at IKEA."

"Really?" Freeman eased back again. "Those dudes usually have really messy apartments. Trash everywhere. Like, six computers always downloading stuff. Industrial rock playing way too loud."

"Nope," Phoenix said. "Total opposite. Although..." His voice trailed off.

"Although what?"

"Well, there is one thing you need to know about Vincent."

Zeke flashed a mischievous grin to his friend in the back.

"What?" Freeman pressed. "What is it?"

11

LONDON

"How did he escape?" Jordan demanded.

The two men stood in an old billiard hall in North London. It was close to the stadium where Tottenham Hotspur played their home games, though no football fans would ever realize it was there unless they already knew about it.

The billiard hall was one of the old places in North London where people went to avoid other people. That often meant a collective of celebrities would gather there in the evenings for a bit of a break from the paparazzi and passionate fans. Through the years, though, the hall fell into ill repute, and after an alleged murder in the alley out back, its doors were closed for good. It was the perfect location for Jordan's underground operation.

The walls remained dingy, and there was still a hint of ancient tobacco smoke mixed with old wooden panels to make the place feel like it was still an operational billiard hall. Only now, super fast computers lined the wall, each with two monitors connected, constantly downloading information.

His second-in-command reflected the stern expression on his employer's face. "We don't know, sir," he groused.

The response made him uncomfortable, and for good reason.

Jordan Bradley paid handsomely and expected commensurate results. The team had worked for Jordan several times in the past. Some missions were similar to this one, others were of a more delicate nature—occasionally involving family members of a target.

This mission should have been like any other—a quick in and out. Securing the target for transport was made more difficult due to the Interpol security systems and strategies in place. The agents within the secret facility were no pushovers. They were hardened assets—at least most were. Maybe a few among their ranks weren't as skilled, but it didn't matter. They all died anyway.

Jordan's men were consummate pros. Once the power was down in the Interpol facility, the people inside didn't have a chance.

And that is why the prisoner's escape was so baffling.

The agents defending the facility were operating almost completely blind. They'd quickly mustered the lights on their phones, but it did little good, only offering spot illumination as they desperately gripped their weapons—if they had them when the attack began.

Despite the thorough planning and perfect execution—or so Jordan believed—the prisoner had somehow slipped through their net. It made no sense.

Fine. These things happened now and then. There were always proverbial bumps in the road.

The signal they'd tracked led them to an apartment and what Jordan hoped would be a connection to the apparent jailbreak. When they arrived, though, the place was empty. The only evidence someone had been there was an unmade bed, a falafel wrapper, and a half-empty basket of fries.

Now there were no leads.

If someone had been there, as Jordan's head technology officer claimed, it made sense the person would still be there. Unless they'd been tipped off or spooked. Sure, there was the chance that the person who'd hacked into the video feed had planned on leaving at a specific time. That wasn't out of the realm of possibility, not by a long stretch. Still, it was frustrating.

"Where is he?" Jordan asked.

"Or she," his second corrected.

"What?"

"It could be a woman, sir. You never know these days."

"Are we...seriously, are we having this discussion right now? You know what I meant. It doesn't make a difference to me if it's a man or a woman. We need to find who hacked that video feed."

"Yes, sir. Right. It's just that...I don't think you should have such a narrow search focus, is all."

"What?"

"It just...you know, sounds a little sexist. That's all I'm saying. A woman is just as capable as a man when it comes to most jobs."

Jordan crossed his arms and arched an eyebrow. He considered reaching into his jacket, drawing his pistol, and ending the conversation right then and there.

"You know, don't you think we should focus on the matter at hand instead of solving the world's issues?" Jordan asked. He tightened the reins on his instincts to kill the man.

"Fine. I'm just saying—"

"Sir," another man interrupted their conversation just as Jordan was about to lose control and blast a crater in his second's skull.

"Yes?"

Jordan turned to the man sitting at a monitor nearby. He looked like the stereotypical military man with short black hair, mostly flattened on the top. His eyes were dark and serious, ever alert under shadowy brows.

"We have something."

Jordan stepped away from his confounding right-hand man and stopped short of the computer station.

"What?"

"Three guys are leaving the apartment now. Our man we left on the scene just called it in."

"Zoom in on them," Jordan ordered as he watched the men leave the apartment building and cross the street to a black sedan.

"That car," Jordan said, the realization hitting him hard.

"Yes, sir. I think we just missed them."

The group watched as the sedan pulled away and disappeared around the next corner.

"I can't keep up with the cameras, sir," the man at the desk said. "We only had eyes on those in the immediate area."

Jordan shook his head. "It's fine. Run it back until you get a clear view of each of their faces. I want to know who they are and what they did with the hacker Zeus.

The guy at the desk worked quickly, cropping out huge sections of the images until he had a single image of the first man. He cut that and saved it to his desktop before going on to the next man in the sequence. He repeated the process until he had clear images of all three men.

"Run them through the facial recognition database," Jordan ordered.

"Yes, sir."

The process wasn't a fast one, even for the more advanced computers in the world running state-of-the-art quantum AI processors. It took nearly half an hour to confirm the first match, and the other two followed soon after, though the information they provided remained vague.

Jordan leaned over the table and pressed his hands into the surface as he scanned through the first page of information regarding a man named Zeke Marshall.

Zeke was the son of a Global Intelligence Commission legend and had, apparently, followed in his old man's footsteps. From what Jordan could glean, he wasn't a chip off the old block and had been a career disappointment until recently when he was promoted. To what, the dossier didn't say. It was as if his position had been covered up.

That meant Zeke had probably been placed in some kind of special operations unit.

After reading through the information on Phoenix Underwood and Gary Freeman, Jordan reached a similar conclusion: that all three men were part of some larger undercover operation. But for what?

The answer was with the target he'd been sent to retrieve: Zeus.

Did the United States and its allies know about the virus Zeus had taken and improved? It was doubtful. Everything Jordan had heard suggested that the perpetrator of the prank had already been apprehended, though the name of the person was never released—likely never would be. Doing so would make the hacker a folk hero of sorts, and would only serve to further the person's career once they were out of prison. Even though the bank virus hadn't resulted in any thefts, there were still plenty of charges to be thrown at the perpetrator.

Jordan knew that whoever the police had in custody was probably a puppet, someone they could put on display for the media to make the public at large sleep a little easier at night knowing their money was safe. Relatively speaking.

The real designer was either dead or locked away in Perses' basement. Jordan couldn't be sure which. While he had the impression the man who'd employed him had the potential to kill, it was possible he needed to keep the original programmer around, just in case.

Jordan realized he was allowing his mind to wander.

"So, these guys are GIC," he stated.

"It would appear so, sir," the man at the station confirmed. "I'm not sure what happened to their records for the last year, though. It seems they went off the grid. You think they went AWOL?"

"No, Jimmison. I don't think they went AWOL. I think they're working undercover, deep if I had to guess. This was all you could find on them?" He held up the sheets of paper.

"Yes, sir. Aside from the usual boring stuff about their childhoods and all that."

"I want that, as well," Jordan said. "Give me everything on them. I want to know all about those three."

"Of course, sir. Right away."

GIC involvement was a bad sign, and Jordan knew it. He turned back to his second and offered a smug grin. "Looks like you were wrong, Corporal." He used the man's previous rank in the military to emphasize his irritation.

"I'm sorry, sir?" The second looked confused.

"It was a man after all."

"Oh, yes. Well, that isn't really the point, is it?"

Jordan had heard enough. He drew the 9mm at his side and squeezed the trigger the moment the barrel was aligned with the top of his target's chest, just below the neck.

The muffled shot was nothing more than a low snap from the short suppressor on the end of the weapon. Everyone in the room turned to see what happened as the second-in-command toppled over onto his back, grasping at his neck through the thick red liquid bubbling from the wound. His legs kicked for a dozen seconds and then began to slow to a wobbly, uncoordinated flop. Within sixty seconds, the body stilled, eyes fixed vacantly on the ceiling directly overhead.

"Someone clean this mess up," Jordan ordered. "I'd do it myself, on account that I made the mess, but I have a little research to do."

An eager-looking redheaded man, probably in his early twenties, hurried next to Jordan and handed him a sheet of paper. There was a picture of a young girl fixed to the top with a paper clip. Beneath the image, a similar picture above a series of paragraphs.

"What's this?"

"That's how we draw Zeus out of hiding," the redhead said. "That's his daughter."

"Daughter?"

"Yes, sir."

Jordan took the paper out of the man's hands and turned his back to them as he read the dossier. The girl was nine years old. This time of the year, she would be at home since schools were on holiday. Of course, assuming she was home was a big leap. If Zeus knew someone was coming, he'd have sent the girl elsewhere to hide her.

He couldn't be certain that Zeus knew who, if anyone, was after him, but his actions certainly indicated paranoia.

"Where is she?"

12

LONDON

The door swung open, and Vincent stared at the three Americans standing in the hallway.

"Hello again, Vince," Zeke said cheerfully and started to enter the apartment.

The host held up a hand preventing Zeke from taking another step, leaving him hovering over the threshold.

"Hold on a second," Vincent said. "Who's he?"

"That's Gary Freeman, our communications guy."

"I'm also an expert in other forms of technology," Freeman said, though it came out less confident than he might have hoped.

"Is that a fact?" Vincent asked.

"Just let them in, Vincent," Philipe chimed from inside the apartment. He was sitting on the end of a couch in the living room, craning his neck to see what was going on in the doorway.

Vincent turned his head and fired a scathing look at his friend. "It's my bloody house, Zeus. So if you don't mind, I'd like to vet whoever comes in here. All right?"

Philipe rolled his eyes and turned back to the television.

His rights reinstated, Vincent turned back to the men in the doorway. "Now, what's your specific area of expertise, Gary?" He said with sardonic venom.

Gary sighed. "Other than communications, I'm proficient with computers, certain forms of code—though not like what you guys do —and I'm best with signal tracking and manipulation."

"Ah, is that it?" Vincent almost sounded disappointed.

"Pretty much. What's your expertise other than hacking, doing the Charleston?" Freeman eyed the inquisitor up and down, noting the zoot suit and matching hat that seemed way too over the top for someone just hanging around his home.

"Good one," Phoenix said in a whisper over his shoulder.

"A wise guy like these two, eh?"

"Look," Freeman said, "I'm not here to cause trouble. But if you want to sit around and listen to Cherry Poppin' Daddies and Louis Armstrong all day, that's fine by me. But just so you know, both the 1990s and the 1940s called, and they want their apartment back."

Freeman could only see a fraction of the décor inside, but it was enough.

"You have some nerve, boy," Vincent sneered.

Even Phoenix and Zeke blushed, suddenly concerned their friend's unforeseen outburst of humor might leave them out in the hall. Although, to be fair, that would be far worse for Philipe than for any of them.

"Boy? What, are you, like four years older than me? I just have one question for you, Vincent."

"Oh yeah?"

"Who will win the World Series this year? Because I think the Yankees will do it easily, what with that lineup of Yogi Berra, Joe DiMaggio, and that crew."

"Deep cut," Zeke muttered.

Vincent stared at Freeman for a moment, one that felt like years.

Zeke and Phoenix couldn't tell what their host was thinking, but his eyes projected both anger and curiosity.

A smile abruptly creased Vincent's face, and he stepped aside, opening the door wide for the visitors to enter. "I like you," he said, jabbing a finger at Freeman. "You're not like these two patsies."

"Wait, what?" Zeke said as he stepped into the apartment.

"Patsies?" Phoenix wondered.

"Thanks," Freeman said and shook Vincent's hand.

"I have to respect a man who knows his baseball history," Vincent said with a broad grin, "and a man who isn't afraid to play dirty. You pass the test."

Freeman shrugged. "I didn't know you guys cared that much for baseball over here."

"Some of us do," Vincent said as he closed the door behind Freeman.

The group gathered in the living room. Zeke sat in a club chair in the corner, facing the television. Vincent stared at him and shook his head.

"What?" Zeke asked.

"That's my seat."

Zeke stood up, exasperated. "Aren't they all your seats? We're in your home, after all."

"You make a good point, Zeke. Maybe you should stand."

The host slid past Zeke and eased into his chair, crossing one leg over his knee, and rested his elbows on the armrests.

"Fine," Zeke said and wandered over to a barstool near the kitchen.

Having made no offense, Phoenix was permitted to stay on the couch next to Philipe.

"Did you run into any trouble when you went to get your friend?" Philipe asked.

"Yeah," Phoenix answered first. "Hit squad was there. I guess we just missed them."

"I hid in the elevator motor room," Freeman explained. "I didn't get a good look at them. I was hiding and doing my best not to soil myself."

"So, they went there to kill you?" Philipe asked; a measure of guilt laced his tone.

"Not sure. That or they were going to abduct me." The thought sent a shiver down Freeman's spine. He still wasn't used to this aspect of being in the field. Both he and his partners were unaccustomed to having their lives threatened. To say it was a big pill to swallow was an understatement.

"All because of me." Philipe lowered his head, enveloped by guilt.

"Hey, don't worry about it," Zeke said from the stool. "That's our job—to be in the line of fire. Won't be the last time."

"You sound so callous about it. Don't you have families, loved ones who would be devastated if something happened to you?"

"Nope," Zeke said. "Not really."

"Me either," Phoenix agreed.

"Crap," Freeman chimed in.

The others all turned to face him.

"I forgot to tell my house sitter to swing by this week and check on my cat."

"So, your cat is just sitting there at your house without food or water?" Vincent asked.

"Yes. I know, I'm a horrible person." Freeman fished his phone out of the right-hand pocket of his pants and began typing a text message to his house sitter.

"Anyway," Zeke said, trying to steer the conversation back to a more purposeful course, "you're safe now." He glanced at Philipe. "But Interpol and MI5 are going to start looking for you soon. They're probably investigating the site where you were being held, trying to figure out what happened and who's gone missing."

"Then it's only a matter of time," Philipe said, dejected. "They'll track me down. I'm a fugitive."

"Maybe, but not if we can stop this Perses guy and his cronies before they do anything serious," Phoenix offered.

It was a small sliver of hope, one that Philipe quickly dispelled. "Don't you see? I'm the one this guy wants. He won't stop until he gets me."

"He's right," Vincent said. "Whoever this man is, he's powerful—very powerful. I'm a good hacker, probably one of the best in Europe, but I can't do what Philipe does. He thinks about things differently, sees the code differently than anyone I've ever met."

"Looks like the ghost of Duke Ellington has a soft spot for you, Philipe," Zeke quipped.

Vincent leveled a warning gaze at his guest and then continued. "He's next level is all I'm saying."

Philipe blushed at the compliment but said nothing.

"So, it would seem our friend here is some kind of a savant, a genius among geniuses," Phoenix said.

"That's exactly what he is," Vincent agreed. "He can do things with code at a speed unlike anything I've ever witnessed."

"Explain that to me," Zeke said, putting his hands out wide as if to beg. "I mean, I can understand how some people type faster than others. I type slowly, so naturally I hate doing reports."

"You hate doing reports because you're lazy," Phoenix corrected.

"And because I'm lazy," Zeke confirmed with a dramatic nod. "But that doesn't mean reports don't suck, and being slow at typing doesn't help with that. So, what makes Philipe here so much better than everyone else?"

Vincent's face turned to stone as he stared across the room at his friend. He'd watched Philipe since he first got started in the world of code manipulation. Vincent had tried to coach the younger man into doing things that could help the planet and its people, subtle manipulations here and there that would steer the course of events toward a better tomorrow.

Philipe, however, had never wanted to do that. He enjoyed hacking, but it wasn't his life. He had a day job as an accountant, which Vincent believed was a blatant waste of the man's talents. It was his life, though, and there wasn't much Vincent could do to change Philipe's mind.

So, the hacker known as Zeus—a tribute to the great God of Ancient Greece—remained almost invisible in the hacker world, only dipping his toes in the pond from time to time to play a prank, which Vincent knew was merely for Philipe's own humoring.

He'd dipped his toes in too many places, though, and now he was a known commodity.

Rumors flew around the hacker network about a new guy with capabilities unlike any other, talents that would make even the darkest, most sinister coder wet their britches. Vincent knew that some stories were fabricated, exaggerated to the point of urban legend status, but he let them go. If the myth of Philipe Gaston—Zeus—took on a life of its own, so be it. Maybe it would keep some of the others in check.

Philipe spoke up, answering the question before Vincent could offer his own explanation.

"I see the code in a very visual way," he explained. "Not like images of people or places or things. I still see the numbers and letters, the commands, all that. But I see all of it as the framework for everything. I don't know how else to describe it. I just...feel my way through it like a maze."

"Yes, but he finds his way through those mazes quicker than anyone," Vincent added. "For a hacker, the faster you are, the better. If you're going to infiltrate an ultra secure site or account, or say, a series of banks, you have to know that the security systems will be watching for you. If you get past the initial steps, the systems don't stop. They will chase you until you're purged from the system. If your target is big enough and you get caught, you won't have to wait long before you hear a knock at your front door."

"And then it's a long, boring stretch in a jumpsuit behind bars," Freeman said.

"Exactly. And our friend here has never been nabbed, except by you two idiots," Vincent motioned to Zeke in particular.

"Okay, seriously? That's like the third time someone has called us that. Frankly, I'm offended you would say that to Phoenix. He's a very smart guy."

Vincent ignored the comments and went on. "But this Perses guy, he must have known about Philipe. I don't know how." He said it with a hint of humor in his voice.

Phoenix had been listening with rapt attention, and his brain was running a million miles an hour. He recalled the first conversation with Philipe, earlier that day in the Interpol holding facility. It was there, in the interrogation room, that the prisoner had told them about Perses and another mysterious hacker who worked for him.

"You said you couldn't find Perses," Phoenix blurted, diverting the conversation.

"That's correct," Philipe admitted. "Believe me, I tried. When the man approached me about trying to tweak his little virus, I was curious as to who he was, why he wanted such a thing. I never found anything about him."

"You said you might be able to find the hacker he used to create the bank virus, though, right?"

"Possibly," Philipe said with a slow nod.

"Possibly?" Zeke echoed. "You seemed pretty sure of yourself when you were desperate enough to get out of Interpol's fungeon."

The others looked at him with annoyed curiosity.

"Fungeon," he said again. "You know. Fun dungeon?" Every eye in the room stared at him, begging him to stop talking. He relented when he realized he would receive no applause or laughter for his joke. "Fine. Go on."

"The hacker Perses used implemented a pretty common strategy for his program. The virus was built on a series of protocols that most decent coders can understand."

"But?" Phoenix asked.

"But there were a few pieces to it that only a handful of guys have used before; at least that I've seen."

"Which guys?" Freeman asked.

"Three that I know of. Two of them are here in London. The other is based in Bulgaria. Last I heard, he was working on some devious scheme to scrape a government site for most of the country's private data."

"You think he might have been behind this?" Phoenix pressed.

"No." Philipe shook his head. "That guy is busy, and he's difficult to find. Not impossible, especially for a person with the resources this

Perses fellow has, but I don't think it was him. I'd say it was one of the other two."

"Who are they?"

A knock at the door interrupted his answer.

Everyone in the room exchanged worried glances, their eyes darting from one to the other.

"Are you expecting company?" Zeke asked Vincent as he reached for his pistol.

"No. I'm not. Friends of yours, perhaps?"

"Doubtful. We don't have many friends."

"You know, I actually believe that," Vincent said, pointing a finger at the American.

"I have friends," Freeman said under his breath.

"No one cares, Freeman," Zeke chirped. He turned and stalked to the door with the gun in his hand, finger resting gently on the trigger.

"If you don't mind," Vincent said, standing, "I'd like to open the door to my own home."

Zeke stopped short at the far end of the kitchen counter and waited. "Fine," he said, extending a hand toward the door. "Be my guest."

"Actually, that's the point, isn't it? You're the guest. Now do me a favor and sit down over there."

Zeke sighed and whimpered like a chastised puppy, though in truth he didn't feel bad at all.

He skulked back to his stool and plopped down, though the gun remained at the ready, his grip firm.

Vincent looked though the peephole in the door and turned around to face the others who were huddled together, anxious about who was calling.

"It's a woman," Vincent said. "She's pretty. Definitely not here for the likes of any of you."

He started unlocking the door.

Zeke's mind raced. "Woman? What woman? What does she look like?"

Vincent finished with the final lock and flung the door open. "Have a look for yourselves."

Three of the men in the room recognized the woman immediately. Her hair had been colored a deep amber, which only made her emerald eyes radiate that much more against her soft, creamy skin.

She wore a black dress that reached to just above the knees and clung to her slender, athletic physique. The V-neck folded over itself and appeared to be kept in place at her waist by the matching black belt. In one hand, she held a badge and an identification card, in the other, a black 9mm pistol.

"Uh-oh," Freeman said.

"Thank you for that, Freeman," Zeke quipped. "Aptly said."

"Jessica," Phoenix said, then corrected himself. "I mean, Director Benson. What a surprise."

13

LONDON

J essica stepped into the apartment, barely regarding the host as he stepped aside and closed the door behind her.

"Do you have any idea how difficult it was to find you idiots?" she asked.

"We prefer to be called imbeciles," Zeke said with a nod and a wink at Philipe.

"Unbelievable. You do realize that you two are wanted now, right? Interpol is all over you."

"Not Freeman?"

"No."

"Well, that's just racist," Zeke said with a glance at the man who could have been his brother.

"Shut it, Zeke. You never learn when to just shut it."

"Oh, so you have the same take as me," Vincent chimed, cutting into the conversation.

"And who are you?" she asked, turning her ire toward the host. "And what's with the costume? Are you going to a swing party or something?"

Zeke let out a belly laugh and slapped his knee. "Good one, sir.

Ma'am. Whatever. Although I think one of us already used the swing party thing before so maybe try a different one."

Vincent and Jessica both turned to him and shouted, "Shut up!" at the same time.

Then Vincent faced her again, though with his cheeks radiating red. "My name is Vincent Vera."

"How alliterative of you. You a hacker, too?" she asked.

"Depends on who's asking."

"The director of the GIC," Phoenix offered. "I'd be honest with her."

"I'll get to you in a second, Phoenix," she warned.

"Yes," Vincent said. "I'm a hacker, but I haven't done anything wrong—not lately, anyway."

"I'm not here for you and don't care what you've done. I'm here for them. And specifically for Philipe Gaston."

"Do you have a warrant or something?"

She held up the pistol and pointed it at his right temple. "Will this work?"

"That'll do," Vincent said quickly. "Zeus, I believe your ride is here."

Philipe looked at him, surprised at how quickly and easily he turned. But he said nothing and didn't budge from his place on the couch.

"I'm not taking him," Jessica said, a comment that caught everyone in the room by surprise.

"What do you mean?" Zeke asked, expecting a catch.

"Interpol is looking for all three of you. Not you, Freeman," she reiterated. Freeman eased back in his seat and spread his arms across the back of it to get comfortable, a show for the other three. It received an eye roll from Zeke.

"They had cameras on the entrance of the building," Jessica went on. "They saw you two go in. Then the blackout happened a few minutes later, nearly everyone in the building ended up dead, and they're pinning it on you. At least they're trying to. I told them you had nothing to do with it, that you were there to interrogate the prisoner that we brought in."

"You went to bat for us?" Phoenix asked, pleasantly bewildered.

"Don't think I'm getting soft on you two. But I know you're not killers."

"Hey. I resent that. We've killed people. Terrorists even." Zeke's protest fell silent after another warning glare from his boss.

"You're not cold-blooded killers," she reinforced. "You just happened to be in the wrong place at the wrong time, which I intend to address later. Right now, though, there are a lot of people looking for you, and I don't think they just want to talk. They blame you for the deaths of several agents and cops at the Interpol facility. I wouldn't be surprised if they shoot first and ask questions later."

A chill shot through the room and caused the hairs to rise on the arms of the two agents in question.

"So, why are you here?" Zeke asked, sounding sincere for the first time in, well, maybe ever.

"I followed you," she said.

"How?"

She pointed at Freeman. "He was in trouble. He sent me a text message while he was hiding out in the lift motor room atop the elevator shaft. When I got there, the hit squad was gone. Then you two showed up. I knew you were up to something, so I decided to wait outside and follow you."

"Stalker," Zeke said with a chastising turn of the head. "How dare you!"

"Better me than one of the Interpol agents looking for you."

"So, what now?" Phoenix wondered. "What are you going to do?"

"That's a good question, Agent Underwood. I should turn you over to the police, but I don't think that's a good idea. I know you two didn't kill those agents at the facility, though based on the fact you're here in some hacker safe house with two known cybercriminals, I'd say that's not a good look for you, no matter what your plan is."

"But we do have a plan," Zeke interrupted.

"I suspected as much. You have thirty seconds to impress me. Otherwise, I'm taking you back to the States, and I'm taking that guy"— she pointed at Philipe—"back to the authorities here in London."

Fear shot through the man's eyes. "But I didn't do anything."

"He's not lying," Phoenix said as he stood up. "I don't believe he created the bank virus. Someone else did."

"Who?"

"We were just trying to figure that out when you knocked on the door," Philipe said. "There are only two hackers I can think of who use the methods implemented in that virus."

"Well, three," Zeke corrected, "but one of them is apparently working on posting Tinder profiles for a few million people in Bulgaria right now, so I guess he's out."

Philipe ignored the stupid comment and continued. He relayed everything he knew about the man who called himself Perses, the offer the guy had made, and the fact that any information about him was simply not available, not even through Philipe's extensive channels.

Jessica listened intensely as the Frenchman told her everything he knew, then he explained that the two agents had saved his life and helped him escape.

"So, you're saying that the attack on the Interpol facility was an attempt to abduct you and get you to build this virus some guy named Perses wants to use to disrupt the global economy?" She sounded beyond skeptical.

"Yes," Philipe said. "Well, not build it. It's already built. I replicated the virus and then created one that would actually work."

"Wait. You did what?" Her voice escalated.

"It's safe. I hid it somewhere only I can find it. The files are encrypted at a level most of the world's best crackers couldn't access. I alone know how to get to it."

"Why on earth would you create a virus like that if you weren't going to use it? I'm sorry, Philipe, but I'm having a bit of trouble believing that."

"I know. And I don't blame you. I just wanted to see if I could do it. I never used it, though."

Then it hit Zeke. Philipe wasn't outright lying, but he'd misled them, although for a good cause.

"You made it to protect your daughter," Zeke said.

Everyone in the apartment turned to face him.

"What?" Phoenix asked. "What are you talking about?"

"Don't get me wrong, Philipe, or Zeus, whatever you prefer. Still don't really get that, and I don't care. I think you created that virus as a failsafe, in case this Perses guy ever got to your kid. It's the ultimate trump card. The ace in the hole."

"Are you going to keep using card game analogies, or are you done?" Jessica asked.

"Fair enough," Zeke said with a curt nod. "Doesn't change the fact that's why you did it. I'm sure there was some kind of Edmund Hillaryesque motivator that made you do it because you wondered if you could, but deep down you knew that if that man ever got ahold of you, you'd need that virus at the ready."

Philipe inclined his head, assessing the agent's assertion. "You don't know what you're talking about."

"I think I do," Zeke said. "And I don't blame you. When we first met, you started asking questions, and the only thing you cared about was your kid. You didn't care what we did to you, which makes you a great parent, by the way. So great that you'd be willing to send the entire planet back to the Dark Ages with the press of a button just to save your daughter's life."

After a moment of contemplation, Philipe shrugged and put his palms up. A tear formed in his right eye. "I would do anything for her, even if it meant destroying the world. I would do it without hesitation."

Every eye in the room was locked on him.

One question kept boiling in Phoenix's mind, and he was pretty sure it was the same question Zeke had on the tip of his tongue.

"Where is your daughter again?" Phoenix asked.

"Like I said before, with my mother. In the country near Cambridge."

"Your mother?" Jessica asked. "If this guy is half as powerful as you say, he will find her."

"No," Philipe said. "I took precautions. My mother's place, it was purchased under a corporate entity's title. There is no connection to me or my family."

"Unless he already knew," Jessica said.

"What do you mean?" Philipe asked. Fear filled his wide eyes.

"Guys like that, they cover all their bases. The hit squad that came to the apartment looking for Freeman, they were pros. The way they took down an entire Interpol black site was surgical and terrifying."

"Almost sounds like you admire them," Zeke chirped.

She ignored him.

"Philipe," her voice flickered with urgency, "we need the precise address of where your daughter is hiding."

He took a deep breath and sighed. "Sorry," he said, realizing what she meant. He gave the address and the agents took notes, both in their phones and in their heads.

Zeke looked to Jessica. "I guess we need to get moving?"

She glared at him, still angry about pretty much everything they'd done up to this point regarding this case. But at the moment, she needed every able body she could find, and none of the other assets from GIC were in the area. Jessica had no choice.

"I guess so, but keep in mind this is strictly off the books, and this changes nothing about your suspension. Understood?"

"Got it," Phoenix said.

"I knew you'd come around," Zeke added.

She rolled her eyes. "I'm already regretting this."

14

CAMBRIDGE, ENGLAND

J ordan stood outside the farmhouse and stared at the door. The place was quaint, a relic from bygone days, simpler times when villages like this one operated exclusively based on what their local agricultural economy could produce.

He'd seen homes and property like this in magazines or on the occasional mission to the countryside, which was infrequent at best. Growing up in the city, Jordan had missed out on scenes such as this: the weatherworn, unbleached stone walls, the dilapidated roof, the twin chimneys. He drew in a breath of cool, damp evening air. The scent of rain was still in the air from a shower that had passed through an hour or so before. Trees dripped the remnants of the storm onto the soggy turf, illuminated by dim yellow lights attached to the exterior of the house on either side of the doorway.

A few lights glowed inside, telling Jordan that the occupants were still awake.

He held up a hand and turned to look over a shoulder at his men. Six of them stood behind him, awaiting orders. His new second-in-command, Jimmison, stood closest.

The young man was clearly eager to please, not wanting to face the same fate as his predecessor, though to be fair, from what

Jimmison had heard the man had a problem with his attitude. His reward had been a hollow point through his chest.

Jordan rarely resorted to such extreme measures–doing so could result in attrition or downright mutiny. His former second, however, had pushed too many buttons, and everyone in the crew knew it. The guy was a good fighter, a strong soldier, capable of multiple forms of hand-to-hand combat, and an expert with almost any kind of firearm you could name.

But he didn't know how to shut his mouth. And he flapped those gums right up until the point Jordan put a bullet in him.

"Jimmison," Jordan said after a moment of silent thought.

"Yes, sir," the younger man stepped up and stood stiff, ready for his orders.

"Take two men and go around back. I don't want anyone sneaking out the rear of the building."

"Right away, sir."

Jimmison spun around, motioned to two of the men closest to him, and then led the way to the rear of the house by way of a rock wall that surrounded the front yard, two side areas, and a larger back-yard. They stayed low, keeping their heads below the top of the wall in case someone in the house looked out.

The nearest neighbor was some way down the narrow road, if it could be called that. It was little more than a roughly paved path in urgent need of repair. No one would notice the three SUVs parked in front of the country cottage. They were as secluded as possible, which should have allowed for an easy extraction.

Having allowed Jimmison and his men time to reach the rear, Jordan glanced at the remaining mercenaries. He ordered two of them to hang back with the vehicles, and to stay out of sight. Despite the cover of darkness that came with nightfall, and the additional gloom provided by the overcast sky, he didn't want to take any chances. They may already have been spotted, but it would take too long for first responders to arrive on the scene. It would be a quick job. Get in. Get the girl. Get out.

He strode toward the front door, and as he passed an ancient oak tree to the right, he motioned for the last of his men to take up a position behind the thick trunk.

The gunman nodded and shuffled behind the tree, pressing his left shoulder into it. He held the submachine gun securely and hugged the trunk tight, ready to spring into action.

That left Jordan alone as he approached the front door.

He glided up the steps and stopped short of the threshold to take one last look back. The men he'd left with the vehicles were nowhere to be seen, and the man behind the tree had concealed himself well enough to go undetected.

Jordan drew a long breath and then rapped on the door several times. There was no answer, and after waiting thirty seconds, he knocked again.

This time, a woman's voice responded. "One minute. I'll be right there."

It was easy to recognize her accent as French, which made sense since the woman was Philipe's mother, based on the intel Jordan could gather.

Philipe Gaston had been clever in his concealment of the ownership of the home. He'd hidden it under a shell company, making it difficult—though not impossible—to find.

Philipe, while extremely resourceful and intelligent, wasn't exceedingly savvy when it came to using shelters in the tax system. Locating the real purchaser of the property required only a few more steps in the process. Once Jordan navigated through the minutiae, he discovered the true owner's identity.

It was only a small leap to assume that this country cottage just outside of Cambridge would be the place Philipe, the infamous hacker known as Zeus, would choose to hide his precious daughter.

Jordan thought about his own life, the life he wished he could have had. He'd always wanted a family, a wife and kids of his own, but it never materialized. That life wasn't for men like him. His kind were resigned to the lonely rigors of the road, and the dangers that lurked around every corner.

It was his choice, and one that regret only dared to scratch at now and then—like now, when he was standing on the doorstep of what he imagined life could have been.

Once he hit his number, thirty million in the bank, perhaps he would buy a quaint little cottage like this one, perhaps somewhere near the coast of Spain or France. He just wanted to be somewhere warm where he could drink away the memories of a life full of death and suffering.

Maybe then, after all of this was over—the jobs, the killing, the servitude to others—he could settle down. Would he ever find a woman that would settle down with him? He doubted it. There were too many ghosts in his past, too many skeletons in his closet for Jordan to pay any more attention to the living.

Jordan pushed all of that aside and focused his attention on the red door in front of him. The paint was peeling in spots, reflecting the age the home displayed.

He heard footsteps inside, and then the deadbolt turned. The door creaked open, and he found himself face to face with an older woman. She was shorter than he was, though that wasn't a difficult feat to accomplish. He found most people were shorter than him, save for those who were of professional athlete stock.

He looked down at her kindly face and offered the same warm smile he'd given to dozens of people he'd eventually killed. There was no way for Philipe's mother to know that the man before her was a viper in sheep's clothing.

"Yes?" she greeted him in an irritated voice. Her accent teetered precipitously on the edge of exotic and annoying.

"Hello. I'm terribly sorry to bother you. My name is Jordan Bradley. I work for MI5." He flashed a fake badge that looked real enough to probably fool someone who really was an MI5 agent. "We are looking for your son, Philipe, in connection with something that happened earlier today in London."

"Philipe?" she asked. Her face flushed as worry filled her mind. "What has he done?"

"Nothing," Jordan said. "Not that we know of. We received word that he was helping with an investigation of some recent cybercrimes.

He disappeared earlier this morning. We aren't sure what happened to him, but we thought he might have come here. It seems there are some bad people trying to find him, and this place would make a logical spot to lie low for a while. Is your son here? Or have you heard from him?"

A drop of rain struck his shoulder and splattered into dozens of micro droplets, some of which rolled down the side of his neck. If Jordan noticed, he didn't show it. He'd been trained to not let the elements get to him. Much like the Marines at Parris Island and the sand fleas that nip at their skin on hot summer days, Jordan had endured similar rigors that rendered him nearly invulnerable to natural distractions. A drop of rain was no more than a cool breeze through his hair.

Philipe's mother looked up into his cold eyes and searched for the truth. She may have been an ordinary person with no formal training in psychology or reading body language, but age was a better teacher than even the highest-ranking universities. She narrowed her eyes, continuing her probe for any sign of deceit, but she found nothing, and that was what concerned her the most.

"You're a liar," she spat.

"Excuse me?" he said with a nonchalant laugh. His reaction was meant to disarm her, but he could tell within seconds that it didn't work.

"You are not who you claim to be," she declared. "I'm sorry, but there is no one named Philipe here."

She swung the door to close it, but Jordan put up his hand and caught the door with his palm.

The woman gave him an angry look, the kind that said "how dare you" without having to say a word.

"Ma'am, I'm just trying to locate your son. We don't want anything to happen to him. His safety is my primary concern, and at the moment, it's my job. Please, may I come in?"

He glanced over his shoulder at the SUVs more out of show than anything else. He hoped the official-looking vehicles would be enough to sway her suspicions, but as he turned back to face the woman he realized that wasn't going to happen. She still pressed the door firmly against his palm. It wasn't much force, though it was likely all she could muster. To him, it may as well have been a child attempting to prevent his entry.

"Grandmama," came a child's voice. "Is everything okay?"

Jordan tilted his head at an angle until he could see the girl standing atop the landing on the second floor. Her frail body was shrouded in baggy pajama pants and a white T-shirt with a big cartoon elephant in the center.

"*Oui*," the older woman said. "Go back to your room. This man was just looking for someone."

"Who?" the girl asked.

"Your father," Jordan said, "have you spoken with him recently?"

"Please leave," the grandmother said in the sternest voice she could gather. "You're not welcome here. Now go before I call the police."

"Didn't you hear me, ma'am? I thought I made it clear when you opened the door that I *am* the police."

The woman paused for a moment and then pushed the door harder. She leaned her shoulder into it and used every ounce of weight she could, but it wasn't enough, not for a strong man like Jordan.

He taunted her for a moment, holding the door in place with nothing more than his right arm and a little muscle tension.

"Call the police, Theresa!" the woman shouted in French, but Jordan understood them perfectly.

"There is no need to do that, Theresa," Jordan countered.

The girl had already spun away. His words caused her to pause at the top of the steps, but she didn't turn back toward him.

"I'm just here to make sure your father is okay," Jordan said. "Now, if you want, go call the police. But it will only waste their time, and they're overworked as it is. It will take them forever to get here, and for what? For them to see that I am who I say I am?"

He stared up at the girl, her back still turned.

"Just...come down, and we'll talk about this. I just want to make sure your father is safe. Okay?"

"Theresa! Don't listen to him. He's a liar! Call the police!"

Jordan took a deep, irritated breath. He was done with this woman. He'd tried to deal nicely with her, and would probably have let her live if she'd been even slightly amicable. But she wasn't. She chose to cause trouble, and that choice would cost her, her life.

Jordan shoved the door back hard enough that the inner edge struck the older woman in the head.

Her vision blurred, and she stumbled backward in a daze, her grip on the door lost. She tripped on a pair of slippers sitting near the entryway and fell on her backside, almost striking the back of her skull on a bookshelf built into the wall.

"Grandmama!" Theresa screeched.

The young girl moved toward the stairs, perhaps thinking she needed to rush to her grandmother's aide, but then thought better of it, recalling the last order the older woman had given.

Theresa jolted toward one of the upstairs bedrooms and disappeared from sight. Jordan's lips creased slightly at the thrill of the hunt. It wouldn't be as fun as some he'd experienced, but it made things interesting. This one was cute. The young girl thinking she could find safety in her room or on the phone with the cops was almost adorable, except that it made things inconvenient.

Jordan didn't shy away from a challenge—he enjoyed it. He embraced difficulties because he knew they would often make him better at everything he did, but this one wasn't like that. The girl running to perceived safety would accomplish nothing, which is why he was both amused and annoyed.

He climbed the stairs like a serial killer in a movie: deliberate, steady, focused. His wet boots pounded on each step, a deep metronome signaling the young girl's impending doom.

"Hello? Hello? Someone answer!" Her panicked voice came from behind a closed door on the right side of the narrow upstairs hallway.

She was already on the phone, but it wouldn't do any good. The cops couldn't help her. They wouldn't arrive in time; if they showed up at all. And they wouldn't.

He arrived at the door and paused. Then kicked it open.

The flimsy bolt did little to resist his powerful leg muscles, and the frame splintered into chunks of jagged wood.

The girl screamed at the sudden explosion of the door bursting open and the sight of the man in the corridor beyond. Jordan's thin smile made him look like a deranged clown—without the makeup. It was a terrifying visage to the young girl.

"The police can't help you," he said as he stepped into the room. "Put the phone down."

She swallowed hard and shook her head violently back and forth.

"Fine. Then I guess we do this the hard way."

"Katros is dead," Vincent said. The flurry of activity in the cabin dwindled to the cold silence of a morgue.

"What?" Philipe asked from behind a laptop in the third row.

"Katros," Vincent repeated. "They found his body on the shore of the Thames a few hours ago."

"You're sure?"

"Yeah. I'm sure."

"Katros?" Zeke asked, looking up from the floor for the first time in twenty minutes. He was exhausted, just like everyone else, but sitting there with his hands between his legs and nothing to do only made the fatigue worse.

"He was one of the hackers I thought could have given us information on Perses. Remember?" Philipe answered.

"Friend of yours?" Freeman asked from the front passenger seat.

Jessica had made it clear before they left Vincent's apartment that the only one she trusted to ride shotgun was Freeman.

"Friend is a loose term," Vincent answered for his friend. "Katros was a good hacker, but he wasn't very ethical."

"Sounds like a contradiction in terms," Zeke commented.

"I'm sure it does to you." Vincent eyed him with disdain. "To outsiders, people who don't understand, all hackers are considered criminals."

"Pretty much."

Vincent snorted. "Exactly. You don't realize there are lots of us out there who aren't thieves trying to ruin people's lives or steal their identities. Some of us try to make things better, even the playing field for those who never had a chance."

"He's telling the truth," Philipe added. "There are some of us who live by a code of honor."

"Playing pranks on the banking system or other important pieces of digital infrastructure isn't innocent," Phoenix said. "It affects people. People like your mother, your daughter."

Philipe considered the statement and searched his mind for a response. He'd heard similar arguments before but never at such a personal level.

Phoenix saw his opening and continued. "Imagine your mother going to the bank to get some money to buy groceries. Or worse, she's at the supermarket with a pile of groceries and gets to the register, where she can't use her debit card because the system is down. Or maybe she couldn't even use cash because the store's computers are down."

The Frenchman nodded. "I suppose you're correct. I never really considered it that way before, that it could affect the people in my own life."

"Don't take it so personally," Vincent refuted. "Zeus here is a good guy. I doubt anything he's done has ruined anyone's day at the market. Most of what he does is an attempt to raise awareness for areas of need, like the environment or the poverty epidemic that seems to be sweeping the world. You only did the one prank, Zee. I wouldn't worry about it."

"I know. But they're right. Even one is too many. You make a good point, Agent Underwood. I will remember that."

The car became silent again as Jessica turned left down the narrow country road. She pulled off to the side where the shoulder widened toward a grassy ditch.

"What are you doing?" Philipe asked. "The house is just around the bend."

"I know," Jessica said, glancing to the back of the vehicle. "But when we get there, we may encounter trouble."

"Trouble?" Vincent asked. "What do you mean, trouble?"

"She means there might be some hired goons there waiting to kill us," Zeke said casually.

"Wait. Seriously?"

Zeke chuckled. "Yeah, what kind of trouble did you think she meant? Blocked plumbing? A kitchen fire? A lawnmower gone sentient?"

"*Maximum Overdrive*," Phoenix said. "That's a deep cut."

Zeke smiled at his partner. "Yeah. I knew you'd catch the movie reference."

"Shut up. Can you two just shut up for one second?" Jessica's frustration radiated from red cheeks and pleading eyes. "This is serious."

"Well, no kidding, lady. I have no intention of getting shot at. And if you expect me to do some shooting, you got the wrong guy." Vincent crossed his arms, the display made more dramatic in the pale glow of his laptop monitor.

"Really?" Freeman asked. "You don't have a Thompson hidden under that suit somewhere?"

"Oh, you're hilarious, mate. Keep 'em coming." Vincent waved his fingers, begging the roast to continue.

"All of you. Shut up." Jessica was over it. "Seriously. This is a life-and-death situation, and it feels like the only one taking it seriously is Philipe, who just happens to have a pretty big investment at stake. This is his daughter we're talking about. So please, pretty please, be ready in case we run into trouble."

Zeke and Phoenix nodded and reached for their weapons. The move was instinctive, a subtle check just to reassure themselves the guns were there, even though they could feel the bulk against their hips.

"Yes, ma'am," Zeke said and raised a finger to tip a cap that wasn't on his head. "We'll be ready."

She didn't seem convinced but stepped on the gas and steered the SUV back onto the narrow road.

The pavement was cracked along both sides near the shoulders, and potholes riddled the main portion of the thoroughfare. Jessica imagined the road had been neglected for decades, only used by the occasional farmer who drove an old, beat-up pickup truck or possibly did things the old-school way with a horse-drawn buggy or wagon. She wasn't sure if the latter was used in this part of the country, but it certainly would have fit in with the surroundings.

She guided the vehicle around the next curve. The road was shrouded in thick bushes lining both sides. Short, squatty trees dotted the meadows beyond, only vaguely illuminated by the head-lights of the SUV.

When they came around the apex of the turn, lights appeared up ahead. They emanated from the windows of a small stone cottage on the right. A rock wall wrapped around the property. As the SUV neared the home, the group could see that the lights were on in the kitchen and upstairs.

Jessica let out a short, inaudible sigh of relief when she realized there were no other vehicles parked in front of the house. She didn't say anything, partly because she hadn't known what to expect. She had also considered the killers might have arrived first.

She stopped the SUV in front of a pathway leading to the front door and switched off the ignition.

"Looks like we're in the clear," she said.

Zeke and Phoenix glanced at each other but said nothing. Their hands remained close to the weapons at their hips. They opened the doors and stepped out into the cool, damp evening.

The stars twinkled between intermittent clouds that sprayed across the sky in small clusters. The moon hung over a collection of hills to the east where lights from the city of Cambridge filled in the darkness with a permanent, pale glow.

Jessica climbed out of the car and then ducked her head back in as the two in the back with the laptops were about to get out.

"Vincent, you stay here," she said, pointing a finger at him.

"What?"

"Stay here. I need someone to stay with the vehicle. Freeman, you're here, too."

"Why me?"

"Because the only person I'm taking in there is Philipe. I'm thinking it might scare his daughter if a bunch of strangers shows up and walks into their house unannounced."

"What about us?" Phoenix asked, jerking a thumb at his partner.

"You two go around back and make sure this isn't an ambush. If there is anyone waiting on us, they'll have covered the rear exit. Clear the area and then return to the SUV to wait with the others."

"Yes, ma'am." Phoenix gave a nod and then took off along the outside of the rock wall.

Zeke waited a moment, as if expecting some thanks, then followed his partner.

The two stayed low as they skirted the edge of the property, keeping their heads down so no one in the house would be spooked at the sight of them. Then again, if there really was someone covering the back door, keeping a low profile could save their lives.

They made their way to the back easterly corner and then scanned the rear portion of the wall to see if there was a way in. Behind the wall, a narrow patch of grass separated the residence from a field of wheat that, from the height of it, seemed nearly ready for harvest. A dark hill rose straight ahead. The surface was devoid of rock outcroppings or trees but marked instead with a gently waving patch of tall grass.

"Wheat fields," Zeke whispered, motioning to the field to the right and the one on the hill.

"Actually," Phoenix hissed, "the one to the right is wheat, but the one on the hill is barley."

"What?"

"They grow lots of different grains in this part of the country. Potatoes and carrots, too. But that field up there isn't wheat; it's barley."

"Why in the world do you know that? And why do you think it's imperative to point that out at this moment in time when we're trying to sneak into this backyard?"

Phoenix shrugged. "You were wrong. I thought it important to correct you."

"You're a mess. You know that, right?"

Phoenix snuffed a laugh. "You and me both, Brother. Come on. I see a gate up ahead."

"What, you think we're going to just announce our presence by going through some creaky old gate?"

"Well, what do you want to do?"

"I was thinking we vault over the wall. That way, if there's anyone on the other side, we catch them by surprise." Zeke almost looked proud of his idea.

"If there's someone on the other side of the wall, they can probably hear your entire plan right now."

The two men fell silent and waited for a good minute. When nothing happened, Zeke went on. "I'm going to go over to the other corner. You take this one, and when I give the signal, go over the top."

"Fine. What's the signal?"

"I'll wave my finger like this and then point to the wall." He twirled his finger around and then made the gesture.

"Okay. I still think this is stupid."

"So is getting dead, Phoenix. Watch for the signal."

Phoenix grumbled something under his breath but gave a nod.

Zeke crouched low and made his way toward the other corner of the wall. He was halfway to the gate when he tripped over a rock and went sprawling face-first into the mud.

It was all Phoenix could do to keep from laughing out loud at his friend's clumsy misfortune.

Zeke pressed his palms into the wet earth and pushed himself up. His face was covered in mud, and his shirt didn't look much better. He blinked away the grime and wiped his face a couple of times with the bottom of his shirt. Then he continued on, making his way toward the far corner.

He was mere feet away from his destination when a man's voice broke through the silence.

"Oy! What are you doing back there?"

Phoenix blinked slowly. They were in trouble.

16

CAMBRIDGE

J essica stopped at the front door and waited for Philipe to knock. His keys, his phone, everything had been left at the Interpol facility when he escaped with his two new...accomplices.

She shuddered at the thought. What were those two idiots thinking? That they would just waltz into a secure Interpol black site and flash their badges around? She had to fight off the urge to smile at their moxie—it was a pretty gutsy move. But that didn't mean it was right. They took a big gamble, and it could have cost them their lives. Then again, if they hadn't, Philipe might be dead right now, or in the hands of some mysterious villain who would force him to unleash a virus so dangerous it could cripple civilization. They'd gone with a hunch, and as wrong as that was, she was glad they did it; though she still didn't quite understand how. The only explanation she could come up with was that their security clearance was still active.

She made a mental note to have that corrected when she got back to HQ. There was clearly some delay in the chain of command. Part of her wondered if Zeke and Phoenix knew that.

The door cracked open an inch and then stopped. Philipe and

Jessica cast concerned sidelong glances at each other as she drew her weapon, ready for trouble.

Philipe swallowed hard and stepped forward, nudging the door with his right hand.

Jessica waited as the door swung free. She lowered her weapon as the face waiting on the other side of the door was an older woman.

"Mama?" Philipe asked. Then he saw the knot on her head, one that wasn't dissimilar to the one on his own forehead. "What happened? Are you okay?"

Tears welled in the woman's eyes. "I'm sorry, Philipe. I'm so, so sorry. I tried."

"Sorry? For what? What happened? Where's Theresa?"

"She's right here, Zeus." The man's sinister voice sent a chill through the room.

Jessica immediately twisted, raising her weapon and training it on the source of the voice.

A fire crackled in the stone hearth to the man's right. His hand was on the shoulder of the young girl positioned between them as a human shield. He held a pistol in his other hand, propped on her shoulder and pointed casually at her head.

"Don't you dare hurt her!" Philipe shouted.

"Philipe, step back," Jessica warned. "Let me handle this."

"No, you won't," the gunman said. "You're going to put down that weapon and step into the house. Then we're going to have a little talk."

Jessica hesitated to obey.

"Look, you can do what I say, or I kill the girl right now, which will not get anyone what they want. I shoot her, you try to shoot me— unlikely—and then my men cut you down."

Men? What men?

Jessica's eyes stayed locked on the villain, but in her mind she knew they'd been way too careless when they approached the house. She wondered if Zeke and Phoenix were positioned out back, and if so, had they stumbled onto any of these men the blond stranger was talking about?

"I can see you're thinking it over," the man said. "Please, don't make me do the whole countdown thing. It's contrived, and quite frankly, I don't have the patience. So, put down your gun, or I kill the girl right now. Your choice."

"Do what he says!" Philipe shouted. "Do it or he'll kill her!"

The Frenchman faced Jessica with pleading, tear-filled eyes and a face drawn long with anguish.

"Fine," Jessica relented. She removed one hand from her weapon and held it up. "I'm putting the weapon down now. Okay? Just like you asked. When I do, you need to let the girl go."

The gunman cracked a grin and offered one laugh in response. "No," he said plainly.

"No? You have to give me something, man. I'm putting down the only thing keeping all of this in balance."

"Very well," the man said. "I'm holding all the cards anyway. If you try anything, say anything I don't like, I kill the girl and both of you at the same time."

"If you hurt her, I swear," Philipe sneered. The bravado carried no weight at all. He wasn't a threat, not physically. While Philipe was brilliant with computers and in fair shape, his physique and demeanor hardly struck fear into the hearts of would-be combatants.

"Save it," the blond said. "Your friend here was just about to put down her gun.

Philipe turned to Jessica again and begged her to put the weapon on the floor.

"Fine," she said. Then she bent at her waist, slowly lowering her hands to her feet. Then she let go of the pistol. It hit the hardwood floor with a gentle thud. She stood erect again and stared at the gunman with her hands up, palms facing him.

"That's better," he said. "Please, come in and close the door."

Philipe took the first step toward his daughter. Jessica eased the door shut and then followed.

The two stopped on the edge of a burgundy area rug. In its center stood an old wooden coffee table. The sofa to their left appeared to be an antique. Philipe recalled the day he bought it at an antique store, along with the coffee table and the two other chairs in the living room. Beyond the sitting area, the kitchen was similarly decorated in old, farmhouse chic-style cabinets and barstools. The white cabinet façades were detailed with dark brown accents and matching dark metal hardware.

Through the kitchen, a small dining area was next to a series of windows that wrapped around the table in a hexagon shape. The windows gave a view out into the expansive backyard and the hills and farms beyond.

"Sit," the gunman said. He wagged his weapon at the couch.

Philipe was relieved that he wasn't aiming the gun at his girl anymore.

Jessica sat down nearest the gunman, and Philipe took a spot close to her.

"You try to run, she dies, then you die. I have men surrounding this entire property." He could see the doubt in their eyes, so added, "We figured we might have company, so I had my men move the vehicles around to the side to avoid detection. It seems our little trap was perfectly executed."

Philipe's nostrils flared, and his eyes blazed with an inferno that would have made the Great Chicago Fire look like a slow flame.

"Let her go," he sneered.

"Oh. Yes, of course. My mistake." The blond man took his hand off Theresa and nudged her forward.

She dove toward her father and wrapped her arms around him. The tears that had been momentarily stemmed broke free again and flowed down her cheeks.

Philipe also cried, but he let the relief of having his daughter safely in his arms overwhelm his concern.

"What a touching family reunion," the gunman said.

"What do you want?" Jessica asked, venom dripping from her lips.

"You know what I want, Director. And so does Philipe here, or Zeus as he's better known in the hacking community. We want the virus. More importantly, *he* wants it."

"He?" Jessica asked.

"Please. You think I'm doing this for me? I'm a hired gun, same as you, Director. I just get the job done and go on my way. None of this is personal."

"You're nothing like me," she seethed. "You're a criminal. Probably a murderer."

"I disagree. You get paid to take out people you deem bad, yes? You work for a government agency, but many of your tactics are the same as mine. We both carry weapons, have likely both killed people —I know I have—and all for someone above us who tells us what to do. We are their puppets, and for that we are well paid." He paused for a moment. "Pardon, I'm well paid. You work for the United States government, so it's anyone's guess if you make good money. I'd say probably not, based on what I've heard."

"I make a living. And I can sleep at night knowing that I didn't threaten children or innocent people."

"Innocent?" he asked. "That's a funny way of putting it. Who amongst us is truly innocent? I say none. Not even this young girl." He motioned to Theresa. "We've all sinned in our own ways, Director. I know you certainly have."

The accusation sent Jessica into a doldrum of silent contemplation for a moment.

"I'm certain you already know who I am, Director; otherwise, it would seem they picked the wrong person for your job. But I don't know if you've told your friend Zeus here who I am."

Philipe peered at the man angrily as he continued to hold his daughter tight.

"My name is Jordan Bradley. Yes, I'm a contractor. Sometimes I have to...well, you know, eliminate people. Sometimes I bring them in. Depends on what the employer wants. In this case, Zeus, you know exactly what he wants."

"I can't give it to him!" Philipe exclaimed.

"You don't have a choice, Philipe," Jordan said. He hoped using the man's real name would help strike a chord. "Let me tell you about the man I work for now."

He sidestepped to the nearest chair next to an end table and eased into it, sitting on the edge while he let his hands hang over his knees, the right still clutching the gun, albeit loosely. The way he was positioning himself made it seem like Jordan was attempting to disarm the others' concerns, but that was an exercise in futility. They weren't going to let go of their fear, not until they were safely far away from all of this.

"I know you probably tried to find information on him when he first approached you," Jordan began. "Likely, you came up with the same intel as me, which wasn't much."

Philipe arched an eyebrow, his curiosity piqued, though he still trembled with an avalanche of emotions.

"I can see I've caught your interest. My employer is a ghost, Philipe. I come from a world full of ghosts. Sometimes, that's what they called us in the special ops divisions. There have been books written about men like me, referring to us as ghosts. I'm telling you something right now, and I'm being truthful when I say, I am nothing like this man. I'm sure that Director Benson here," he motioned to Jessica, "could easily dig up information on me. She may even have a dossier back in her office. Men like me are easy to find, by comparison, to the man I work for."

"Why are you telling us all of this?" Philipe asked. "You're going to kill us anyway."

"Actually," Jordan said. "That's up to you."

Philipe shrank back, he didn't like the way their captor had made that statement. It gave away a hint at what was probably a huge catch to the forthcoming deal.

"Up to me?"

"Yes. If you come with us willingly, here's what will happen: Two of my men will stay here with your daughter and with Director Benson here. Once you have completed the task for my employer, I will call my men and order them to leave. Your daughter and Director Benson get to live. No harm will come to them."

"You lie," Philipe spat.

Jordan dismissed the accusation with a snort. "I may be a lot of things, Philipe. I'm certainly a killer, cold-blooded at times. I've done things that would make an inmate on death row cringe. I don't deny that. But I don't lie."

"A killer with a moral compass," Jessica groused.

Jordan shrugged and tilted his head to the left for a second. "Call it principle. We all have them, Director. But I'm not lying. I will make sure your daughter is safe, and you, too, Jessica." He used her first name to show off a little more.

"And if I don't?" Philipe grumbled.

"Do you really have to ask? I think you know what will happen, and honestly, I would prefer not to discuss it in front of your daughter. It might distress her."

The girl looked over her shoulder at the man. Her face was flushed red, and her eyes were swollen from sobbing. Despite all that, she managed an angry glare that would have sent chills through a dragon.

"Look," Jordan said finally, "you seem like a nice guy. I can't say what the boss will do once you've done your job, I truly can't. Maybe he will let you live. Maybe he brings you on as an employee, like me. Think of that. We would be coworkers."

"You can shove that idea right up your—"

"Easy," Jordan cut him off. "Your daughter is right here, after all. Let's keep this civilized. I was doing my best to be. You should as well, for her sake."

Every fiber of Philipe's being wanted to leap across the room and rip the man's head off, but he knew he possessed neither the strength nor the know-how to do something like that. Besides, Jordan would cut him down in a flash of bullets. Philipe believed his fate was sealed despite the pandering offer of employment that Jordan made. Philipe was a dead man walking. The only question was how and when. He could not, however, die right now. Not in front of his daughter.

"I know you already have the virus ready," Jordan said. "Don't bother asking how I know that. Let's just say, we've been watching you for a while now. The point is, we know. So, it will be easy for you to come with me to see my employer, drop the virus where he wants it, and then see what happens. I know you have no reason to trust me on this, but you also don't have a choice."

Philipe thought about it for a long moment. His fingers continued to squeeze his daughter's hand as he held her in a tight hug. He drew a deep breath and exhaled slowly. The gesture overflowed with regret, but Philipe had no other choice.

"I will come with you. And I expect you to keep your word. No harm must come to her."

"None will, Philipe. You have my word."

17

CAMBRIDGE

"Can you please turn the air on?" Vincent asked from the third row. "It's burning up in here." He tugged at his collar and cricked his neck in both directions, as if that would somehow dispel the heat in the vehicle.

"No. I can't turn the air on," Freeman blathered. "They told us to sit tight, and that's what we're going to do."

"What does that have to do with being comfortable?"

Freeman sighed. He'd already tired of being stuck in the car with this guy. The conversation had gone from bad to worse, starting with Vincent's constant proselytizing about how swing music was due for another comeback, and when it did, he'd be ready.

"Because we're trying not to attract attention," Freeman said. "If we turn the engine on, the lights will come on. The lights go on; we attract attention."

Vincent thought for a second and then shrugged. "So, turn the lights off."

"It will also be loud. It's so quiet here, the noise would be heard for miles. Besides, if you're hot, why don't you just take off that ridiculous suit jacket? I can't believe we're even having this conversation with you wearing that stupid thing the entire time." He turned back around to face the front of the car and resumed his watch on the farmhouse.

"What did you just say to me?" Vincent sneered.

"I said if you're hot, you should just take off your jacket."

"No," Vincent's head turned slowly back and forth. "That's not what you said. You said it was ridiculous."

"And stupid," Freeman said.

"Yeah. Stupid."

"Look. I'm sorry. Can we just focus on the job at hand?"

"Which is what? Sitting here broiling?"

"You know what? Fine. I will turn on the engine and the air conditioning if it will shut you up."

"Thank you," Vincent said. "Although I'm still mad at you. Wouldn't kill you to be a little nicer."

Freeman rolled his eyes. "Really?"

"Well, yeah." The man paused for a moment, reflecting on memories of long ago. "I used to get picked on as a kid. The other kids would make fun of the way I looked. So, I thought to myself, *Who were the toughest guys in history?* I came up with some mobsters from the States, you know, real tough guys. It worked out because I played the trumpet and really enjoyed swing music. For a long time, I thought I was the only one. Then the 1990s hit, and it made a huge comeback for a year or two. It was the first time in my entire life that I fit in, that I was one of the cool people."

Freeman stared back at the guy and then shook his head. "That was lame. You know that, right?"

Vincent swore at him and then laughed. "Ah, it was worth a try." He waved a dismissive hand. "Truth is, I like my style. And if you don't like it, that's your problem. I don't have a problem with knocking a fellow out, though, if they make fun. See? So, keep at it, and we'll find out where that leads. My prediction is bloody nose and a short nap for you."

Freeman nodded, pressing his lips together at the threat. "Okay, then."

He turned the key, and the engine revved to life. Cool air poured out of the vents. Freeman tilted them toward the back despite there already being vents near the rear seats. It was more to keep the chilly air off his skin than to help Vincent cool off faster. Before long, Freeman was shivering, but he didn't say anything. Instead, he used the cold to keep his senses on high alert.

"What do you think is going on in there?" Freeman asked absently.

Vincent continued staring at his screen. "I'm sure I don't know. Probably packing up some clothes, or maybe supplies."

"Yeah, I guess," Freeman said, unconvinced. "They've been in there a while, though."

"It's been ten minutes, mate. Give it a rest. They'll be back in a jiff."

"Only ten? It feels like they've been gone an hour."

Vincent rolled his eyes. "That's because you're worried. Stop worrying. They have it under control. That woman, your director or whatever, she doesn't strike me as the bad-decisions type. She knows what she's doing."

Freeman thought he detected a hint of admiration in the man's voice.

"She's smart, that's for sure," Freeman agreed.

"And gorgeous. What's the matter with you three, anyway? None of you tried going after that?"

"She's our boss, first of all. And second, try being a little more respectful. Okay?"

"Oh," Vincent said, taking a few seconds to get the word out. "I see. You're interested, but you don't have the guts to make a move."

"No. That's not it."

"Sure it is."

"No, I'm telling you it's not."

"Oh okay. Into guys then, are ya?"

"What?" Freeman scowled and took his eyes off the house for a moment. He turned around and glared at the hacker, who was intensely focused on his laptop's monitor. "No, I'm not. Not that I judge that lifestyle. I'm just...No, you are infuriating. You know that, right?"

"Yep," Vincent agreed. He offered a sly grin, still avoiding eye contact.

Freeman grunted and twisted around again to face forward. He watched the front door of the house for another few seconds. In the silence of the vehicle's cabin, the stream of air flowing from the vents became a distraction, causing him to focus solely on how cold he was.

He looked at the internal temperature of the SUV, then reached over and adjusted it so that at least his little area would be slightly warmer than the rest of the car.

"Oy. What did you just do?"

"Climate-zone technology. I'm cold. Just adjusting my zone. If that's okay with you. Don't worry. Your area will still be like the North Pole."

Vincent smirked again. He knew he was pressing all of Freeman's buttons, and it was the only thing that seemed entertaining at this point.

Then his laptop pinged, and his eyes opened wide. "Got him," he said. It was the first time Vincent sounded excited about anything.

"Got who?"

Vincent looked up, his eyes bright in the white glow of the screen. "Marilyn."

Freeman blinked for a moment, bewildered as to who he could possibly mean. "Who's Marilyn?"

Vincent rolled his head around in a wide circle and then sighed. "Seriously, mate? The whole reason I've been on this thing for the entire night is so we can track down the one hacker who can help us."

"You mean, you and Philipe can't do it?"

"Okay, you don't have to be like that. We're good at what we do. But Marilyn..." He let out a whistle. "She's something different, my friend."

"All right, I'll bite. What's she going to help us do?"

"If anyone is planning something big in the hacker world, she'll know about it. Marilyn keeps tabs on everything in the digital landscape."

"Sounds like you admire her."

"I respect her," Vincent corrected. Then: "And maybe she's pretty. Still, that doesn't change anything. If anyone can help us, it's her."

"You don't think this guy who came after Philipe is going to see what she can do for him?"

It was a good question and one Vincent had rattling around in his brain since the onset of his search for the mysterious woman.

"It's possible," Vincent admitted. "All the more reason we need to get to her first. Although I'd say she's exponentially tougher to find than any of us."

"How did you find her?"

"Email."

Freeman's eyebrows lowered, sending lines across his forehead. "What?"

"She uses several emails, dozens of them. And only a handful of people have access to the ones she uses for communication. She almost never looks at them, and if she does, she rarely responds to requests."

"Okay...so why would she respond to you?"

"Because she likes me," Vincent said.

"Oh, so you do have a thing for her."

"That's neither here nor there. Did we spend a romantic weekend off the coast of Croatia a few years ago? Maybe. That's neither here nor there. The point is...she's agreed to meet with us for ten minutes."

Freeman looked skeptical. "Only ten minutes? What's with the time slot?"

"She's very busy," Vincent said.

Freeman detected a hint of boyishness, or was that regret?

"Okay, fine. We go meet this Marilyn person, and she helps us locate Perses so we can take down whatever he has planned. Where is she?"

The door to the farmhouse burst open and a man emerged forcing Philipe ahead of him at gunpoint.

Vincent noticed the movement first and pointed through the windshield. "Um, Gary, I don't think the place was empty when we arrived."

Freeman turned and stared through the glass.

A blond man held a gun at Philipe's lower back as they marched toward the road. A bright glow appeared on the road ahead, and a second later, two headlights appeared. Then two more emerged from the darkness just behind the other.

The SUV skidded to a stop in front of the farmhouse. The driver climbed out and opened the back door then helped shove Philipe in. The blond climbed in after him and slammed the door shut. The second the driver was behind the wheel, he gunned the engine, and the SUV shot past and back into the night.

The two men ducked down to avoid detection then looked back at the SUV as it disappeared around the turn.

"What was that?" Vincent asked.

"Looks like we have trouble."

"Who were those guys?"

"I'm guessing they work for Perses. But he's the one in charge. I doubt he was with the hit squad that came after me. Not sure about the driver, but it's likely he was with them."

"And what about those two?" Vincent asked, pointing through the windshield.

Two men climbed out of the remaining SUV. They both carried multiple firearms, including submachine guns slung over their shoulders and pistols in their hands.

"That doesn't look good," Freeman said.

"What are they doing?"

"Looks like the blond guy—the one I figure is the leader—doesn't have the stomach to kill our friends."

The gunmen passed through the gate in the wall and moved methodically toward the entrance to the cottage.

"We have to do something," Vincent said.

"I know."

Freeman thought fast. Then it hit him. The car was already running. He knew what he had to do.

18

CAMBRIDGE

Phoenix watched as the patrol guard stepped toward him with just a waist-high rock wall separating them.

"Stand up so I can see you. What are you doing back there?" the guard repeated.

Zeke deftly tucked his pistol in the back of his pants and stood up, wavering slightly.

"What's wrong with you?" the guard asked.

"I'm sorry," Zeke said in a terrible English accent. Fortunately, he was slurring, so it covered up his inability to mimic the locals. "Have you...seen my car around here? I know I left it here somewhere." He added a hiccup for good measure, which was probably overkill, but at this point Zeke figured he was probably screwed anyway.

"What? Your car?"

"Yeah, mate. I left...I left it here somewhere to go into the pub and have a drink."

"Your car? Here? For a drink?"

"Whoa," Zeke said, flinging his hands around like a man possessed. "Did you hear that echo in here? Hold on a second. Let me see." He cupped his hands to his lips. "Hello?" he whispered, then listened with one hand over his ear. "Nope. Nothing. Maybe I shouldn't whisper. You think that's it?"

He stumbled toward the wall, and the guard pointed his weapon at Zeke's head. "Stop right there."

"Wow!" Zeke exclaimed. "Is that a gun? That is awesome. Are you some kind of cop? Because I don't know anyone here with a gun. I've seen one before, but not in a long time." His slurring was probably the only thing saving him from catching a bullet.

"Yes," the guard lied. "I'm a cop. And I was called in to investigate a disturbance. Seems there was some drunkard lurking about. I'd say I found him."

"Really? Where?" Zeke made a show of twisting his head around dramatically, as if he was searching for this drunken fool. "Let me help." Then he cocked his head to the side and squinted. "You sure don't look like a cop. Where's your uniform?"

"I'm undercover," the guard said in a condescending tone he was certain the trespasser wouldn't catch. "You say you went into the pub for a drink?"

"Yep. And I didn't drive, Occifer," he embellished. "Mainly because I can't find my car, but maybe you can help me."

"The nearest pub is a few miles from here, mate," the guard said.

"Hey, what are you doing, man?" Another voice entered the conversation from the other side of the wall.

Phoenix crouched lower for a moment as he heard the soft sound of boots against grass and damp earth nearing his position. Then the second patrol guard veered away, toward the ruckus. Phoenix risked a peek over the top of the wall and saw a second man, this one with an American accent, walking toward Zeke and the other guard.

The second guard had dark skin and a shaved head. His torso was easily twice as wide as Phoenix's. The guy was big enough to forklift a small car with his bare hands, and his black T-shirt looked like it was about to stretch to the point of disintegration from his bulging muscles.

"This moron is drunk. Says he's looking for his car. I think he wandered a little too far away from the pub."

"Pub? The closest pub is a few miles from here," the second guard said. "You're telling me that he stumbled all the way out here to the sticks from one of the pubs in town?"

The first guard rolled his shoulders. "That's what he said. You want me to kill him?"

The second stopped next to the wall, right beside the gate. He stared at Zeke, who was standing with his feet wide apart. He wobbled in place as if a swirling wind blew him back and forth.

Phoenix watched with wide eyes, trying to think of a plan. He drew nothing but blanks.

Think, man. Come on.

He didn't work well under pressure, hadn't since college. He hated procrastination for that very reason. Putting assignments off for later when he could get them done early made no sense.

Now was a moment Phoenix wished he were more skilled and able to act in these situations. He could take the two guards by surprise—they were clearly unaware of his presence. Even so, if Phoenix was able to take out the closest guard, the second would react instantly. That could be bad for Zeke if the guy chose to shoot him before defending himself.

Phoenix wiped that idea off the chalkboard and tried to think of something else as he watched the interaction between the guards.

"Well, what do you think we should do with him?" The first guard was sounding irritated. "Take him back to town?"

The American guard spat a laugh. "Are you off your rocker? No, we're not taking him back to town." He let out a slew of profanity, mostly directed at the idiocy of the question.

"Well, what then?" The first guard's annoyance had reached boiling point.

"I already told you," the American said, elongating each word. "Kill him."

"And then what? Where are we going to put the body?"

Phoenix felt sick to his stomach as the men casually discussed his partner's fate. For all his flaws, Zeke was a good guy, and the two men had become friends in their short time together. Now, they were a team, inseparable—except for the span of grass between them now, anyway.

Phoenix knew what he had to do. He would climb over the wall and call the only play he could muster. The nearest guard would be his primary target, and then he would try to take out the second. Phoenix was accurate enough with his weapon, though hardly an expert. Taking out even one of the guards would be difficult.

Still, it was his only play; he was out of time. The least he could do was get a little closer to minimize his chance of missing the targets.

Phoenix stayed low as he moved along the wall another ten feet before stopping at the sound of voices. He thought he saw Zeke notice him out of the corner of his eye, but he may have been imagining things.

"Gentlemen," Zeke said, interrupting the conversation of the two bickering guards. "May I make a suggestion?"

"No," the two said simultaneously.

Zeke leaned back at the hips in shock. He nearly fell over, and Phoenix hoped he would to give himself space for the imminent attack, but Zeke kept his balance by waving his arms around in a circle.

Once he was steady again, he pushed forward with his incursion of the discussion. "I just think your friend here has a point," Zeke slurred, motioning with an unsteady finger at the first guard. "There is no way you should kill that guy. I mean, what did he do to you? Huh?" This time, Zeke leaned forward and looked as if he might topple over onto his face and pass out, but again, he corrected and stayed upright. "And where would you put the body? Like he said, that sounds like a lot of work. I hope you two aren't expecting me to help, by the way. That would make me a successory...sexcessory...ax murdery..."

"Accessory, you moron!" the first guard shouted. "An accessory to murder."

"That's what I said." Zeke raised his finger to the sky as if trying to make his point to the heavens.

"Would you two shut up?" The American guard's voice boomed, and the other two instantly fell silent.

Zeke even looked as though he might sober up but then began to teeter in all directions.

"You're the one we're talking about, moron," the second guard said to Zeke. "You're the one we're going to kill." He raised his weapon and aimed it at the drunken man.

Phoenix had no more time. He had to act or his friend would die. He swallowed hard and accepted his fate, one that involved him being riddled with bullets and dying in a patch of grass in the middle of the English countryside.

"Now, hold on just a second," Zeke protested. "If you two would just let me pay you to take me back to my car, I'd be happy to do it. I got two suitcases of money in my trunk. You guys can have some of that?" He curled his lips into a goofy smile that matched the silliness in his wide eyes.

"What?" the first guard said. Then he turned to the second. "Wait a second. Hold your fire."

"He's lying," the American guard said.

"Who is?" Zeke asked.

"You, you idiot."

"Me? Why would I lie? And why do people keep calling me idiot and moron and—"

"I wonder." The second raised his gun again, tensing the trigger with his finger.

"Hold on, I said," the first guard ordered. "Let's hear him out. No sense in not getting a little extra bread and honey while we're here if it's not out of the way."

"Thirty seconds," the American guard said.

"Fine." The first turned back to Zeke. "What money? Why do you have suitcases of money?"

"Ah," Zeke said, raising his index finger again. "Are you two cops?" He lowered the finger and waved it at both of them, sweeping back and forth in a wide arch.

"What? No, we're not cops."

"Oh good. For a second there, I thought one of you told me you were cops."

Phoenix would have cracked a smile if the circumstances were less dangerous. His friend was playing these two the best he could. But that could only last for so long. He raised his weapon and propped it on the wall to keep it steady, then lined up the second guard in his pistol's sights. Then he leaned into the rock wall to brace himself. He would only get one chance at this.

"Like I was sayin'," Zeke went on, "if you're cops, you gotta tell me. Or this is entrapment."

"We're not cops," the first guard said.

"Twenty seconds," the second reminded in a sinister tone.

"What are we counting?" Zeke asked.

"He's going to kill you in twenty seconds," the first said in a begging voice.

"Oh. Well, that's rude. I suppose I should talk faster."

"Yes, please."

"Right. What was I saying?"

"You have money in your car? Suitcases? Yeah? Why do you have it?"

"Oh yeah," Zeke said. "I'm a heroin dealer. We only deal in cash. No checks or money orders, you two." He wagged a warning finger in front of them.

"That's it," the American guard said. He tightened his grip on the weapon, ready to kill.

"No, wait," the first insisted. "He's telling the truth. Heroin dealers only deal in cash."

The second rolled his eyes. "Of course they do. Everyone knows that. You can't pay for illegal narcotics with a debit card."

"Well, when did you become such an expert on narcotics, Frank?"

The American, apparently named Frank, turned the weapon from Zeke and lowered it slightly.

"It's common knowledge. I don't know who's dumber, you or this drunk guy. At least he has an excuse."

That was the window Phoenix had been waiting for. He didn't

want to risk taking a shot at the gunman while he had his weapon aimed at Zeke, but now that it was pointed away from his partner, Phoenix had his opportunity.

He pressed his shoulder into the jagged rock wall and tensed his finger on the trigger. Suddenly, he felt the top of the wall give way. Gravity pulled him toward the backyard amid a crumbling pile of rock. His elbow struck something hard and his trigger finger responded involuntarily, twitching twice as he tumbled head over heels before hitting the ground and rolling to a stop.

As Phoenix clumsily crashed through the wall and rolled forward, he didn't see what happened when he accidentally pulled the trigger.

Thirty-five feet away, the two bullets smacked into the American guard, one striking him in the right butt cheek. The other blasted through the back of his head. The second shot, the mortal one, sprayed red on the first guard's face, momentarily blinding him.

Zeke reached to his lower back and drew his weapon. He extended it toward the first guard and stalked toward him. "Don't move," Zeke commanded, suddenly sober and equally as suddenly, no longer an Englishman.

The first guard was wiping his comrade's blood off his face when he heard the order. He turned to see the drunk now holding a weapon and coming toward him.

"Wait a tick," the guard said.

Zeke stepped through the open gate and was about to tell the man to drop his gun when he tripped on a metal strip that ran across the ground. His trigger finger tensed, and the weapon discharged. The bullet had sailed wide to the right of the target, but the guard appeared startled. His eyes widened and he dove head first to dodge the bullet. He hit the ground and rolled to a stop, then didn't move again.

Zeke clambered to his feet and hurried to the body. He realized what had happened. His shot had indeed gone wide, and bounced off the wall before dying impotently somewhere on the floor. The guard, in his desperation to avoid being shot, dove clear of the round, but on his way to the floor, struck the hat of a garden gnome with his head.

The hard point punctured the man's temple only slightly. The blunt force did the rest, knocking him out cold.

Zeke nudged the guy's face with the tip of his boot and immediately regretted it as he noticed the obvious absence of life in the man's limp, unresponsive repose. He glanced over at the garden gnome and laughed. "Good thing the French love those weird statues."

"Good shootin' there, Tex," Phoenix said. He shook his head in disdain.

The unexpected comment startled Zeke, and he nearly jumped out of his pants as he spun around with the gun still in hand.

"Whoa," Phoenix said, hands up high with his own weapon gripped in the right. "It's me, buddy."

"Oh. Good," Zeke said. He looked over his friend's shoulder at the pile of rubble and then back at the bodies. "Not bad yourself. If I didn't know any better, I'd say you meant to do that."

"And yours was total skill? I saw you trip."

"Hey, what is this? A witch hunt? Come on. Let's get inside and get Jessica and Philipe out of there."

An abrupt series of muffled pops came from the front of the cottage. It was difficult to tell, but it sounded like suppressed gunfire.

Then a motor roared and was followed by two hard clangs from a crash, then the peal of tires screeching.

"What was that?" Phoenix asked, turning his head slowly to face his friend.

"I have no idea, but we'd better get inside."

19

CAMBRIDGE

The two agents rushed toward the back door. They reached the steps leading onto a wide landing that stretched into a patio. Zeke reached for the doorknob as the door burst open.

They involuntarily stepped back at the sight of another guard, this one towering over the two and holding a submachine gun leveled at their chests.

His icy blue eyes pierced Zeke and Phoenix, striking renewed fear in both of them. The man's dark hair and eyebrows made the eyes appear even more menacing.

He was about to squeeze the trigger and cut the two Americans in half when his body shuddered and a confused scowl cascaded down his face. The mountain of muscle dropped to his knees with a crack and fell onto his side. A steel kitchen knife protruded from the base of his skull.

Zeke and Phoenix turned their awed attention back to the door as Jessica emerged holding two more knives, one in each hand.

"Whoa! Nice!" Zeke exclaimed. Then he paused and looked around, assessing the situation. "What's going on?"

"They took Philipe," she said. Her tone echoed regret, pain, and fear.

"The girl?" Phoenix asked, hoping for something positive.

"She's still here."

"At least she's safe. What happened?"

"I'll explain later," Jessica said. "I heard a crash in front of the house. Or something like a crash. It happened right after we heard the gunshots out here. Glad to see you two came out on top."

There was a sarcastic tone in her voice. Or was there? Was it just a hint of jealousy because they were so lucky?

"Of course we did. Get the girl. We need to move...if it's not too late already."

The two men hurried into the house and found Theresa huddled deep in the couch. She was shaking and tears welled in her eyes.

"Theresa?" Zeke asked, holding out his hand. "My name is Zeke. This is my partner, Phoenix. We need to get you out of here to somewhere safe?"

She looked up, uncertain if she could trust the strange man.

"Sweetie, you have to trust me. Okay? I'm a friend of your dad."

Jessica stepped back into the room after a quick sweep of the kitchen and the adjoining hallway. "He's with us, honey. It's okay."

She extended her hand. Theresa looked at them both for a moment, still uncertain, then reluctantly reached out and placed her fingers in Jessica's palm.

"Atta girl," Zeke said. He turned and found Phoenix floating toward the front window.

"Um, Zeke?" Phoenix said. "Is that our SUV in the front yard?"

Zeke stepped closer and peered through the glass. "Yeah, it is. But why is it there?"

The partners burst out of the front door with pistols drawn. They caught a glimpse of Freeman sitting behind the wheel, his face glowing in the dim white light given off by the dashboard. His eyes were wide with surprise, fear, or both. Vincent was nowhere to be seen, but he'd been in the back before, so it was possible that's where he remained.

What was even more shocking were the two bodies splayed out on the grass with arms, necks, and legs bent in various awkward directions.

The gunmen didn't move, not even a flinch. One was facedown on the wet turf; the other was on his back, eyes staring lifelessly into the cloudy night sky.

The driver's side of the SUV was scratched and partially dented, but it seemed the vehicle was still in working condition.

Zeke and Phoenix followed the vehicle's path, tracing it back to where Freeman had deftly piloted it though a side gate, bursting through the wooden barricade and knocking down a portion of the rock wall on either side.

Jessica rushed out of the house and appeared next to the two men as they stared at the scene of death and destruction before them. She had both Philipe's mother and daughter with her.

"What did Freeman do?" she asked, seeing the man behind the wheel.

Freeman rolled down the window. "Come on!" he shouted. "They have Philipe!"

"We know," Zeke said as he stepped over one of the bodies. Then he turned, reached down, and plucked the submachine gun from the man's shoulder. "Better take that," he said to Phoenix. "May come in handy."

"Good call."

Jessica threw open the back door and ushered Theresa and her grandmother into the SUV.

Phoenix struggled to free the weapon from the second dead man's body, but he finally tugged it loose and found the strap covered in thick blood.

"Gross," he said with a scowl.

"Stop being such a sissy. Just unclip the strap and let's go."

Phoenix winced as he did his best not to touch the sticky liquid. He unclipped the first end of the strap and then the second, though it took way longer than it should have.

"Come on, man. They're getting away."

Phoenix dropped the strap onto the man's back and then followed behind his partner. "I didn't see you having to deal with a bloody strap. You should have let me have the clean one if it wasn't a problem for you."

"Yeah, maybe. But I enjoy watching you squirm."

"You're a—"

Freeman honked the horn, and it drowned out whatever choice word Phoenix had selected.

"Hurry!"

The two scrambled around the SUV and climbed in. Phoenix took the back seat while Zeke claimed the front.

In the back, the cabin was cramped with the new passengers, but there was just enough room for everyone.

"Who is this?" Philipe's mother asked, pointing at Vincent.

"Hello, I'm Vincent. A friend of your son. We're—"

"Work associates?" she asked dubiously.

"Yes, something like that."

She scanned him up and down before saying, "I like your outfit."

"Thank you," Vincent said with a condescending glance toward Freeman in the rearview mirror. "I'm glad to see someone in this world still has good taste."

Theresa shifted into the back seat near the hacker and stared at his clothes. "You're like a real-life cartoon."

"And we're back," Vincent sighed.

The doors shut, and before everyone was buckled in, Zeke ordered the driver to step on it.

Freeman already had it in reverse and stomped on the gas pedal. He expertly whipped the vehicle around, shifted into drive, and mashed the pedal again. The SUV shot through the gap in the wall, scraping the sides of the truck again, and slid out onto the road.

Philipe's mother stared at the destruction to her property, but said nothing; her forlorn look saying it all.

"They went this way?" Zeke asked.

"Yep."

"You're sure?"

"Pretty sure," Vincent chimed from the back. "They drove right by us."

"And they didn't spot you?"

"We were staying low. Didn't want them to see us."

"Oh," Zeke said. "I guess...that makes sense. Good job, you two."

Freeman touched the brakes and then pounded the gas again as he spun the steering wheel. The back end of the SUV whipped around. The rear tires dug into the pavement, tearing loose chunks of rock from the surface and spitting them backward.

The vehicle lurched forward and sped toward the town of Cambridge. The SUV climbed a short rise and then descended the other side. Fields of wheat and barley lined the road, along with thick stretches of shrubbery, but ahead there was no sign of the enemy's vehicle.

Freeman slowed and peered through the windshield. There were no headlights for miles ahead, and from this vantage point, they would have seen something.

"What are you doing?" Jessica said, louder than necessary. "Why are you stopping?"

"Because they're gone," Freeman said. He surprised himself at how loudly he'd answered and immediately regretted it. "They're gone," he added in a softer voice.

"So drive faster," she insisted.

"We don't know if they went this way," Freeman said. "They could have gone the other direction. If they were anywhere up ahead, we'd see them from here. Too much time has passed. They're long gone now."

An overwhelming pall of gloom settled into the vehicle.

"Where did those men take my daddy?" Theresa asked, the grief in her little voice cutting into the silence like a katana.

"We don't know, honey," Jessica said, reaching back to pat the girl's knee.

"There's only one person who can help us now," Vincent blurted.

Everyone turned to look at him. He was cramped in the back row with his laptop on his knees. The glow from the screen cast the same eerie white glow it had before, but now that light seemed to give the rest of the passengers the slightest glimmer of hope.

"Who's that?" Phoenix asked.

"Some woman he has a crush on," Freeman answered.

Everyone turned to face the driver and then looked back to Vincent.

"A woman you have a crush on?" Zeke asked.

"Thank you for that, Gary. I appreciate it." Vincent sighed. "Her name is Marilyn, and she's the most powerful, most connected hacker I know. If anything sinister is going on in the digital world, she knows about it."

"Sounds like you do have a crush on her."

"Here we go."

"Did she break your heart?" Phoenix asked.

"Or did you break hers?" Jessica wondered out loud.

"Very good. Can we please get moving? Last I checked, this girl's father was just taken by some bad people, and you lot are wondering about my dating life."

"Right," Freeman said and steered the truck back onto the road. "So, where are we going?"

"She runs a nightclub in North London. We can find her there. She said her security people will let us see her."

"Okay," Freeman said. "What's the name of the club?"

20

LONDON

The group stood outside the entrance to an old brick building with a gray wooden door. The only indicator that this was the correct place was the small image of a medieval knight on his steed carved into stone and placed above the doorway. That...and the muted deep bass pounding from somewhere inside.

"Seriously? It's called the Knight Club? That's what she called it? Doesn't seem very creative."

"I think it's clever," Phoenix argued.

"You would."

"What's that supposed to mean?"

"I don't think it's so bad," Freeman offered.

"You know what doesn't matter, guys?" Jessica interrupted. "The name of the friggin' club. Now can we please, for the love of all that is good and decent, get off the street and into the building so we can find this Marilyn person and get what we need?"

The three men glanced at each other, then their boss. Vincent stood off to the side, giggling.

They'd left Cambridge and driven south toward London, making a short detour into the small town of Harlow where Theresa and her grandmother were left with a friend, a woman about the same age as Theresa's grandmother.

Satisfied that they hadn't been followed and that Philipe's family would be safe, at least for the short term, the group returned to the road and continued toward North London.

"I don't like it," Jessica confessed. "It's after midnight. Nothing good ever happens after midnight."

"I thought it was two o'clock," Zeke arched an eyebrow at her.

"It's both. Come on. We need to stop hanging around out here on the street. People will notice."

Jessica stepped to the door and pulled it open. The muted sound of bass thumping inside immediately swelled as the door swung wide. She stepped to the side as a drunken reveler stumbled by. The young woman was scantily clad and pulled an equally drunken young man by the wrist.

The group watched in rapt curiosity as the two staggered to the side of the building where they began ravenously making out.

"At least someone will have a good night," Vincent quipped.

No sooner had the words escaped his lips than the young woman pushed the guy away and heaved violently, expelling the contents of her stomach into the alley. At the sight of it, the young man joined in, adding to the concoction now coating the sidewalk.

"Or not," Phoenix said.

"That. Is. Disgusting," Zeke said, horrified. He felt bile creeping up into his throat and had to fight off his own sudden urge to puke.

"Come on, boys," Jessica said. "Show's over. We have work to do."

She stepped through the door and into a different world. Zeke held the door open as she passed and allowed the others to enter first, then he pulled up the rear, giving one final look around to make sure no one was following them.

Inside the club, the throbbing sounds of electronic dance music filled the narrow hallway. The walls were lined with black sconces holding electric candles. The paint on the walls was such a dark blue that it, too, looked almost black. Up ahead, at the end of the corridor, flashing lights bounced off the corner wall where a bouncer stood blocking the entrance into the club.

He was just shy of six feet tall with bulging, veiny muscles sprouting out of a black T-shirt that was easily a size or two too small. He glimpsed the approaching visitors and turned to face them.

Jessica stopped short and motioned for Vincent to step in front. "You wanna do your thing?"

"Certainly," Vincent said, and he sidled by the others. He looked up at the bouncer with no small measure of anxiety but forced himself to speak as confidently as he could. "Hello. We're here to see Marilyn."

"Who are you?" the bouncer asked. His voice was deep and matched the exact imaginings of everyone in the group.

"Um, well, my name is Vincent. I'm a friend of Marilyn's. She's expecting us."

"What's with the suit?"

Vincent bit his lower lip, holding back a lashing he wished he could give the bigger man. "I...like the style. That's all. So, if you could just point the way to where we meet her, I would greatly appreciate it."

"Marilyn doesn't take meetings. With anyone." He leaned forward so that his nose was just a few inches away from Vincent's.

The bouncer's breath reeked, but Vincent didn't back down.

"She takes meetings from me," he said defiantly. "I suggest you tell her we're here, or when she and I speak, I'll be forced to tell her you delayed us. I assure you, you don't want to delay us. Especially my friends here." He motioned back toward Zeke and Phoenix, who were putting on their most intimidating faces. Their expressions wouldn't have frightened the attendees of a child's birthday party, much less the seasoned bouncer, but something in Vincent's voice must have swayed the man.

"All right. Tell you what I'm gonna do." The bouncer scanned the group, unimpressed by any except Jessica. His gaze clearly lingered on her for a few seconds too long. "I'll ring the boss and see what she says. If you're lying, I'm going to get my boys to come escort you out."

"Thank you," Phoenix said. "We appreciate it."

The bouncer looked at him as if he was crazy. "You won't appreciate it if my boys have to escort you out. You see, they have a knack for finding all the right ways to hurt a person. They'll take you to the alley 'round the corner and work you over a bit. They won't kill you, but you might wish they would before they're done with you."

"The alley next door?" Zeke asked. "Not to be a bother, but I think it's occupied right now. There was a young couple making out over there before we came in. Of course, they ended up vomiting everywhere, so they might be passed out on the sidewalk. Either way, it might be rude of us to intrude."

"Shut your mouth," the bouncer snapped. "What's with him?" he asked Vincent. "Some kind of wise guy?"

"I don't know. We all get tired of it."

Zeke started to defend himself, but Phoenix grabbed him by the elbow and shook his head.

"Fine," the bouncer continued. "I'm calling Marilyn. Last chance to get out of here in one piece." He took a phone out of his pocket and began dialing the number. He held it out as a warning to the group before he hit the green button.

Behind the man, the dance floor raged with people jumping up and down, arms flailing in all directions. There were hundreds of patrons, all writhing to the beat of the music. Two cages hung above the bar to the right, each with a female dancer in a bikini.

The bar spanned nearly the depth of the room. Three bartenders manned it and appeared to be perpetually busy slinging drinks to the thirsty dancers. The line at the bar was three deep nearly the entire way across, and Zeke couldn't help but think maybe they should have hired more help.

"All right, then," the bouncer said. It was easy to tell he was trying to call Vincent's bluff, though it was more difficult to tell if the man wanted Vincent to be lying or not.

The big man almost sounded like he would enjoy watching the guys in the group get the crap beat out of them, though it was unclear what role Jessica would play in such an event. More than likely, she would be sent on her way, but there were also other possibilities that caused Zeke's stomach to turn.

"It's ringing," the bouncer said as he pressed the device to his ear. "Tell the boss she has some visitors. Some guy calling himself Vincent is here to see her."

Vincent swallowed hard as he waited to hear the reaction.

"You're sure she's expecting us, right?" Freeman whispered into Vincent's ear. The uncertainty in the question was palpable.

"Far as I know," Vincent answered.

The bouncer watched them suspiciously as he listened to the other person on the line. "Yeah," he said, "he's wearing one of those suits that looks like it's from the 1920s or something."

"Forties," Vincent corrected involuntarily.

The bouncer tightened his eyebrows into a scowl but didn't comment. Then his expression softened into one of outright embarrassment.

"Yes, sir," he said. "I'll send them right up. Please, apologize to the boss for me. I didn't know."

He ended the call and slid the phone into his pocket. The bouncer's demeanor had changed dramatically, and he stepped to the side. "I apologize, sir. It appears you were telling the truth. I'm sorry for any inconvenience I may have caused. I didn't know it was you, you see. I had no idea. I'm new here, just started last week."

"You're lucky I don't drain your bank accounts right now," Vincent threatened. It was a hollow threat and he knew it, but the bouncer didn't. He was a sheep, just like most of the people in the club, or in the world for that matter. That's what hackers called people who had no clue what went on in the seedier side of the digital underworld.

"Thank you, sir," the bouncer reiterated. "I appreciate your patience. Won't happen again. Right up the stairs over there to the left." He motioned to a metal staircase that ascended toward the back wall and disappeared behind the elevated DJ booth.

Vincent nodded. "See that it doesn't." He strode by the bouncer and didn't exhale until the man was safely ten feet behind them.

When he reached the stairs, he continued up, though at a more deliberate pace.

"That took guts," Freeman said. "Well done, sir."

"Thanks," Vincent said, finally catching his breath again. "Good thing Marilyn really is waiting for us."

"Wait. You didn't know? I thought you said you spoke with her."

"I did. But she's...fickle."

They rounded the first landing and continued toward the second floor, where an elevator waited with doors open and an even bigger bouncer standing in front. He was taller than the first, and twice as menacing.

"Fickle?" Freeman hissed. "What's that supposed to mean?"

Vincent shrugged. "Let's just say that Marilyn is prone to changing her mind...rapidly."

They climbed the last step and proceeded to the elevator. The guard stepped aside and motioned them in. Then he pressed the button for the fourth floor and returned to his post outside the lift. Two seconds passed before the doors slowly closed and the elevator started to rise.

"Good one back there," Zeke said. "I thought you were gonna piss yourself for a second." He slapped Vincent on the back, and the force of the blow caused the recipient to rock forward.

"Yeah, well, it's not what you know...it's who you know."

"I'm just glad this Marilyn person knows you. Otherwise, we'd be up a creek."

"I'm sorry?" Vincent said.

"Up a creek?" Zeke repeated. "You know. Without a paddle?"

The blank stare told him Vincent didn't know what he was talking about.

"What creek?"

"It's an expression, Vincent. Jeez. Do you ever get out...of the 1940s?"

Jessica interrupted the bickering before it escalated. "This Marilyn person. What's she like? You think she will help us?"

"That depends on her mood," Vincent said honestly. "If she feels like helping us, she will. If not, we'll end up next to the pools of vomit in the alley."

"That...doesn't make me feel better about all this."

"It'll be fine," Vincent said. Then he lowered his voice to just above a whisper. "I just hope she's forgiven me."

"What was that?" Phoenix asked.

"Nothing. Nothing." Vincent spoke the words with less conviction than a politician. He didn't mention to the others that they'd just walked right into the lion's den. And if the lioness was hungry, they wouldn't be walking out.

21

LONDON

Philipe awaited his fate as would anyone unaccustomed to the idea of dying young. His eyes darted back and forth even though there was nothing there to see. A single lightbulb screwed into the cinder block wall next to the door illuminated the 200-square-foot space. He wasn't tied to the metal chair and had gotten up several times to pace around, but the thick steel door was locked from the outside, leaving no avenue of escape. The makeshift prison cell was a dungeon.

It had been over an hour since the men had brought him here, Philipe's watch the only thing he had in his possession connecting him to the real world.

The men had covered his head with a pillowcase. Not that it mattered; he wouldn't be escaping, and no one was going to come to his rescue. He had no idea where he was, and the disorientation was causing him to feel a range of foreign emotions, especially claustrophobia, despite the fact he had more than ample room to move around in the cell.

He knew he was a dead man. The only thing he could control was when it happened. His daughter was safe, though, and that was all that mattered. It was the sole thought that gave him comfort in the face of certain death.

In his solitude, his mind played fanciful tricks on him. He imagined that the man behind everything might reward him for his efforts. Perhaps a private beach, somewhere he could retire to and disappear.

But that was beyond fantasy, and Philipe knew it. He forced himself to focus on the safety of his daughter. Once the virus was initiated, events would transpire quickly: Banks would shut down within hours, and governments would be forced into emergency mode. Public panic would follow. It would begin with looting and riots, then spill over into more personal violence. Angry citizens would start hurting each other, and eventually it would lead to murders on a grand scale. Police would often be overpowered, and in some nations the cops might well be tempted to cease any resistance to the raging mobs and join in the violence.

The anarchy would be global. Cities would crumble, and millions would die in the initial wave.

His thoughts returned to his daughter. She wasn't in London, and that brought him a smidge of comfort, though eventually the violence would spill into the countryside and rural areas. All he could do was hope that his mother would take Theresa somewhere safe, keep her on the move until things died down and order was restored.

The virus wouldn't cause permanent damage to the world's electronic infrastructure, but it would do enough to alter the course of history—it was that powerful. And because of that, Philipe had already decided he wouldn't cave in—no matter what they did to him. His daughter was out of reach, and unless they somehow located her again, he would hold out as long as he could. Even in the face of torture.

Philipe's nose twitched, and he rubbed it with the back of his hand. There was no real odor in the room save for a mild scent of dust and perhaps a dash of mildew; he'd smelled much worse. He considered the idea that he might well die in this place, but it didn't frighten him, not as much as it had initially. His main emotion was sadness: sadness that he wouldn't get to see his daughter grow into a woman, to see her finish school and get married. He regretted that part, and that she would have to grow up without her father in her life. All he could do was hope that she'd learned enough from him thus far, that he'd been a powerful enough influence on her and helped shape who she would become.

A tear welled in the corner of each eye, and he used his thumbs to wipe them back.

Footsteps echoed in the corridor outside, and he stiffened. Philipe wasn't sure what to expect, but he figured at least one of the men— the blond guy, most likely—would make an appearance. As the door swung open, he wasn't disappointed.

The blond man stepped through the door, a pistol in his right hand. He wore a gray trench coat with black buttons. Behind him, the second man from the farmhouse entered. He had been the driver who brought them here.

Then a man who appeared to be older than both stepped into the cell. He wore an expensive suit, black with silver pinstripes and shiny black shoes. His dark brown hair was streaked with a few strands of gray and slicked back with pomade that kept it rigidly in place. The man's skin was tanned a dark bronze, evidence of years on the beach or by his private pool. He walked with an air of confidence and command, yet behind all of that Philipe detected a hint of insecurity. Perhaps his appearance was one big compensation.

Behind him, two more security guards stepped in, both wearing tight black T-shirts and matching cargo pants, their weapons holstered on their hips.

The four guards surrounded Philipe, and the man in the suit stepped directly in front of him. Philipe had nowhere to go. Even if he'd had some kind of superhuman ability, he wouldn't have known how to get out of this compound, wherever and whatever it was.

"The mighty Zeus," the suit said. "Finally, we have you here."

Philipe said nothing, biting back a flood of both English and French expletives he wanted to sling at the man.

"Do you know who I am?" the suit asked.

For a moment, Philipe didn't respond. He merely stared at the man's shoes and fought to keep control of his urge to leap at him and pummel his face until the guards either pulled him off or shot him dead on the spot. He doubted the latter would happen. They needed Philipe alive, and that was the lone card he had to play in his back pocket.

"Perses," Philipe muttered and raised his eyes to meet those of the man before him.

"Very good." The man nodded slowly. "I understand that some of your friends took out most of Jordan's team." He motioned to the blond man. A look of embarrassed irritation crossed his face.

Philipe regarded him casually then returned his gaze to Perses.

"That's not something easily done," the man went on. "Jordan has some of the deadliest men in the world working for him. Well, he did." The man chuckled as though the deaths were of no consequence. In fact, that was precisely the case. This was a man who was accustomed to getting what he wanted, and everyone, both against him and for him, was expendable.

Jordan didn't appear amused, but he kept his lips pressed tight. The repeated clenching of his jaw, though, betrayed his feelings.

"You must be wondering why I chose such a strange moniker," Perses continued.

Philipe scrunched his face in a confused scowl.

"Actually, I hadn't given it a second thought," Philipe lied.

"Ah," Perses tilted his head back and laughed. "Well, that's fine. I'm going to tell you anyway." He crouched in front of the Frenchman and rested his elbows on his knees as he peered up into Philipe's eyes. "You see, I come from an ancient family, one of eight ancient families who ruled this planet long ago."

Philipe failed to see the connection, so he allowed the man to go on.

"Many years ago, two of the families emerged as the most powerful on the planet. You've probably heard of them. I won't say their names, quite frankly, because they disgust me, and to even utter them makes my blood boil. And when my blood boils, I just want to...

do horrible things," he sneered. Spittle shot through his clenched teeth.

He stood again and flattened out the bottom of his suit jacket. "You see, what those two families did was...well, it was a betrayal of the highest order. Before, the eight families were on an equal footing. We decided the course of human events together, as one, and guided humanity on the right path. We controlled elections. Monarchs bowed to our rule. The global economy was under our direct influence. We could sway booms or depressions with the snap of a finger."

"But those two families got greedy, didn't they?" Philipe said.

The man's face stretched into an almost mocking grin, impressed that his captive had connected the dots.

"Very good, Zeus." He looked to Jordan. "See? I told you he was smart."

His attention returned to Philipe. "Yes. They got greedy. They concocted a plan to out the other six families, essentially minimizing our power and influence on the global scene. Oh, we remained some of the wealthiest families in the world, and still had a considerable amount of influence on regional and local scales, but nothing like what we enjoyed before. My family was stripped of our most of our power, along with the others."

Philipe tried to play along, to keep him talking, all the while formulating a plan in the back of his mind. He didn't know why this man was telling him his life story, but he had to assume it was because Perses needed him to sympathize with his mission, or whatever he called it.

"Why didn't you fight back?" Philipe asked. "Surely, the six families combined could have overthrown the other two, set the balance back to the way it was."

"Again," the man said to Jordan, wagging a finger, then turning back to face Philipe. "This one is so astute. Yes, Zeus. That's right. You'd think that six powerful and wealthy families could have pooled their resources to overthrow two interlopers. Unfortunately, their resources were considerably more vast than the rest of us. They'd grown tired of splitting profits and decision making, so they cut us and the others out. And that, my young hacker, is why I am called Perses. My sole purpose is to shake up the current hierarchy, tear down the global financial structure, and reset everything to the way it was meant to be...so my family and the other five can reclaim our seats at the table, and push out those who betrayed us."

Philipe listened to the man finish and sat on his thoughts for a moment as he considered his next question. The guy was clearly trying to win him over to his banner, to get Philipe on his side in an effort to avoid any...unpleasant coercion. Philipe wanted to avoid that, as well, but not at the cost of millions, possibly billions of lives. And not to wreck the world his daughter lived in.

"I have to admit," Philipe said finally, "the name seems a tad...contrived."

Jordan snorted a laugh for the first time since coming into the room. It was actually the first sound he'd made.

The man in the suit snapped a scathing look at his mercenary commander, firing darts of flame at him from his eyes.

Jordan wasn't afraid of the man, but it was apparent he respected him enough to settle down. Maybe it wasn't even respect, simply a show for the man who wrote the checks.

"I've heard of the eight families," Philipe said, interrupting their unspoken dispute.

"You have?" Perses sounded impressed.

"Hearsay mostly, nothing but rumors. There are forums, though, websites that exist in the shadows that discuss such things. I've seen a few of those. Most of the time, they're full of fanatical conspiracy theories. For what it's worth, I regarded them as nothing more than that. Hearing your story, though, I have to say you have changed my mind on the issue. You're either legitimately one of the six who fell from power, or you're a lunatic with delusions of grandeur." He watched his captor carefully to see if the insinuation would sway his fiery mood one way or the other.

It didn't. Instead, the man simply stood there listening.

"I know the stories about the two families you speak of," Philipe continued. "I've heard the things they do, the lives they've destroyed, and the massive scale they work on that shifts the balance of all life on Earth." He cocked his head to the side. "Based on your appearance, you're not one of the families from North Africa or Asia. Your accent is not from the New World. That only leaves three European families."

"I see you're a man of truth," Perses said. "And have wisely discerned the truth."

Philipe disregarded the comment. "My guess is you're of the Bannister line," he said flatly. "How's that for truth?"

The man's face flushed pale for a moment, exposing the secret he'd kept from everyone for so long. But then the shock on his face turned to relief, as if he were finally able to share the truth with another person for the first time in his life.

"Leopold Bannister," the man said with a slight bow.

Jordan's jaw nearly hit the floor. "Seriously?" he asked. "All of that is true?"

Bannister turned to his hired help. "Yes. It's true," he confessed. "Until this point, I've never heard that name outside of my family's estate. Even when I was sent to one of the most expensive private schools in the world, I was known by an alias, a ghost that no one could find. The Bannisters—indeed, all of the six families—take similar precautions to protect our own against the threat of the other two. We know they're always watching, always keeping us in check.

There is a particular Irish family in America who tends to be punished more frequently for stepping out of line. Although I believe they are treated worse than the rest of us due to certain...prejudices."

Philipe knew who the man was talking about but didn't say the name. His mind was spinning with a plan. It wouldn't get him out of here, and would almost certainly result in his execution, but it was the only way to stop this madman from wreaking havoc across the planet.

Jordan was still trying to process the information. His head swam, though try as he might, there was no conclusion he could reach that would counter what Bannister had just told him. It all added up. This man who'd managed to remain anonymous, while at the same time amassing a fortune, had spent considerable resources to keep his identity a secret from the world, including him. Jordan's experience in intelligence and counterintelligence was vast, yet he'd never been able to dig up anything on this man who called himself Leopold Bannister. Jordan couldn't recall anything about a powerful family named Bannister, or any of the so-called eight families he was talking about. Truth be told, he didn't know as much about mainstream history as he probably should have, but he figured it was too late for that and he honestly didn't care.

This revelation, however, had him curious.

"Of course," Bannister went on, "we can't have any loose ends." He turned to face Jordan, who was still holding his gun.

"No, we certainly can't," Jordan agreed.

Three muted clicks interrupted the silence. Jordan's face contorted in agony as the realization set in. He looked down at his chest—and the three holes in his shirt. Then he raised his gaze to meet Bannister's as he fell to his side.

Jordan's guard spun to retaliate against the shooter, but he was cut down by Bannister's second guard, taking two rounds to the chest and one to the gut. Jordan's man stumbled backward against the wall and crumpled to the floor in a heap. Dark crimson pooled behind him and under his legs as his head slumped to the side, eyes staring blankly at the floor.

Philipe shuddered at the sudden and callous murder of the two men.

Bannister looked through the smoky haze and waved some of it away as the acrid odor seeped into his nostrils.

The two guards continued to aim their weapons at the downed targets, making sure the men weren't getting up. Thin trails of smoke trickled out of the suppressor muzzles, adding to the macabre feel that now permeated the space.

Bannister smiled and clapped his hands together. "Now that that's over, we should get to work, yes?"

Philipe looked up at the man as if his head was on fire. "You just killed your own men," he said, clearly disgusted, confused, and slightly agonized at the thought he could be next.

"Zeus, Philipe, whatever you want to be called. These aren't my men. They're just hired guns. That's all. I needed them to find you for me, and they did. Now I don't need them anymore."

"And when you're done with me and don't need me anymore, you will do the same to me."

Bannister's lips creased and stretched deep across his cheeks. "Oh, Philipe. I knew you would think that. You're not a loose end. No." He shook his head and wagged a finger to reiterate. "I'm going to need you, probably for a long time. You see, taking down the global financial infrastructure is just the first step."

"First step?"

"Yes," Bannister said with a slow nod. "Once everything has come crashing down, the people will need a hero, someone who can rebuild and reestablish order from the chaos."

"You want me to fix the issue once the job is done?"

"Something like that." He leveled his gaze. "What I want is for you to move some of the world's wealth into my possession while the virus is doing its thing."

Philipe blinked rapidly. "So...all of this is just an elaborate heist?"

Bannister's head bobbed in multiple directions. "Don't diminish it like that. When the people of the world look for answers, I will not only be the leader they need, but I will have the resources to bail out entire nations, help them get back on their feet. I will be the bank, and everyone will have to come to me for a loan."

Philipe's eyebrows tightened. This man was crazy. There was no way a plan like this would work. Was there? There were too many moving parts, too many ways it could go wrong.

"I know, I know," Bannister interrupted his thoughts. "It's a lot to take in. Look"—he said, placing a hand on Philipe's shoulder —"you're just going to have to trust me. But if you pull this off, Zeus, you will be one of the most powerful men in the world. You will be able to go anywhere, do anything. You'll be my right hand. Imagine the good you will be able to do."

Philipe had to think fast. The two guards still held their weapons at the ready. Were they going to shoot him if he said no? That seemed to be the obvious conclusion. What else could he do? At the very least, Philipe needed to buy himself some time. For what, he didn't know, but if he agreed to help without having to be tortured, it could give him the opening he needed to implement the plan that had been festering for the last few minutes.

"Yes," he said with a nod. "Let's do it."

22

T he doors opened, and the group was greeted by a guard, this one shorter than the others and with dark brown skin and a black beard that ran up to the sideburns. He had a triangle tattooed under each eye, which made him look even more menacing.

"She's waiting for you," the guard said in a dense Arabic accent. He stepped to the side, and they found themselves in a vastly different place than they'd been just an elevator ride ago.

Zeke blinked for what he thought was an hour as he took in the sight.

Phoenix caught himself staring as well.

They had expected to exit the elevator into a corridor that led to an apartment or an office. Instead, the group stood in a wide-open expanse that stretched fifty feet to the far wall and another eight to the other end of the massive room.

Old-school arcade games lined the walls to the left and ahead. To the right, pinball machines were the décor of choice. In the center of the room, foosball tables, two air hockey tables, and domed ice hockey machines filled the space.

Speakers in the corners blared Def Leppard's "Pour Some Sugar on Me." Red neon lights ran along the ceiling line. Above the video games and pinball machines, posters of popular 1980s bands and movies hung as a tribute to the decade.

"Um, Phoenix? Are you seeing this?" Zeke asked.

"Yes. Yes, I am. And it is awesome."

Vincent continued through the center of the room toward what looked like a living room set up in the back-left corner. Two more guards stood with their backs against the wall, arms folded across their chests, a pose that seemed to make guys like that appear tougher—as if they needed it.

All those bulging muscles made each of the visitors feel immediately inadequate, bordering on threatened. Except for Jessica. She appeared to be the only one in the group who remained unimpressed.

The guards were on either side of a black leather couch. In the center of the sofa, a blonde woman sat with her legs crossed, the short red miniskirt revealing most of her pale legs—all the way to her upper thighs. She wore matching red heels and a black halter top. Her hair was teased up to shoot off in every direction. Her bright red lipstick could have been seen from the space station. She stared at the group with icy blue eyes wrapped in dark eye shadow and thick mascara.

"Just let me do the talking?" Vincent whispered over his shoulder as they approached.

"To Cyndi Lauper over there?" Zeke said a little too loudly. "Sure. No problem."

Vincent's eyes widened in horror, and he turned quickly to face their host. They stopped beside a metal coffee table with a glass top.

"Hello, Marilyn," Vincent said. "Long time."

She stared at him for what felt like minutes, her head cocked lazily to the side and leaning against the couch cushion. Marilyn loosely held a red lollipop in her right hand. The candy dangled as if it might fall. She blinked, which slightly unnerved the visitors since —for a moment—they wondered if she was made of wax. Then her right hand moved, and she popped the lollipop into her mouth. She sucked on it for a moment and then gradually removed it, letting the red sphere slowly emerge from between her lips.

"Who are they?" Marilyn asked, pointing the all-day sucker at the other guests.

Vincent cleared his throat and shifted uncomfortably, then stepped to the side. "This is Phoenix, Zeke, Jessica, and Gary." He motioned to them with one hand.

"You can call me Freeman. Everyone else does."

The hostess rolled her eyes. The gesture was more than enough to tell Freeman that she truly didn't care.

He quickly bit his lower lip and took a step back.

Marilyn uncrossed her legs and then slowly recrossed them as she sized up the group.

"You," she said, pointing at Phoenix. "Your name is Phoenix?" Her British accent was sharp and pointed, much like her question.

"Um," Phoenix looked at the others for answers, then bobbed his head. "Yes, ma'am. That's my name."

Her right eyebrow remained skeptical for another five seconds. Then her lips creased, and she wagged the lollipop at him. "I like that name. That's a cool name."

"Thank you," he said.

"You didn't make that up, did you? Like some of these people who legally change their name to something cooler because they didn't like the name their parents gave them? Or is your family from Arizona?"

Phoenix nodded, pressing his lips together. They were questions he'd heard before. "No. My real name is Phoenix Underwood. Mom and Dad were big fans of River Phoenix. And we're not from Arizona."

"Ah," Marilyn said, her eyes brightening. "I loved him. Of course, I was too young to remember when he was alive. I may have seen him in the third Indiana Jones movie."

"*Last Crusade*," Zeke interjected.

All eyes turned to Zeke, each casting their own scathing rebuke for interrupting when he wasn't spoken to. Even the guards shook their heads slowly as they glared at him.

"It...it was the *Last Crusade*. Sorry," he said. "Just...I'm a big fan of that one. You know, the whole Holy Grail pursuit and all that. Cool story." He could see he wasn't winning anyone over with his blather. "Sorry. I'll...I'll stop talking."

"That would be good," Marilyn said, then redirected her attention back to Phoenix. "Your parents have good taste," she said.

She uncrossed her legs again and planted her feet on the ground, then stood deliberately, letting her hands fall by her sides, the right still clutching the red candy. She strode over and circled him, one slow step at a time, running her eyes over his form as if she were eyeing a new dress she might purchase.

Marilyn stopped behind him, and Phoenix shifted uncomfortably, unaccustomed to this kind of attention from...well, any woman. She let her eyes wander to his heels and back up again, then dragged her free index finger across his shoulders until she reached the other side and faced him again.

Marilyn gazed into Phoenix's brown eyes as she spoke. "What do you want, Vincent?"

Vincent shifted awkwardly. "We have a problem."

"We?" She snapped her head at him. "We don't have a problem, Vincent. You have a problem. Any *we* there might have been walked out the door with you two years ago."

"I know. And I'm sorry, but it was for the best. There would have been trouble if we'd stuck together. You know that. They were onto us. We had to split."

"Maybe. Or maybe we would have been stronger together. We could have fought them off, you and I. But you got scared."

"That's true," Vincent admitted. "I did. And I'm sorry. I never wanted to hurt you." He lifted his head and looked into her eyes.

Jessica and Freeman watched the exchange in silence.

Zeke, as usual, couldn't keep his yap shut.

"Look, you two..."

They slowly turned their heads and gazed at him with irritation.

But still, Zeke kept jabbering. "I'm sure whatever happened before can be worked out. Okay? Every relationship goes through some tough spots." He glanced over his shoulder at Jessica, who merely rolled her eyes and mouthed what he thought was the word *idiot*. "But you guys can work it out. I mean, Vincent, clearly you just wanna sing, sing, sing. And Marilyn?" He looked at her. "Girls just wanna have fun. I get it."

They both glared at him, deadpan.

"But you have to work out your differences. Trying to make Vince here jealous by flirting with Phoenix isn't the way to do that. What you've still got? It's good enough."

Vincent and Marilyn scowled at him.

"I'm just saying," Zeke went on, "It's good enough, guys."

"Okay, I'm just gonna stop you right there," Marilyn said. "I see what you're doing with all the Cyndi Lauper references."

"Do you? Because you two seem like you're caught up in circles."

"She's my sister, you twit," Vincent blurted.

Everyone in the group turned to look at him. Then their eyes switched to Marilyn, then back again.

"Sister?" Freeman asked.

"Yes. She's my bloody sister. All right? We got into some stuff a few years ago and thought the cops were onto us. I moved away to throw them off the trail."

"And you never came back," Marilyn pointed out.

"Right. I didn't come back. And I'm sorry for that."

"Now you're here, and you need my help."

Zeke's head spun as he tried to catch up. "Okay, so, just to be clear, you two are brother and sister? And you're both hackers?"

"Yes," they replied simultaneously, annoyance in both their tones.

"I don't mean to break up this little family reunion or...whatever this is," Jessica said, stepping forward, "but we have a serious issue."

"Who are you?" Marilyn asked bluntly.

"My name is Jessica Benson. I'm the—"

"She's a new friend," Vincent cut her off. "A new friend I picked up at a bar yesterday.

Marilyn's suspicious eyebrow inched up again. "New friend? At a bar? That doesn't sound like you, Vince. And she doesn't strike me as your type."

"What? Why don't I? No," Jessica realized she was being sucked into a conversational black hole that would end up going nowhere. "I'm the director of the GIC, and we are trying to stop a catastrophic virus from infecting most of the world's financial systems."

All eyes shifted to Jessica. Even the two guards who'd been like statues widened their eyes slightly.

Marilyn turned to face her brother. "Is that true, Vincent? You're here because you need my help to stop another hacker?"

Vincent sighed dejectedly. He was the boy who got caught with his hand in the cookie jar. "It's bad, M. It's real bad." That was all he could offer in way of an explanation.

Marilyn folded her arms and gazed into her brother's eyes. "We're hackers, Vincent. That's what we do, what other people call bad. We level the playing field for everyone. We bring equality to the masses. We bring fairness to an unfair world."

"Do we?" Vincent asked. "Because it feels like the lines are a little blurred here, Sis."

"Blurred? Obviously, your brain is blurred because you brought the director of the GIC here. To my club." Her voice escalated until it reached the point of shouting.

Vincent cringed with every syllable.

"Hey, now," Zeke said with an unsteady voice. He put up his hand to calm down the situation, but the gesture caused the guards to take a step forward. "I'm not going to hurt her, guys. Go do another cycle of 'roids and let me talk." He faced Marilyn with a sincere expression. "Listen. Maybe your brother has had a change of heart. We drove all through the night to get here."

He flicked a side-glance at Phoenix to make sure he was paying attention.

"That was a deep cut. You're welcome. Maybe your brother is showing his true colors now. But money changes everything— another deep cut—and if we don't stop this guy, you and your club here," he waved his hands around, "the city, the country, and most of the world will be plunged into the Dark Ages. You ever tried to run your laptop without electricity? I'm here to tell you, time after time, it is a huge pain in the butt."

Marilyn clenched her jaw.

"I'm sorry I can't work in a 'Sally's Pigeons' reference," Zeke said. "But a guy named Philipe is in trouble, and someone is about to force him to unleash a virus that will do all that bad stuff I mentioned, including possibly destroying everything that Cyndi Lauper stands for. I'm talking orphans. Habitat for Humanity. ASPCA. All of it."

"Okay, that last one was Sarah McLachlan," Phoenix corrected.

"Whatever. My point is...we need your help. Leveling a playing field is one thing. I get it. I really do. But this will destroy our entire way of life. All of civilization could collapse."

Marilyn listened to his rant with a disinterested, vapid stare. When he finally stopped to take a breath, she cut in. "Are you done?"

"I think so. Maybe. I don't know. Do you feel convinced?"

She licked her lips and then looked at her brother. "So, Philipe is in trouble? You say someone is forcing him to create some super virus?"

"He's already created it. If they make him think his daughter is in danger, he'll unlock it if he believes it will keep her safe."

"Oh," Marilyn said and spun around. She paced toward the couch and then spun around dramatically. "Philipe is one of the best."

"True."

"If he built something that powerful, odds are no one will be able to stop it. Maybe not even him."

"I'm sorry," Phoenix said, stepping forward. "What do you mean by that, not even him?"

"Some viruses get out of control. They almost become sentient, though not completely. Philipe is one of the brightest hackers I've ever met, if not *the* brightest. If he made this thing unbeatable, then it very well might be even for him. My only question is, why did he do it?"

"He said he didn't create it," Zeke offered. "But he took the design and improved it."

Marilyn inclined her head. "The bank virus?"

The four Americans exchanged knowing glances.

"Oh dear," Marilyn added.

"Oh dear? That...that doesn't sound good," Freeman noted.

"Since you boys are with the GIC, I have to assume that's why you're all aware of what the virus did. Correct?"

"That is accurate," Zeke said without overplaying his hand. He didn't want her to know that he and Phoenix were the ones who'd arrested Philipe under the belief he was the one who'd initiated the virus attack.

"Well then, you know that if that thing is unleashed, there isn't much anyone can do to stop it, if it's weaponized properly. And if Philipe has already coded the thing...we're running out of time."

"That's why we're here," Jessica said, stepping forward. "Vincent here says you may be able to help us track down whoever has Philipe and stop this before it gets sent out into the world. You say you want to level the playing field? Well, how about you level it for us? Tell us where we can find Philipe, and we'll hold off Armageddon for a little while longer."

Marilyn's eyes twitched as she contemplated the problem. It didn't take her long to come to a conclusion. "All right," she said. "I'll help."

"Thank you. We owe you a tremendous debt."

"Yeah, I know. That's what I was going to address next. I don't want the GIC, MI5, MI6, CIA, or—if you can control them—the KGB interfering with my business. I want full immunity."

"You know I can't do that."

"Not forever, love," Marilyn said, placing a hand on Jessica's shoulder. It was the first time she'd noticed the hacker's tattoo of an ace of spades on the back of her hand. "Just six months. I just want six months of operating in peace without having to look over my shoulder. Don't worry, I'm not going to do any harm to anyone. You have my word."

Jessica considered the offer, but she had no real play here other than to cooperate with Marilyn's plan.

"I'll do everything I can," she said finally.

"Good." Marilyn smiled pleasantly and extended a hand. They shook for a moment. Then Marilyn turned to one of the guards. "Open it."

The nearest guard immediately sprang to life. He strode over to a bar in the opposite corner and stepped behind the counter. Dozens of liquor bottles gleamed in the red neon light. The shelves were fully stocked with whiskey, tequila, vodka, gin, and rum. The guard reached up to the top shelf and pulled down on an empty Pappy Van Winkle's 23-Year bottle. Immediately, the wall to the man's left slid behind the bar and revealed a secret room. The space was filled with the white glow of multiple computer monitors.

Marilyn stepped over to the open door and looked back at the others. "Welcome to my secret lair," she said.

"You used a Pappy Van Winkle's 23-Year bottle as your secret lair's entrance mechanism?" Zeke asked.

"Of course."

"I prefer the Fifteen-Year, but I tip my hat to you, lady. You have good taste. I assume you drank the contents?"

She grinned, winked, then sashayed into the secret room.

Zeke turned to his friend. "She's a keeper, buddy."

Phoenix rolled his eyes and followed her into the room.

Vincent nudged Zeke on his way past. "She's my sister, mate. Don't forget that." The menacing tone in the man's voice had returned.

"Right." Zeke nodded and squeezed his lips together. When Vincent and the others were safely in the other room, Zeke brought up the rear, and the last guard closed the door behind them.

23

LONDON

The secret computer room looked more like a military command center—a low-budget one, but a command center nonetheless.

Computer monitors lined tables set against all four walls, each screen hooked into custom-built towers beneath the tables. Three 70-inch flatscreens hung from the back wall. The far-left screen displayed the BBC News channel, providing updates of the latest breaking news from around the world. The other two screens showed maps of the world, the Eastern and Western Hemispheres, respectively.

A narrow table in the center of the room was unoccupied, but it was clearly a conference table, no doubt used during operations.

"What is this place?" Jessica asked. It was a question they all had running through their heads.

"This," Marilyn said, twirling around a full 360 degrees, "is where I monitor what's going on in the world."

All eyes looked toward the screens. There were zoomed-in areas around some major cities; others appeared as text.

"You monitor what's going on in the world?" Freeman asked. "What does that mean exactly?"

"Cybercrime," Marilyn said bluntly. "From this room, I can locate the epicenter of every major viral attack."

"That's...impossible," Jessica protested. "No one, not even well-funded government agencies, have that capability. No one can catch all of it."

"You would be right if we were having this discussion two years ago. Now, though, the rest of the world has fallen behind. Governments included. And before you ask, I'll just go ahead and tell you. I designed the code. I call it Birdie."

"Birdie?" Zeke asked.

"Yes," she said, her head snapping in his direction. "Is that a problem?"

"Nope. No problem. Just curious."

"My grandfather hunted ducks when I was little. He had a bird dog named Birdie that retrieved his prizes." She turned toward the monitor. "This program can detect system anomalies within seconds of them striking."

"And...you've just kept this to yourself for the last...two years?" Jessica wondered. Her voice drifted.

"Yes," Marilyn answered, putting her hands on her hips. "I created it. I can do with it as I please."

"But...why did you create it?"

"That's the big one, isn't it? Why would a hacker want to monitor what other hackers are doing? Simple. I'm not like them." She turned to her brother with disdain. "He's not, either, though he's dabbled in the past."

Vincent lowered his head like a chastised child.

"I'm not sayin' I'm a saint," Marilyn continued. "I'm a sinner, same as the rest of you. But now I'm on a different path. I still gotta pay the bills, though. So, I hunt cybercriminals and sell their information to the highest bidder."

"You're a digital bounty hunter?" Phoenix asked, sounding like more than just the new information intrigued him. There was a look in his eye that Zeke hadn't seen during their short friendship. He knew what it meant, too. Phoenix liked this Marilyn chick.

"You could say that. Tech companies pay big money to catch the people tampering with their systems. They also pay well for anyone who can crack their stuff in a contained environment. I don't really get into that anymore. Turns out, CEOs will pay generously for justice."

"Justice?" Jessica asked. "You mean revenge. You're taking those hackers to the slaughter."

"Look, love, I don't know what happens to most of them. And I really don't care. You ask me, the companies would be doing the world a favor by taking out some of those miscreants. Most of the time, I know they turn them over to the cops. Know what happens when they do that?"

Jessica blinked and waited for the answer.

It was Zeke who gave it. "They go free," he said solemnly.

"That's right. They go free. And for what? Lack of evidence? Lack of motive? Who knows? Most of these hackers are so connected, within hours of their arrest they can make a phone call and have everything set up online to look like someone else was behind it. So, truth is, it's probably better for the world if the less-ethical tech giants take them out for us."

"So, that's it? You're some kind of saint? That's how you justify what you do?"

Marilyn grinned proudly. "No, love. I don't have to justify anything I do. I'm justifying it for you, 'cause I can tell something about it bothers you." She held up a finger. "But I can also tell there's a part of you that appreciates it. You know the system is broken. Can't always play by the rules."

Jessica wanted to refute her statement, but she held back. Her comments weren't going to change anything, and the truth was Marilyn was right, about pretty much everything. As long as Marilyn was on the right side of the law, which she appeared to be, Jessica wouldn't push it.

"Now, if you don't mind. We should probably get back down to business. Our boy Philipe is probably in dire need of rescuing, and us standing around gabbing on about it isn't going to help." She picked up a remote from the center table and pointed it at the map of Europe. She pressed a button, and the view zoomed in to a specific area of London. "This is our best bet." The circle encompassing the zone was dark red.

Phoenix took a step forward to get a closer look. There was a name in black letters in the center of the red circle. "What's Brompton Road Station?" he asked.

"Brompton Road Station," Vincent fielded, "is an Tube station." He stepped forward as well and turned his head toward his sister. "They're using an abandoned Tube stop for their operation?"

"Looks like it. I know this: There's a massive mainframe working there, and probably a ton of servers. Whatever it is, it's big. The heat signatures and data streams going in and out are off the charts. I haven't seen one this big outside of Moscow."

"Moscow?" Zeke asked.

"You don't want to know." She eyed him down off the ledge before he dove into a conversation that would take up more of their valuable time.

"But Brompton was bought years ago by some big company. They came in and built flats there, some of them pretty expensive, from what I hear."

"It's an apartment complex?" Freeman asked. "Would that account for the huge bandwidth and the other readings you're getting?"

Marilyn chuckled. "That's cute. No. What we're seeing out of that area," she jabbed her finger at the screen again, "is way more than a few hundred tenants streaming their favorite television shows." She looked at Vincent. "You don't happen to know who owns that company, the one who built the flats?"

"No," he answered with a shrug, "but I can find out."

She nodded. "Do it."

Vincent snapped into action and slid into the nearest empty seat. His fingers flew across the keyboard as he rapidly entered search terms. Results popped onto the screen, and he clicked the first relevant article. The others looked over his shoulder as he scanned the paragraphs. He shook his head and went back to the search results, clicked on another article, and started reading again.

"You won't find it," Zeke said.

Everyone in the room whipped their heads toward him.

"What?" Jessica asked first. "Why not?"

"Because Phoenix and I saw the look in Philipe's eyes when he told us about this guy, Perses, the one who's behind all of this. You won't find the name attached to the corporation." He pointed at the screen. "Do you see the name of the company that bought the property?"

"Yes, but—"

"You will find the CEO, the members of the board, all that, but they're all puppets. A man like the one Philipe described doesn't plaster his name and title on anything. He keeps a low profile. Real low. We're talking about someone who's been playing a long game for a while now. He's bent on something. Maybe it's revenge. Maybe it's some other motive, like greed. Or perhaps he wants the power of knowing he can hold the world's financial systems by the cojones. I have no idea. But one thing I do know is that guys like him can't be found with a quick Google search."

Zeke turned and faced Marilyn. "You say this Brompton Station is where we'll find what we're looking for?"

"Yes. I've been watching it for some time, but since we haven't traced any malicious attacks coming from there yet, I haven't checked it out personally."

"The bank virus didn't come from there?" Phoenix asked.

Marilyn smiled at him. It seemed he was the only one who could crack her icy exterior. "No. But that is good thinking. That virus was dropped in from somewhere else. We tracked it to a hotel. More than likely, they used that as a neutral place because it's not tied to the company or person who bought Brompton. Lots of people use hotels. It could have been anyone. This, however," she motioned to the screen, "is built for a much larger attack. It would take a while to do something like that from a hotel."

"Okay," Zeke said. "I guess we're going to the subway."

"Tube," Vincent corrected.

"I'm sorry?" Zeke asked.

"We call it the Tube. Sometimes the London Underground."

Zeke rolled his eyes. "Fine. Whatever. It's a train that goes under the city. Can we just get going? We have no idea how much time we have, so it's probably best to assume we're up against it."

"He's right," Jessica said through obvious existential anguish. "We need to move. If you're sure that's the place, then we need to be there ten minutes ago."

Marilyn gave a nod. "Okay, then. Follow me."

24

LONDON

The façade of the old Brompton Road Station had worn fairly well considering how long it had been closed. The glossy, deep red Leslie Green tiles on the exterior looked almost new, and the white window frames contrasted with the dark crimson color.

Perhaps the new owners of the building had taken the time and resources to spruce the place up a little for the tenants. The upstairs flats appeared to be much like any others in the area...save for the fact they were built on top of an abandoned Tube station.

It was the perfect cover-up for a massive underground criminal operation.

"This is the place?" Zeke asked, staring at the building from across the busy street.

"This is it," Marilyn responded. Her eyes remained locked on the building.

At first glance, it didn't appear to be well guarded, if it was at all. Zeke and Phoenix immediately scanned the rooftops for snipers or men with guns sweeping the perimeter. Their eyes fell to the entrance and panned the sidewalk and adjoining side street to the left, then the alley to the right. Again, there were no signs of any guards.

Vincent trotted up to the group and slowed to a halt. He panted for breath for a moment and then grinned. "Sorry about that," he said. "Just had to make sure there wasn't anyone watching us." He'd circled the block parallel to the Brompton Road Station entrance, though he seemed hardly qualified to do any kind of recon work. The others had humored him while they searched the immediate premises.

"All clear," Vincent said once his breathing returned to normal.

"Does it bother any of you that there isn't a single security guy guarding the place?" Phoenix asked.

"It's definitely odd," Jessica answered. She'd noted the same peculiarity and wondered if they were being led on a wild goose chase. She turned to Marilyn. "How sure are you that this is the place?"

Marilyn sighed. "Is it possible that we've been thrown off track by some kind of decoy system? Is that what you're asking?"

"I...honestly, I don't know."

"Well, it would take an immense amount of effort to set up something like that. It would hardly be an efficient use of someone's time. And the fact that these heat and data signatures are larger than anything we're currently seeing on the map means that there's something huge going on down there. Don't worry," she said with a smirk, "I'm sure there will be more than enough security for you to deal with once we're inside."

"Yeah, about that," Freeman said. He looked exceedingly uncomfortable with the pistol tucked under his jacket, and kept he shifting nervously. "How do we get in, exactly?"

"That door right there," Vincent said, pointing at the entrance to the red building.

"Yeah, but it's blocked off."

"I guess it's a good thing you have a couple of criminals with you then, innit?"

Traffic stopped at the lights on either side of the group, clearing the street momentarily.

"Come on," Marilyn said. "We may already be too late."

Marilyn stepped onto the street and trotted across. The others followed hesitantly and reached the sidewalk just before the lights turned green again.

The group stopped at the door and lingered for a moment as Vincent reached into his daypack and removed a small black cylinder. He stuck his hand back in the pack, removed a silver cylinder, and screwed it onto the black one. The two pieces combined were no longer than his hand from the heel to the tip of his middle finger, barely over two inches in diameter.

"What is that?" Freeman asked.

Vincent looked up with eagerness in his eyes, like a child who'd just opened a new toy at Christmas.

"Breaching torch," he said. "They make these for the military and law enforcement, but theirs are about twice the size of this one. Way too clunky for my tastes."

"Wait," Jessica said. "You have a breaching torch? Why would you have that?"

"You never know, love," he said with a wink. "Pays to be prepared, though, don't it?"

"Yeah, but those things aren't exactly subtle. They produce a ton of heat, a bright orange glow, and a cloud of smoke. Everyone within view will notice."

Vincent held out the device and pressed it to the thick deadbolt keeping the door to the London Underground locked. He looked at his sister and nodded.

She removed a small black box from her jacket pocket. There was a silver switch near the top and a red button under a plastic sheath beneath it.

"What is that?" Zeke asked.

"A diversion," Marilyn answered.

"Diversion? What diversion?"

Vincent looked over his shoulder at Zeke. "My little jog I took a minute ago? I wasn't just having a go for some fish and chips, mate."

Concern filled Zeke's face with a red hue on his cheeks as he watched Marilyn flip the arming switch and then tilt up the plastic sheath. She pressed the button, and a moment later a loud boom erupted from somewhere amid the buildings across the street. Within seconds, a pillar of smoke plumed up above the rooftops.

Pedestrians on the sidewalk froze for a moment and then started running in a panic, fleeing for safety. People abandoned their vehicles and followed the pedestrians down the next street.

"Bomb!" Marilyn shouted. The word seemed to urge on the slower folks, and they picked up their pace.

Screams echoed down the street as people fled. It took less than a minute to clear the street. Sirens blared in the distance, a sign that first responders had already been contacted.

"What did you do?" Phoenix asked with a stern tone directed at Marilyn.

"Take it easy, love," she said. She stroked his cheek with the back of her right hand, still holding the detonator. "Just some fireworks is all. Nothing dangerous."

"Yeah," Vincent said as he repositioned his torch against the door. "Mortar in a rubbish bin. Makes it sound much louder and more violent. Combined it with some smoke grenades, and boom. Literally. When the mortar blew, it popped the top off the dumpster and let all that smoke blow out. Pretty smart, eh?"

"Right, so maybe next time you should let us know when you're going to set off what everyone thinks is a bomb!" Phoenix roared. Then he lowered his voice. "Sorry."

"Seemed to work," Vincent said with a shrug. He pushed the sunglasses on his nose a little closer to the eyes. "You might want to look away. This burns pretty bright."

He pressed the button on the device, and a searing orange light burst from the contact point between the torch and the door. Within seconds, the hard metal glowed brightly and turned into a thick liquid. Sparks flew and smoke burst from the hotspot, shrouding Vincent for a moment before he stepped away from the door and turned off the device.

Everyone else had already taken a step back. The Americans

stared in rapt wonder at the freshly melted hole that replaced the lock. The door swung open on its own, creaking slightly.

Vincent stepped up to the door again and used the side of the torch to push it all the way open. Then he cautiously poked his head in, had a quick look around, and then motioned the others to follow.

"All clear," he said as he took a step into the dark alcove beyond.

His sister followed first while the trained agents held back for a moment, uncertain if they should simply stroll in. Zeke took a deep breath and made his move first, mostly because he already felt emasculated that Marilyn had gone before him.

Once all six were in the building, Vincent pulled the door shut again. The group drew their weapons and switched on the attached lights. The area was dark though not pitch black. A dim yellow glow emanated from a concrete spiral staircase ahead.

Each member of the group twisted and scanned the immediate area to make sure they hadn't walked into a trap. There were still no signs of security; all they found were the remnants of the abandoned Tube entrance. Old signs hung from the walls, some emblazoned with safety warnings, others there to direct passengers along the Piccadilly Line.

The room smelled of dust, the absence of moisture or mold striking considering its age and the lack of upkeep or use.

"Down the stairs," Marilyn said, pointing at the staircase that twisted down into the bowels of the city.

"Okay," Zeke said. "Let me take the lead."

Marilyn huffed but stepped aside to let him pass.

Zeke tiptoed by a retired ticket kiosk and shoved his weapon into the space over the first steps. He pointed the light down through the shaft, silently praying there was nothing or no one waiting below.

Then he took his first step, keeping his back to the wall. He let his pistol lead the way as he took one step after the other in deliberate, slow movements. His boot's sole hit the fourth step, and he was about to take another when he slipped. Zeke's arms shot up. His fingers loosened, and the gun slipped away a moment before his balance.

He snatched at the weapon as he fell after it, desperately trying to catch it. He struck the steps three feet below with his upper back, a blow that sent a sudden jarring pain through his nerves. The weapon bobbled in his hands as he tumbled head over heels down through the spiral staircase. His shoulders hit the wall, then his knees, then the back of his head—thankfully not hard enough to do more damage than was already done. The entire time he rolled down the stairs, he fumbled with the pistol to regain control.

The light below rapidly grew brighter as he neared the bottom. Zeke had lost all concern regarding his stealth and was now focused on not breaking any bones, particularly his skull. Zeke hit the last step with his tailbone at the exact second he snatched the pistol out of the air. His fingers grabbed the weapon so tightly that he accidentally squeezed the trigger.

The gun discharged and the suppressor clicked. Zeke was about to cringe, anticipating the ricochet bouncing all around the basement area, but instead he looked up to find a guard dressed in black and standing six feet away.

The man was holding a Heckler & Koch submachine gun slung over one shoulder. His skin was tanned golden and his eyes were a bright, piercing blue. His head was shaved clean, and he bore a barbed-wire tattoo around his neck.

Zeke nearly panicked and was about to squeeze the trigger again, this time on purpose, when he realized the guard was immobile. Seconds ticked by, though to Zeke it seemed like minutes. Then the guard unexpectedly dropped to his knees. Blood trickled from the corner of his mouth, his vacant eyes stared straight ahead. That's when Zeke noticed a small hole in the center of the man's black shirt. The bullet had entered the man's heart, rupturing the organ instantly.

Footsteps echoed down the stairwell, and Marilyn appeared with the others in tow. They found Zeke holding his weapon with arms extended and a guard lying facedown on the concrete floor, a pool of blood swelling around his torso.

Zeke heard them arrive and rose quickly, a little too quickly. His head spun, and he wavered for a moment, disoriented and dizzy. He reached out and braced himself against the nearest wall. Jessica rushed to his aid, wrapping an arm around his back and holding him tight so he wouldn't fall.

"You okay?" she asked.

He wasn't sure if he was hallucinating from the fall or if she really was holding him up and actually asking about his well-being.

"Um. Yeah. I think so," he grunted. The truth was, everything hurt. He knew that the next day he would have bruises over pretty much all of his body. His right shin, the left knee, both elbows and the forearms below them, his back, at least two ribs, and the back of his skull throbbed from the blows they'd taken on the edges of the steps and against the wall. He hoped it was nothing more than bruises, but he doubted there were any mortal internal injuries. Although if there were, he wouldn't have known it. Zeke decided it was best not to think about that.

"That was quite the tumble you took," Phoenix said, running up to him while Marilyn and Freeman scoped out the area.

"Yeah," Zeke said. "I'd say I've had worse, but I don't think that would be true."

Phoenix nodded and checked the guard to make sure he was dead, though the sticky puddle under the man's body would have been sign enough for most. As he suspected, there was no pulse in the man's neck.

Marilyn walked to the left while Vincent inspected the platform to the right.

Tunnels leading to other parts of the Tube had been sealed off long ago, some with thick concrete and a tile façade, others with bricks and mortar.

It didn't take long to realize that there was nothing down there, and no way in or out other than the staircase.

"What is this?" Phoenix asked, irritated. "It's just a basement with some mechanical stuff and old Second World War maps."

Freeman was in a corner, analyzing one of the archways that had been sealed off. People had written their last names on it, though he couldn't tell if it was vandals or if the markings originated during the war.

Pipes ran up the wall in one section and then stretched across the ceiling before disappearing above. One strange device in another corner had stacks of what looked like metal funnels, each leading down to another, and another from the ceiling to the floor. No one was certain what it was, but it was interesting.

More warning signs regarding high voltage hung from various points on the walls. The Tube itself stretched the length of the building, as far as they could see, until it ran into a section that had been sealed off—like nearly everything else.

"This doesn't make any sense," Freeman said, standing on the edge of the platform and looking down into the empty rut in the middle of the tunnel.

"What doesn't?" Zeke asked. "That we followed these two down into a dark, abandoned subway in London because they claimed they knew where Philipe had been taken? Or that it looks like everything down here has been blocked off, so if there is something going on it must be hidden behind a secret door or something?"

Freeman stared at his friend for nearly ten seconds before he slowly shook his head, never taking his surprised eyes off Zeke. "Um, actually, I was just going to say that it doesn't make sense that there aren't any tracks here."

Zeke's face flushed, though no one noticed in the darkness. "Oh." He looked down into the rut and realized what Freeman was pointing out. "Yes, that's...that's what I was thinking, too."

"Hold on," Marilyn ordered. She turned toward Zeke and made her way back across the room so she could address him face to face. "What did you just say?"

"That's what I was thinking?"

"No, you twit. The other thing."

"About the no way out or that it is your fault we're wasting our time down here?"

She cocked her head to the side, and even in the dim light it was

easy to tell Marilyn wanted to sock him in the face. "No, you idiot."
She looked at Jessica. "Seriously, what is wrong with him?"

Jessica could only throw up her hands in surrender.

"The part about the secret entrance," Marilyn finished. "That has
to be the answer. Whether you believe me or not, there's definitely
something down here pushing all that power and data. There's no
way it's a mistake."

A metal clunk shocked the blood of everyone standing on the
platform.

"What was that?" Phoenix asked.

"Quick," Jessica snapped, keeping her voice to a loud whisper.
"Everyone down in the Tube."

25

LONDON

Philipe stared at the three computer monitors on the wall behind a sleek wooden workstation. The pale wood surface was made from aspen trees and was propped up by wrought iron legs.

The wireless keyboard felt like warm gloves against his hands and fingers, the comfort of familiarity. Philipe was in his element when he was at a computer. The near-silent whirring of the machines filled him with a sense of peace, at least they normally would. In this case, however, peace was the furthest feeling from his mind.

He knew that behind him two guards were holding weapons aimed at his back—in case he got any bright ideas. As if that was something he'd considered. *Yeah, sure. I'll just stand up, spin around, and charge toward the exit.* The notion was ridiculous. He'd manage one step before they shot him. And these bullets wouldn't kill.

The men were armed with electric pulse rifles. They fire a small pellet at the target, and once it struck, the tiny prongs within the soft tips sank into the skin and sent literally a stunning amount of voltage into the victim. One pellet was enough to cause slight disorientation and momentary loss of motor function. Two, however, had the same effect as a police-issue Taser, capable of dropping a large person.

Philipe wasn't large, so he figured one would do the trick, and he did not intend to find out how it felt.

The guards also carried sidearms, real firearms that would inflict serious damage with their .40-caliber hollow point rounds. They were for emergency use only, or so Bannister had said. But Philipe knew that he was only useful while he was alive. There was no way to tell if Bannister was truthful when he said he'd let Philipe live after the virus had been activated, but he didn't have a choice. Whether or not the man was telling the truth was irrelevant because Philipe wasn't going to send that virus out into the world.

He glanced at the reflection in the monitor on the right and noted the guards' positions again.

The two men had been standing there for ten minutes. They hadn't moved since their employer exited the room. Philipe wasn't able to tell if the guards were paying attention to what was on his screens, though he doubted they could make out the details. The code was small enough that even he had a measure of difficulty reading it as his fingers tapped away at the keys.

He took a deep breath and sighed, then continued to enter the various codes needed to access the location of his virus.

A 3-D hexagon appeared on the screen directly in front of him. One side blinked green, then illuminated.

"That's one," he said. Philipe knew that he only had thirty seconds to get the next code entered, or the first one would disappear and he'd have to start all over again. It was a failsafe he'd included in the process to make extracting the virus even more difficult. The element of time always pressed on hackers, especially those who were up to no good. It was that feeling of knowing they could catch you at any moment. The digital cloak and dagger was every bit as stressful as in the regular world.

Another side blinked with twenty seconds to spare. When it became solid, the timer in the top right corner started over again, counting down from thirty.

Code filled the screens to the left and right of the center. It took every ounce of Philipe's concentration to read it fast enough and pick apart the sections he needed to drop into the encryption.

He typed faster and faster, knowing that every time he filled in one patch of the hexagon, he would only have a second before the timer started up again. The third block blinked and then became solid. This one completed with only twelve seconds to go.

The codes were more difficult with each subsequent success—another reason he was certain no one else in the world could crack it.

Philipe wiped the sweat from his brow with the back of his wrist and set back to work. One by one, the blocks fell into place as he continued to insert the encoded keys until he only had a single block left.

The timer started, and he began again, piecing together the code from memory as he scanned the two side screens for the clues only he would recognize. He felt the pressure mount as the clock ticked down to fifteen. Philipe's heart raced. He knew he would cut this one close. He had to concentrate, eliminating any distractions including those that came from the anxiety in his mind.

"Come on," he whispered. The clock hit ten, and he still wasn't as close as he wanted to be.

His fingers worked faster, and he feared making a wrong entry. He knew it was highly probable he'd have to make several attempts at cracking open the virus; it was irrational to think otherwise. No way could he get it on his first try. Or could he?

He saw the code flashing through his mind as he gazed at the three screens simultaneously. Philipe barely noticed the six seconds on the clock. He swallowed hard and pressed on, fingers a blur on the keys. Then after a last flurry of keystrokes, he tapped the enter key with his pinky and focused on the center screen where the hexagon spun like a jagged globe. The clock read one second. He held his breath.

Then the last block blinked and filled in. He exhaled loudly and clapped his hands together, a move he immediately regretted as it startled the guards.

"What was that?" one guard asked.

Philipe spun around in the chair and grinned at them with hands up. "Sorry. Just making progress."

"Well, keep it down. I almost shot you."

"Yes. Of course. My mistake."

Philipe twisted the chair back around to face the screens and grinned. On the center monitor, the green hexagon continued to spin. The words, "Welcome, mighty Zeus," glowed at the bottom.

He grinned at the greeting. Even though he'd written the code himself, it still made his inner child happy to see a machine say hello and call him by his moniker.

Once more, his fingers set to work as he typed a response to the system. "Hello, Milton. How are you today?"

The computer responded instantly. "I'm fine, sir. How may I be of assistance?" The response might have caused a novice to think it was some kind of sentient AI. Truth was, the virus wasn't far from that, at least the way Philipe had designed it. There were, however, limitations to how much it could grow and learn. The restrictions forced it to focus all of its energy on a certain list of hacking protocols. Putting such a governor on the code would keep it within the fences that Philipe dictated and prevent it from running wild.

Now, though, he had to move the fences. The virus was designed to take down financial centers for a prolonged period, long enough to cause a global economic shutdown. Philipe didn't want that. He knew that if he was successful with such an attempt, both his and his daughter's lives would be forfeit. He'd gotten used to the idea that he was going to die. It wasn't an idea he liked, but what choice did he have?

He glanced at the guards' reflections again and then set to work.

"Initiate new protocol." He typed the words into the computer and waited.

"Authentication required," the screen read.

Philipe sighed. "Here goes nothing." He typed in the word *Theresa*, and the screen blinked. A new set of code appeared on the center screen, replacing the hexagon.

Access Granted appeared at the top of the new screen.

"Initiate BRIARPATCH."

The screen ran dozens of new lines of code within a few seconds. At the bottom of the screen, a new message appeared: Please Direct BRIARPATCH to Specific Accounts."

Philipe looked to the piece of paper with messy scribbled numbers on it. He'd asked for it from Bannister himself, telling the man he needed his account numbers and routing numbers to prevent the virus from erasing his money. There were several accounts listed, and it would take more than a couple of minutes for him to enter the information. That didn't matter. Now that he was in, time wasn't the issue. The only issue would be if Bannister had another hacker watching this computer to make sure Philipe wasn't going off plan.

With a last look over his shoulder, he started entering the numbers.

26

LONDON

Everyone in the group stayed low, just beneath the edge of the platform. They didn't dare take a peek over the top until the two guards who'd appeared in the station noticed one of their comrades lying dead on the floor.

"Oy," one of them said. "We've got trouble."

It was unclear whether the guard was talking into his radio or merely making a comment to the other, but there was no time to waste. On the off chance the man hadn't radioed that message to more guards, this would be the only opportunity for the invaders to take them out and find the secret door.

Zeke nodded to the others, and they popped up from their hiding place with guns extended. In the split second between emerging from the rut and pulling the trigger , Zeke noted where the newcomers had entered—one of the sealed tunnel walls was now open.

Without preamble, the silence of the abandoned station erupted as everyone fired simultaneously, unleashing a deadly volley of hot metal on the two guards.

Zeke and Phoenix fired five shots each to conserve ammunition, and they'd ordered the others to do the same. Jessica did as instructed. So did Marilyn.

Vincent and Freeman, however, emptied their entire magazines at the targets, missing with every single shot. The wall behind the guards took a beating from their wildly inaccurate shots. Luckily, the others hadn't been so imprecise.

The guards shuddered as bullets riddled their bodies. The blizzard of rounds punctured legs, torsos, and one neck. Once the attack was over, the guards lay lifeless next to each other. A thin haze of smoke lingered over the platform, filling the air with the scent of burned powder.

Zeke and Phoenix were the first to climb up. They checked the bodies with rapid efficiency. Touching the necks of the victims told the two all they needed to know. The guards were dead.

"Okay," Zeke hissed. "Come on. Won't be long until more come looking for them."

The rest of the group crested the edge of the platform and hurried over. Jessica held her weapon low, her knees bent, ready for action if Zeke was right about the reinforcements.

She glanced down at the dead men and pointed. "Get their radios."

"Good call," Phoenix agreed. He bent down and took one from the closest guard while Jessica removed one from the ear of another.

Zeke bit his lower lip as he stared down at the lone remaining guard with a radio in his ear. "Seriously?" The question came out louder than he intended, but it expressed the full range of his irritation.

Jessica and Phoenix looked at him with questions in their eyes. "What?" they both asked.

Zeke stared down at the dead man. The earpiece was covered in blood and a few fragments he thought might have been bone. A bullet hole in the side of his head was the cause of the mess.

"It's...covered in blood," he said, holding back a bulb of bile that suddenly lurched into his esophagus.

"Wipe it off. We need to go."

"You know what? You two have radios. We're good."

"Take the radio," Jessica ordered. "Don't be such a diva."

Zeke cringed at the thought, but he also didn't want to appear to be soft, especially to Jessica. Vincent and Marilyn looking on in judgment didn't help.

"Why do I get stuck with the radio with the dude's brains all over it? If it's not so bad, you take it, Phoenix."

"Stop being such a baby," Marilyn said. She stepped over, plucked the bloody radio from the dead man's ear, and wiped it on the side of Zeke's shirt. "There," she said, dropping it on his wrist. Zeke stared in horror at the device as it rested on the back of his forearm. He was so disgusted he couldn't shrink back. Instead, he simply stood there, momentarily paralyzed.

"See? That wasn't so bad," Marilyn added.

"Um, thank you. Thank you so, so much." He grimaced as he took the radio and inspected it like a picky child trying to decide whether to eat a lima bean. Everyone watched as he shoved the still-warm earpiece into his left ear.

"Ugh," Phoenix said once the device was in his friend's ear. "That is disgusting."

"What?"

"Come on," Jessica said with a grin she couldn't hide. Then she started toward the open doorway.

The rest followed close behind, weapons ready. Freeman and Vincent picked up guns from the dead men since the two had spent the contents of their magazines and needed new rounds.

They checked them to make sure there were no signs of blood or gore and then shouldered the guns as they hurried to catch up to the others.

Once everyone was inside the next corridor, Jessica pressed a red button on the wall, and the giant faux seal easily swung shut.

Inside the new tunnel, things looked much the same as they did on the other side. The tiles that lined the curved walls were like the others, which meant whoever was down here hadn't changed the original design. The one change was the fluorescent lights hanging from the ceiling, casting a sterile white glow into the passage.

Zeke took the lead, stepping by Jessica despite her best attempt to keep him back. His masculine ego wouldn't allow it to be any other way. He recalled being beat up by a girl when he was in elementary school, though remembering the event was an unnecessary exercise. It had shaped the way he acted around women, shrouded in a cloak of insecurity that resulted in a humorous self-defense mechanism.

Phoenix remained in the rear, close to Marilyn—by her choosing. She allowed herself to linger while the others pressed forward, forcing her way to the back where she could be near him.

Zeke noted her deliberate movement but said nothing—at first.

He came to a curve in the tunnel and poked his head around the edge, leading with his pistol.

He waved the all-clear and kept moving. The corridor stretched another fifty feet before it reached a set of steps leading farther into the bowels of the city. Hot air wafted up from below, filling that part of the tunnel and pushing away the remaining cool air that had lingered from above.

It reminded Zeke of the subways in New York. He'd visited the Big Apple several times, but he never got accustomed to how hot it could get down in the subway stations, especially during the summer. He imagined winter would be less abysmal.

The group paused at the top of the stairs and looked down to the platform below. What met their gaze wasn't remotely close to what they anticipated. They'd expected an ordinary train platform from the early twentieth century—dark, lifeless, and derelict. Instead, the platform was a hive of activity.

People in similar outfits to the dead guards' buzzed around computer stations set onto the platform that had been extended over the gap where the rails used to be. It also housed the server room.

"Black One."

A man's voice in the radio earpieces startled the three wearing them.

Jessica's eyes widened, knowing she couldn't respond.

"What?" Freeman mouthed, seeing that his three counterparts were clearly frightened by something.

"Radio," Jess pointed at her ear with her index finger. She turned to Phoenix. "Answer them," she mouthed.

His face scrunched in confusion. "What?" he responded with an inaudible question.

"Talk," she encouraged, rolling her hand in the air to egg him on.

"Oh," he said and cleared his throat. "Yes, this is Black One. Nothing to report so far, sir."

"What was that ruckus before? We thought we heard something."

"Just trying to get rid of some rats," Phoenix answered with a shrug, hoping the guy on the other end believed it.

The silence that permeated the channel caused them no shortage of concern, but what could they do but sit and wait?

It might have only been ten seconds, but it felt much longer before the man responded. "Bloody things are such a nuisance. Big ones this time?"

"Uh, yes, sir. Monsters. I think we scared them away." Phoenix spoke in a gruff tone with a bad English accent. He felt certain there was no way they'd buy it.

"All right," the voice responded. "Finish up and sweep the upper area. We have word there might be company coming, and we don't want to get caught with our pants down."

"Yes, sir," Phoenix said.

The channel went dead, and he took the radio out of his ear, found the mute button, and pressed it. A tiny red LED light glowed from within and he put the device back in his ear.

He looked at the others. "Kill yours," he whispered. "They'll hear us talking if you don't."

"Kill?" Zeke asked. He took the radio out of his ear and placed it on the floor, then raised his boot. "You sure?"

"Mute it, dude," Phoenix said, shaking his head.

"Oh right. I knew that." Zeke picked up his tainted radio and found the mute button.

Jessica had complied by the time he silenced his device.

"I count a dozen guards," Jessica said, looking at the group and meeting everyone's eyes.

"Yep," Zeke agreed as he turned back to face the scene below. "That's what I got, too." He hadn't bothered counting the enemies yet but didn't want to look stupid. "You're not counting the guy in the suit?"

"No."

"Why not?"

"He's not armed," she said and turned her head to fling an irritated glance his way.

"You sure?"

She rolled her eyes. "Fine. Thirteen."

Freeman crouched near the top of the steps and looked into the dimly lit space below. Lights blinked on the machines and in the server racks near the wall within the gap's platform.

"That's a lot of servers," Freeman noted. "Probably the heat signatures you were picking up."

"Yeah," Marilyn agreed. "Not the best place to put those things if you ask me. They need to stay cool. Normally, if you got your own servers, you have them in a separate building. You don't ever want to keep them in the same place as your other hardware."

"Why's that?" Zeke asked.

"Those things get hot, first of all. They need to be kept in a climate-controlled environment. Second, they're hosting a ton of data. If something were to happen to your computer systems, those things are your backups. If they go down, you lose everything."

"Unless you're storing stuff in the cloud," Vincent said with a chuckle.

Marilyn snorted a laugh with him. "The cloud," she snickered.

"What?" Zeke asked. "What's so funny?"

The siblings looked at each other and had to hold off the laughter for fear of giving away their position.

"Nothing," Marilyn said, forcing a straight face. "What's the plan?"

"We need to find Philipe," Zeke answered. "I don't see him down there, which means he's probably in some kind of cell or something."

"A cell? In the London Underground?" Vincent asked.

"They filled the gap where the rails used to be," Phoenix countered. "It's not out of the realm of possibility that they made some other modifications."

"Fine," Jessica said, interrupting the conversation. "We need to find him, but we also need to shut this whole thing down. We could shoot the servers, right? That would take their operation offline?"

"It might," Marilyn said. There was an unfinished but at the end of that answer.

"It might also kill us all," Vincent warned. "Could start a fire. I don't feel much like dying in the Tube from smoke inhalation, thank you very much."

"Okay," Jessica sighed. "What then? Pull the plug?"

"That could work," Vincent said. "But we'd have to find it. Cut the power, they still might have backup generators. I know I would."

"He's right," Marilyn said. "This setup will have a backup system. Anyone who spends this kind of money to build something like this will have every failsafe available. And then some. They won't be taking any chances."

"All right, then?" Jessica groused. "What do we do?"

Marilyn and Vincent blinked for a moment, their minds drawing a blank.

"We need to find Philipe before we do anything else," Freeman said. "Find him, and we don't have to worry about the rest."

"True, but we still need to shut down this entire operation." She glanced down at her phone and realized there was no chance she'd get a signal down here. They were on their own. Unless one of them volunteered to go back up to street level and try to hail the cavalry.

That wouldn't work, either. They would only accept an order from Jessica. Zeke and Phoenix were already in trouble. They were suspended, and if they called it in, there would be no help arriving anytime soon.

Then there was the little problem of her going up to do it. Jessica didn't like leaving the group without a natural leader. Zeke and Phoenix were capable agents, despite their numerous shortcomings, but they weren't leaders.

Freeman and the other two wouldn't work, either, which left her zero options. On their own.

"Wonder what's in there," Zeke said, pointing at a red door set into the wall about twenty feet down the corridor.

He'd noticed it on their way in but thought little of it since everyone in the group believed they were supposed to keep going. He stayed low and made his way back down the passage.

"What are you doing?" Jessica hissed. "You're going to get us caught."

"By who?" Zeke whispered over his shoulder. "The three dead guys?"

He rolled his eyes and kept going until he reached the door. He turned the latch, but nothing happened. He frowned then tugged on the handle. Surprisingly, the door broke free and flew open.

"Zeke, get back here," Jessica demanded.

He ignored her and stepped into the opening.

"Jeez, he is infuriating," Jessica said to Phoenix.

"I know. I'll go get him."

"Well, well, well." The new voice came through the radios, causing Jessica and Phoenix to freeze. "I didn't realize so many people had RSVP'd to my little party."

Jessica spun on her heels to locate the source of the voice. She didn't have to look far.

A man she'd noticed earlier was standing in the center of the main floor below. His back had been toward the group as he stared up at a massive screen on the brick wall. It showed a map of the world with several blinking green dots where some of the planet's largest cities were located.

Now, he was staring straight at them.

"Crap," Phoenix said.

"What?" Vincent asked. "What's wrong?"

Footsteps pounding on the hard floor behind them answered the question.

Before anyone in the group could spin and open fire, a man with a shaved head and a Berretta 9 mm ordered them to put down their weapons.

"Great," Jessica said.

The clean-shaven man was accompanied by three others. They didn't need to ask how the gunmen got behind them. It was obviously a trap, and the group had walked right into it.

Phoenix slowly put his gun on the floor next to Freeman's. The two hackers were hesitant, but seeing a pistol brandished in their faces, they reluctantly surrendered their guns.

"That was smart," the man in the suit said into the radios, "coming in through the front door like that. Did none of you realize we have cameras everywhere? What did you think this was? Google?"

Jessica and Phoenix looked over their shoulders at the man. He was older than they were, by at least twenty years. They'd never seen him before, but they knew exactly who he was.

He was the one behind all of this, the one who called himself Perses.

And they'd all just walked right into his web.

27

LONDON

W atching through the gap between the red door and the frame, Zeke swore under his breath as they escorted his entire team down the stairs at gunpoint.

He breathed heavily and let the door close quietly the second the group was out of sight.

He leaned back and pressed the base of his skull against the wall, doing his best to slow his panicked breaths and racing heartbeat.

"What now, Zeke, you idiot," he whispered to himself. There was that word again. Idiot. Now he was calling himself that, and it wasn't the first time. Then again, it quickly became evident that if he'd been out there with the group, he would have been nicked as well. He'd be in the frying pan with the rest of them. Surely, the gunmen would notice one of them missing.

He'd heard the voice through the radio and immediately guessed who it was. It had to be Perses, the villain behind all of this. He'd mentioned cameras, but Zeke saw none on their way into the abandoned station.

But there could have been cameras in a hundred different places and he wouldn't have noticed. That none of his squad had seen them was either an indication of their ineptitude—Jessica included—or of how well hidden the devices were. That didn't matter at this point; Zeke knew he needed to focus on how to get his companions out of this mess, stop a virus from wrecking the entire planet, and, oh yeah, save a hacker.

"Sure. No problem," he muttered. Then he sighed and took inventory of his surroundings.

The best Zeke could tell, he was in a maintenance tunnel of some kind. Old metal pipes ran along the wall from where he was standing until they disappeared into the darkness twenty feet away. Unlike the corridor outside, this one wasn't illuminated. That alone caused overwhelming concern, to the point he wasn't sure if he should go back out into the other passage. That would be a mistake, though, and he knew it. As soon as the men in charge realized one of the intruders had disappeared, they'd come looking for him. There was a chance they wouldn't realize he was missing, but that was an outlier at best. For the moment, Zeke had gotten lucky, but that luck could turn in an instant.

With that last thought, he pressed ahead into the dark tunnel. It was nearly pitch black, and while unnerving, it was also a good sign. It meant he was alone, and if someone else approached, he would see them coming because they'd be using a light, same as him.

He raised the weapon again and shined the light down the corridor, once more revealing the path that led straight ahead until the light waned and he could see no farther. His feet moved almost involuntarily, stepping on the edges of his boots to keep contact with the floor to a minimum.

Farther along, the passage made a sharp turn to the right, continued another twenty feet, and then veered left again. As he rounded the corner to the left, he realized he was probably parallel to the control room, and somewhere above the hundreds of servers racked up on the concrete platform. He tried to remember if he'd seen some kind of ventilation shaft over the servers, but all he could recall were several massive fans blowing a constant stream of air to cool the machines.

He kept moving forward and walked face-first into a spider's web.

The sticky substance stretched across his face and wrapped around his ears. He freaked out and started swatting at the air in case the spider was still hovering in front of him. He pointed his light in every direction hoping to find the arachnid, but there was no sign of it, which—of course—meant the bug was on him somewhere.

Zeke frantically wiped his face and head, arms, legs, torso, everything in a desperate attempt to rid himself of the cursed creature. After nearly a minute of freaking out, he aimed the light at the floor, then on every inch of his body that he could reach, and let out a sigh of relief. He reassured himself that the web was probably very old and hadn't been inhabited for quite some time, maybe years. Yes, that was it. Years. What reason would a spider have for being down here?

He moved toward the end of the corridor and waved the light around one last time to make sure he hadn't missed the eight-legged threat dangling from some unseen portion of the tunnel. Loose strands of the web hung from various points on the ceiling, but there was no sign of the creature, so Zeke forced himself forward, albeit at a more careful pace.

He reached the end of the tunnel where a spiral concrete staircase descended. It looked much like the one they'd used when first arriving in Brompton Road Station.

Zeke narrowed his eyes suspiciously and aimed the pistol around to make sure he checked every possible inch of the staircase. He didn't want to run into any more surprises, insect or otherwise.

He heard no strange sounds and saw nothing to make him linger any longer. So, he took the first step and began his descent. He remembered his fall down the other stairs and took one hand off his weapon to keep it on the railing to prevent another accident. His bones and muscles still ached, and he knew that tomorrow it would be worse.

As long as he kept moving, he'd be fine. Adrenaline and blood flow could stave off the worst of the soreness. He'd learned that when playing sports. The best thing for an injury—if it wasn't significant—was to keep moving.

With that reminder, Zeke kept moving down the staircase.

Moving deliberately took longer, but he finally made it to the bottom and discovered another metal door. The room was only fifty or sixty square feet, and the pipes from above ran down the center of the shaft and into the floor. A huge metal valve was attached to the one next to a dusty pressure gauge. The needle on the gauge remained squarely in the middle.

"I guess there's still something flowing through this old thing," he muttered. Was it water? Gas? He had no idea. Civil engineering wasn't his forte. He wasn't even sure if it was a civil engineering thing or not. Maybe it was a plumbing thing.

He snapped his head to rid himself of the useless thoughts and stepped close to the door, pressing his right ear against it to listen. He heard something that sounded like a constant humming on the other side. Was he behind the server racks? He took a deep breath and decided there was only one way to know for sure.

Zeke gripped the pistol in his right hand and grabbed the latch to the door with the other. He twisted it, expecting it to creak or groan in protest, but was surprised when it only made the slightest squeak.

He paused for a second, still uncertain if he should open it. With his friends captured, Zeke was their only hope to stop global chaos. "No pressure," he whispered to himself. If there was a guard standing on the other side of the door, it would be the shortest offensive in history.

He let out a long exhale through his nose and then jerked the door open.

A blast of surprisingly cool air assaulted him with such force that it almost knocked him backward. His hair blew back for a moment, and he winced against the barrage. In a matter of seconds, the pressure between the room and the outside area equalized, and the onslaught dissipated.

Zeke poked his head out through the doorway and looked in both directions. There was a narrow space between the ten-foot-high server racks and the curved wall of the Tube. The concrete platform extended in both directions, stopping when it reached the darkened tunnels on either side. There was enough space to walk behind the huge collection of servers, probably for service or repairs, and the gap also provided a decent path for airflow behind the racks.

The hum Zeke had heard when pressing his ear to the wall was more pronounced now, and he realized what the source of the noise was after another quick look in both directions.

Several machines that looked almost like pressure washers without the sprayers were placed on the floor behind the servers. Big corrugated rubber tubes extended from the blowers and pumped cold air into the server station. Some tubes were draped from metal hooks above the servers, while others extended under the shelving to add cool air to the lower area. The result was that the server racks were enclosed in a dome of cool air, hence the surprising burst that hit Zeke when he first opened the door.

Vaguely remembering the positioning of the server racks, Zeke moved to his right to try to flank anyone still in the control center. He had no idea where his friends had been taken or what was about to happen to them, but standing around wondering wasn't going to help. He had to take action, and quickly.

He maneuvered around the air blowers and crept toward the end of the shelves. He kept his pistol high, near his shoulder, with both hands gripping it in case he had to use it. The suppressor and the flashlight made it heavier than usual, and as he reached the corner, he realized that the flashlight was still on.

He rolled his eyes at his stupid gaff and switched the light off. "Idiot," he mumbled.

Zeke peeked around the corner of the racks and looked toward the control center. He could only see the far edge of it but didn't see anyone in the area. Five rows of servers stood between him and the main control room, along with a narrow walkway. To the right of the concrete path, the gap opened up, and Zeke could see the old train tracks. He doubted any power went through the third rail but still noted it just in case.

He ducked behind the next row of servers and looked down the length of the aisle to make sure it was clear. It was empty, so he took a second to breathe and slow his heart rate again.

Again, he stepped out from behind cover and worked his way up the next row, then repeated his movements until he reached the row of servers closest to the control station. This time, he peeked out more cautiously, aware that there would likely be someone in the command area.

Zeke wasn't surprised when he spotted the man in the suit standing near the map. And next to him, handcuffed with zip ties and sitting in workstation chairs, were Zeke's companions.

He clenched his jaw in anger as he looked at Phoenix, Marilyn, Vincent, and Jessica. Oh, and Freeman, too.

The twelve guards they saw before were now sixteen, which didn't help. Even if his team hadn't been taken, they would have been outnumbered and up against a dangerous and capable foe.

Zeke would have to do something to even the odds, but first he needed to find Philipe. He stepped back away from the open and pressed his back against the stacks of servers, all sitting in rows atop dark metal shelves. Then he looked down at the base of the racks and realized that they weren't bolted into the ground. The shelving was recklessly put together, as if the thought of them tipping over hadn't occurred to anyone.

That gave him an idea, but it still didn't tell him where Philipe was.

Zeke made his way back to the wall and the narrow gap between the last row of servers.

"Think, man. Where would they keep a hacker down here?" He ground his teeth together as he pondered the question.

Out of the corner of his eye, he glimpsed movement to his left. He frowned and ducked behind the last air blower in the row and crouched to stay out of sight.

A beam of light danced along the wall and the narrow walkway in the Tube to his right. Someone was coming in his direction. But who?

Zeke only had one option: stay put and be ready to fight. He readied his weapon, propping the base of the grip atop the whirring blower. He kept his head out of sight and looked through a small gap in the machine's metal frame.

The person carrying the flashlight turned out to be a man with darkly tanned skin and short black hair. He had tattoos on his face, neck, and arms and carried the light in one hand with a submachine gun slung over the same shoulder. In the other hand, he had an empty bottle of water and a barren plate with ketchup stains.

Food, Zeke realized. The man had been feeding someone. A prisoner? Philipe?

The dots were easy enough to connect—unless this Perses fellow had other people he was holding captive. While not out of the realm of possibility, it was certainly not likely.

If this guard was coming back from a holding cell, there was a good bet that's exactly where Zeke would find Philipe. Once he found the Frenchman, he could lead him to safety and save his friends. Of course, that was the best-case scenario. The kind that rarely happened, especially in Zeke's line of work. Still, it was his only lead, the single opportunity he had to save the French hacker and his entire team.

Zeke watched as the guard diverted his path toward the control center and disappeared around the last row of servers.

Now was Zeke's chance. He stepped out from behind the blower and hustled toward the shadows of the Tube, silently praying that no one would see him but feeling like he'd drawn the attention of everyone in the London Underground.

Each step felt like a mile as he stalked toward the darkness. His mind begged him to look back over his shoulder, but he forced himself to stay focused on the shadows ahead as he took one step after the other. Perhaps looking back would have no consequences. Maybe it was a kind of superstition. Whatever it was, it worked because the second he felt the light wane and the darkness envelop him, he relaxed and finally took a glance back toward the control center.

The group was no longer visible, cut off by the corner of the tunnel. It was only then that Zeke realized he would have been exposed for a short distance, though most of his journey across the platform was hidden. He snorted his derision and moved on.

His eyes quickly adjusted to the darkness. He blinked away the last few seconds of dimness and noticed a door set into the curved wall, centered in an alcove just ahead.

So, that's where he came from.

Zeke's pace quickened. He reached the doorway in two dozen hurried steps, then ducked into the recess in case someone else was coming back from the control area.

He peeked around the corner and saw no one, then turned and checked the door latch. To his relief, it was unlocked.

Zeke took a deep breath, pulled down, and shoved the door open.

28

LONDON

Jordan's eyes creaked open, and the eyelids grated across his eyeballs like cheap toilet paper. He forced himself to blink away the pain, which took nearly a minute. As that irritation began to subside, he noticed a more prominent source of pain in his chest and abdomen. He winced and tried to push himself up with his elbows. The hard concrete bit into his bones and caused another grimace to crinkle his face.

He grunted through the pain, but as he bent slightly at his waist, a new wave of agonizing pain washed through his upper body.

Then he remembered.

Bannister.

His employer had said something about loose ends.

Jordan twisted himself onto his side to relieve the pressure on the worst of the pain. The right side of his head throbbed, too, probably from the fall. His skull must have smacked against the concrete and rendered him unconscious.

He knew he was lucky to be alive.

The thought caused him to look over at the body of the last man from his crew. Jordan knew the guy didn't have a vest on. He wore nothing but a tight black T-shirt. Jordan wasn't so ill prepared. He knew a high-value target could bring unwanted attention and trouble.

He had no idea the trouble would come from the man who was paying his bills.

Jordan had grown accustomed to the idea that anyone who hired him was just as dangerous as him—almost. But over the years, he'd become soft, too trusting of those writing the checks. That much was evident now.

He clenched his jaw, grinding his teeth as he stared at the inert body in a congealing pool of crimson.

The realization hit Jordan with stunning gravity. A lump formed in his throat as he considered the reality of the situation. All of his men were dead, wiped out in the last few hours. They were mercenaries. They knew the game, knew the stakes, knew the risks. He didn't feel bad for them; they were hired guns. They were expendable tools, as he was.

But the mere fact that someone had been able to take out his entire team, at the farmhouse and then here, revealed a serious problem—either in his hiring practices or in his judgment of employers. Perhaps it was both.

Jordan grunted again and pushed himself to his feet. The room spun, and he teetered for a moment as he felt the ground might rise to meet his face. He deftly spread out his legs and bent his knees to give himself a wider base of support while gathering his balance.

A few short breaths, and Jordan felt a little better. The bullet holes in his tactical shirt were haunting reminders of just how close he'd come to death. He pulled the shirt up over his head and examined the areas where the rounds had burrowed into his vest. The crushed metal had knocked him back, shocked him, and undoubtedly bruised his chest and abdomen. He wanted to examine the damage but knew it was best if he didn't. He assumed he'd cracked a rib or two, but he could have himself assessed later—when he escaped this hole.

Jordan had access to a few medical experts around the world and one of them was right here in London. They were discredited physicians, men and women who—for one reason or another—had lost their licenses in their respective countries. Most were guilty of the accusations brought against them. Sometimes it was as simple as incompetence, but mostly it was for indiscretions of a more sinister nature.

Those were the ones Jordan wanted, those with fewer scruples. They were more than happy to take cash for services, and it was fine by Jordan to pay their higher rates just to avoid the hospitals.

He would see the London physician when he left this place—if he found a way out.

His eyes darted toward the door, and he wondered if they'd locked it. *Is there a guard outside? Why would someone be guarding this room? Everyone inside is thought to be dead.*

He glanced around again and realized that Bannister, for all his cocky bluster, had forgotten to take the guns off the dead men. The wealthy boss man must have planned on his busboy taking care of the weapons when he disposed of the bodies.

They could be sold on the black market, but what would be the point of that? A couple of grand in the big scheme of things wouldn't affect Bannister, or his acolytes.

Whatever the reason, Jordan was glad they had left the weapons behind. He hurried back to the spot where he'd fallen and scooped up the pistol. Then he turned and strode over to Jimmison's body. Jordan paused and then bent down. The younger man's lifeless eyes stared blankly at the far wall. A pang of regret singed Jordan's chest; it took a herculean effort to push aside the feeling and stay focused on what he needed to do.

He tugged the pistol loose from the dead mercenary's rigid fingers and examined the magazine, checked the slide that ejected the round in the pipe, and then replaced the round before slipping the magazine back into the base of the pistol.

Jordan sighed; it was going to be difficult to get out of here. He'd helped escort the prisoner down to this level and was all too aware of how many armed guards he'd have to shoot before he could make a break for the exit.

At least he had two weapons and enough rounds to take out most of Bannister's men, if not all of them. One bullet, however, he specifically assigned to Bannister. Jordan hoped it would be the last one in his arsenal; he wanted Bannister to know who was shaking his entire world apart.

A heavy clunk startled him from his thoughts of vengeance. It came from outside the room, down the hallway to the left. Jordan held his pistols out to his sides as he moved toward the door. He crouched against the wall and waited. He positioned the weapons higher, closer to his jawline.

Seconds ticked by. His heart beat steadily in his chest. The fact it didn't race in such a tense situation was a tribute to Jordan's training, his mastery of self-control.

The latch squeaked and then turned. The lock clicked free. Still, Jordan waited. He didn't move when the door swung open. He would wait until his target was in full sight. Then Jordan would eliminate them.

A boot landed, and Jordan knew the intruder was inside the room. Just another two steps, and they would have zero chance of attack.

"Philipe?" A man's voice startled Jordan, but he didn't flinch at the voice, or at the name of the prisoner. The accent, however, caught Jordan's attention. It was American.

Had one of the American agents made it into Bannister's underground lair?

"Philipe?" the voice asked again, this time in more of a whisper. "You in here?"

Jordan eased the door closed and raised his weapons, aiming them at the back of the intruder's head.

"Don't move," he warned.

The man startled, nearly jumping out of his shoes. The pistol in his hand, held a little too loosely, jiggled free and fell to the floor with a clatter.

Jordan grimaced, fearing a round would discharge, but the

weapon remained silent. Then he drew a deep breath through his nose, irritated at the stranger's ineptitude.

"Who are you?" Jordan asked.

"Me?"

"No, not you. The dead guy over there. Of course, you. What are you, stupid?"

The man slowly turned.

"I didn't tell you to move."

"Yeah," Zeke said as his face came into view. "Well, I really don't care. I'm tired of people calling me an idiot or stupid. Do I do some stupid things? Sure. Does it always work out? No. Not exactly. But you know what? I'm tired of it." He wagged his index finger at Jordan. Then he realized who it was and quickly stopped talking, but only for a second. "My name is Zeke Marshall."

"Jordan Bradley." Jordan inclined his head. Every instinct told him to shoot this guy, but he held back. He could be useful, if for nothing else than as a human shield if it came down to Jordan shooting his way out. He figured he might as well pry for information. "What do you want with Philipe?"

"We were protecting him. You took him."

"Yes, I know that," Jordan said, rolling his eyes. "Why do you want him now?"

"I'm trying to get him out of here," Zeke said. "But you work for that Perses guy, so that's why you set up this trap for me. You knew I was coming."

"Bannister," Jordan spat.

"I'm sorry?" Zeke cocked his head to the side, looking like a curious puppy.

"Leopold Bannister. He calls himself Perses. Not important. You're clearly against Bannister."

"Yes. He took my entire team prisoner. They're in the central control area thingy. I don't know if he realizes I was with them or not. If the does..."

"We would know it by now. His guards would be sweeping the area. My guess is they have no clue you're here."

That made Zeke feel a little better.

"So, you're going after the hacker instead of your friends?" Jordan asked.

"First of all, not all of them are friends. I mean, I think Phoenix is, Freeman probably, although he's like the parasite of the group. Jessica is more like a work acquaintance."

Jordan's eyes widened with annoyance, and he finally had to cut Zeke off. "Fine. Shut up. I don't need to know your entire friend list. So, what's your plan?"

Zeke shrugged. "Get Philipe to safety, then take down Perses... Bannister's operation."

Jordan's head inclined slightly, and then a grin creased his face. "Good. Then we're on the same side."

Zeke frowned. "We are? Since when?"

"Since now. Follow me."

29

LONDON

The man in the suit stood before the group tied to the chairs in the middle of the control room. He eyed them one at a time, walking by with his hands folded at his waist. He analyzed each of the prisoners as though they were cattle at auction.

The large digital map of the world loomed over them from the wide projection screen on the wall.

The contingent of gunmen surrounding them was formidable, their mere presence imposing. Escape seemed as good as impossible.

Phoenix did his best to put on a tough poker face.

Jessica looked more incensed than anything else—the nerve these guys had to keep her tied down like this.

Phoenix then smirked, which was a look that didn't escape the man in the suit.

"Something funny?" the suit asked, raising his eyebrows.

"Other than you calling yourself Perses?" Phoenix responded.

The man inclined his head for a second and then crouched back to meet Phoenix eye to eye. "If you knew who I was and what I was doing, you'd think differently. I'm going to shake up the global playground, my American friend. And you all are going to get to see it unravel. When it does, there will be one person left on top, one person to help those in need, one person with the resources to guide the planet toward a prosperous future."

"Whose prosperous future? Yours?"

The man's lips creased on the right side of his face. "Obviously, as the unquestioned most powerful man on the planet, I'll be positioned to continue prospering far more than I have for years."

"I know who you are," Marilyn spat.

The suit turned, surprised at both her comment and that she'd spoken at all. Marilyn had remained quiet since being captured, but especially so upon seeing the man up close.

"What was that?" he asked.

The man with the shaved head and a neck the size of a tree trunk was standing near her. He frowned at the confession.

"I said I know who you are, Leo." She cocked her head to the side and grinned.

He stalked away from Phoenix and over to Marilyn, who sat with her hands bound behind her back.

He stopped directly in front of her and bent over at the waist, lowering his face to where his nose nearly touched hers.

"And who are you?" he asked.

"Doesn't matter who I am, love. I'm just another hacker. But I know who you are. I know all about you."

"Is that so?" Bannister straightened and did his best to pretend that her statement didn't bother him.

"Oh yeah," she said with a slow nod, head cocked slightly to the side. "I know a lot about you. I wouldn't have thought you were the one behind this, though. Wouldn't want the other families to think you've gone rogue, would we? Heaven knows what they would do to you, right?"

Bannister kept his gaze steady, unwavering except for a slight flinch in his right eye. It was almost unnoticeable, but Marilyn caught it. Her smirk widened.

"Yeah, that's right. Innit, Leo? The other families would put you down, and no one would ever find out what happened to you. That's how they do it, innit? They make you disappear—unless they want to shame you. But they usually save that for the more notable traitors in their midst, like that Hollywood producer who got caught up in the sexual allegations. But that won't work for you. You're an unknown. But not to me, and certainly not to the other seven families."

Bannister drew a long sniff through his nose, clearly disarmed by her comments.

"You don't know what you're talking about, girl."

Her left eye winced at the ludicrous accusation. "Why are you blushing then, boy?" The retort earned a sneer, and Marilyn had no plans on stopping. "So, that's what this is all about, huh? Wreck the entire global system so you can have a crack at being top dog? It won't work. You know that, right? Even if you take them down, they'll come for you. They'll know. They always know."

Vincent blatantly stared at his sister as if seeing her for the first time, and uncertain if he liked what he saw. He suddenly had the sickening feeling that he didn't know her. She sounded and looked foreign to him. How did she know who this man was? And if he was part of some secretive, global cabal, how did she know so much about it? If they got out of this situation alive, Vincent had firm plans to have a long discussion with his sister.

Everyone's gaze remained locked on her. Jessica appeared to be the most interested in what she had to say, soaking in every single word with narrow, appraising eyes.

Freeman, too, drank the information in. He'd always been a conspiracy theorist, someone who dabbled in the online forums, read articles from the "less-reputable" news sources. He called those publications the hot sheets, even though he knew most of their content was pure fanatical conjecture. Now and then, though, they hit the nail on the head and produced some undeniable facts.

Phoenix even looked at Marilyn differently. Was that admiration in his eyes or just curiosity? Were the two mutually exclusive? He wasn't sure, but he suddenly appreciated her more than he had before.

Bannister inclined his head again and cracked his neck from side to side.

"Who are you?" he asked. "Tell me and you'll be the first one killed. Resist and...let's just say I'll make sure you're the last."

He didn't have to elaborate further. Marilyn knew, as did the rest of them, exactly what he meant. He'd force her to watch as he tortured and then eventually killed each person in the group before doing the same to her.

What Bannister didn't know was that the only person in the group she had ties to was Vincent. She'd only just met the rest of them a few hours ago. Still, she thought Phoenix was cute. There was something about him she felt instantly attracted to, and that initial feeling had never waned, which was strange for her.

Vincent knew that she might well throw away the lives of the Americans to save her own skin, as well as his. There was a small part of him that was okay with that, but a larger part of him—the part with morals that annoyed him more often than not—wasn't fine with it. He waited to see how she would respond.

Marilyn had secrets, but this new interaction with Bannister seemed more like stalling. Why would the man care who she was? There was the off chance that he believed she might be some kind of government agent, which was ironic since the others in the group were all part of a government agency.

"I'm nobody," she said finally, looking him in the eyes. "I'm just a harvester."

"A harvester?" Bannister asked, his confusion causing his face to twitch and head to tilt to the right.

"Of information," she clarified. "I simply gather what is there and analyze it. Sometimes I sell what I find. Sometimes I keep it for myself."

"So, you are a criminal." The condemnation came as a statement rather than a question. "A common thief."

"There is nothing common about me," Marilyn said confidently. "I assure you. And the information I sell is always about criminals, people like you who are set on hurting others for nothing more than your selfish gain. Power-hungry fools like you deserve to have everything taken from them. I promise you this, Leo, it's going to happen to you."

There was a truth in her prophecy that cut through the room like a broadsword. Bannister narrowed his eyes and motioned to one of his guards. "Very well," he said. "Kill her first."

The guard stepped up without hesitation and drew his pistol. He raised the weapon and was about to put two rounds into her chest when one of the men operating the computers stood up and interrupted.

"Sir?" The man was young, perhaps early twenties, though he may have been closer to thirty. His skin was clean and smooth, but his light brown hair was already thinning at the front. He was thin, clearly more brains than muscle, and he approached his employer with a fear that the guards didn't seem to possess.

"What?" Bannister snapped, turning to face the young man who dared interrupt his entertainment.

"We have a problem."

Bannister looked at Marilyn, then at the young man, then to the guard who was about to execute the woman. "What do you mean, we have a problem?" Bannister was obviously a man unaccustomed to interruptions, especially with potentially bad news.

The young man swallowed hard, and it was obvious to everyone in the room that the information he was about to relay was, indeed, not good.

"Spit it out," Bannister insisted when seeing his employee's hesitance.

"Well, sir," the man lowered his head slightly, keeping his gaze only vaguely on his boss, "it seems that your hacker has uploaded the virus."

"Really?" Bannister sounded hopeful. He squinted in surprise and a satisfied grin crept onto his face. "That's not a problem. Wait. How is that a problem?"

"The virus is doing what it was supposed to do, sir, but...the targets..." His voice trailed off.

Bannister's head shook. "What about them?" He was rapidly losing his patience with the younger man.

"None of them have been affected. In fact, only one account holder was attacked."

"One?" A look of concern crossed Bannister's face. "Which one?"

The young tech guy swallowed again, desperately wishing he could get out of the room and disappear to somewhere far away.

"Yours, sir."

Marilyn let a grin slip across her face. Philipe had just signed his own death sentence, along with theirs, but she knew the rest of the world would be safe and there was nothing Bannister could do about it.

30

P hilipe leaned back in his chair and laced his fingers on top of his head, letting them settle into his thick hair.

He stared at the screen with satisfaction, and with a small measure of resignation. He'd effectively signed his death warrant, but he was okay with it. He had no regrets apart from wishing he could see his daughter, Theresa, one last time.

Philipe could still smell her scent on his clothes from the last tear-filled hug he'd given her. His mind filled with the touch of her hair against his fingertips, and his heart pounded at the thought of her embrace, an embrace he'd never get again. He'd been a good father, as good as he could be. Money had never been in tremendous abundance, though that wouldn't be a problem for Theresa anymore.

The singularity virus he'd uploaded burrowed into the code of Bannister's accounts and distributed every single cent to charitable organizations around the world. There was only one entity that wasn't a charity, one that would provide his daughter with a decent head start on life.

The amount was small considering the vast resources in Bannister's holdings. All told, over twenty billion dollars were taken from the man's accounts and distributed all over the world. Only $250,000 of that went in the secret account Philipe had set up for Theresa. His mother would get an email detailing how to access the funds, but she could only take out $10,000 a year until Theresa was eighteen years of age.

He sighed as he considered what she might look like when she was older, getting ready for college, perhaps even getting married. It caused a dam of tears to form in his eyes, and he had to fight hard to keep it from breaking free.

Hurried footsteps echoed outside the room, and his spine involuntarily stiffened. They were coming for him; it wouldn't be long now. Bannister was likely storming down the corridor with his armed guards.

Philipe figured Bannister would be the one to pull the trigger after what he'd done. Bannister would feel some twisted sense of righteous indignation at killing the man responsible for losing everything his family had built over the centuries.

The footsteps grew louder then came to a sudden halt outside the door. Philipe knew what would come next. Bannister's men would burst through with their boss in tow. Would he see the weapon before Bannister fired a bullet through his head? It was a bold assumption that it would be a headshot, but a swift death was the best Philipe could hope for. He doubted he'd be so lucky.

The more likely scenario was that Bannister would try to make Philipe reverse everything he'd done, put it all back, which was impossible. The damage Philipe's singularity virus caused was irreversible. Bannister wouldn't believe that, of course, not until later.

Philipe snorted at the thought of the future pain he would have to endure for his sins. Sins. It was unfair that they would punish him for doing the right thing, for helping billions of people all over the planet, most of all, his daughter.

It was his path, though, his destiny. There was nothing getting in the way of that now. And his fate stood at the doorway.

Philipe had never been a religious man. He was open to the idea of a god, an all-powerful creator, but he didn't know for sure what to believe. Still, he caught himself whispering a little prayer of protection for his mother and daughter, for the people who helped them, and that he would have the courage to endure the torture.

The door burst open. The back of it slammed against the wall with a loud clank. Philipe swallowed hard. He didn't dare turn to look his killer in the eyes. If Bannister wanted him to do that, he could walk around the prisoner.

"Philipe?" The familiar voice cut through the room, startling him. Philipe spun around in his chair and looked toward the door.

To his astonishment, Zeke was standing in front of the door. Another man, the blond guy who'd abducted Philipe, was behind Zeke, watching the corridor like a guard dog turning its head back and forth.

"Zeke?" Philipe managed, finally able to get the words out of his mouth. "What are you doing here?"

"Seriously?" Zeke asked as he hurried into the room and checked over the Frenchman to make sure he wasn't hurt. "I'm getting you out of here." Zeke pored over the chair and the rest of the workstation with a befuddled gaze. "Are...are you not tied down or anything?"

"No," Philipe said, standing. He felt the circulation return to his legs, feet, and toes. He didn't realize how long he'd been immobile, and now the blood coursing through his extremities stung slightly.

"Oh. Okay, well...let's get moving."

"Why is he with you?" Philipe pointed at the man in the doorway sweeping a gun one direction and then the other.

"Long story," Zeke said. "Well, maybe it's not that long. Bannister, the guy in charge of all this, tried to kill him after using him to get to you. Now Jordan—that's his name—wants Bannister dead, and he's willing to help us to make that happen."

Philipe wasn't so sure. His brow tightened. "You cannot trust this man," he said.

"That's true. However, we don't have a lot of choice right now. And besides, if he wanted me dead, he could have killed me when I let him out of his cell. I think he's telling the truth."

"How can you be certain?"

"I can't," Zeke relented. "You're just going to have to trust me. He wants Bannister dead. And I think he just wants this to all be over." Zeke rubbed the bridge of his nose. "Look. We can talk about it after we get you out of here. Okay?"

Philipe hesitated, but only for a second. "Okay," he agreed with a nod.

"How we looking, Jordan?" Zeke asked as he and Philipe started for the door.

"You two are on a first-name basis?" Philipe asked, once more confused.

Jordan answered Zeke's question. "Clear for now, but we should get moving. The longer we sit around here, the more likely it is we'll have some unwanted company."

"Especially after what I just did," Philipe said.

"What?" The other two asked in unison, snapping their heads around to face him.

"What did you do?" Zeke clarified.

Philipe offered a cryptic smile and shrugged. "The virus."

"You didn't," Zeke hoped out loud. "Tell me you didn't do it."

"*Non*," Philipe said. "I created something I call the Robin Hood virus. It does everything the bank virus does but only attacks a single entity's accounts and all accounts that have been traced to it. It's a singularity virus."

"Okay..."

"I launched it."

"At whose accounts?" Zeke asked, though he had a bad feeling he already knew the answer.

"Bannister's, of course. I dumped about twenty billion of his money into various charities all around the world."

"You did what?" Jordan asked, half chuckling and half worried.

"Bannister is finished," Philipe said. "He has nothing now."

"When did you do this?" Jordan wondered.

"About ten minutes ago."

Jordan's eyes widened. "Yeah, that doesn't give us much time. The second Bannister realizes what happened..."

"He's going to come here," Zeke finished.

"Which means we need to move."

Jordan took off to the left, heading the way they'd come after Zeke found the mercenary in another room, then led the other two back to the door leading into the subway tunnel and paused for a moment.

"This is the way you came in, right?" Jordan asked, hand on the door handle.

"Yes. Come on, we have to go. The others are in trouble."

"No," Jordan said.

"No? What do you mean, no?"

"This is the main way in and out. The second Bannister realizes he's been financially destroyed, he's going to storm through this door with every guard he has and kill each one of us."

"So, what should we do?" Philipe asked.

Jordan motioned back down to the other end of the hall. "We go that way."

"What's that way?"

"I'm not sure," Jordan admitted. "Never been through that door."

"Well, you know what's not through that door?" Zeke asked. "Bannister and his goons. So, come on. I'll take my chances with the unknown versus a small army of bad guys."

"Okay," Jordan said though sounding slightly disappointed. Something about his response told Zeke that the guy was more than okay with a gunfight with Bannister, probably because Jordan was bent on revenge. Vengeance, however, didn't always lend itself to clear thinking.

Zeke spun on his heels and darted toward the other end of the hall, Philipe tucked in behind him. Jordan was about to follow suit when he heard angry shouts from the other side of the door.

"They're coming," Jordan hissed. He put his hand on the door's latch and held it firm.

"What?" Zeke asked as he skidded to a stop and spun around.

"We need to stall them."

"How are we going to do that?"

"Grab the chair from in that room." Jordan pointed to the room where he'd been shot.

"This room?"

"Yes!"

"Well, you don't have to get snippy with me."

Zeke hurried through the open door of the room. He emerged seconds later holding the prescribed chair. "Not sure how this is going to help us."

"Bring it here."

Zeke did as told and carried the chair over to the door. As he set it down, the latch started shaking back and forth. The men on the other side were trying to open it.

Jordan knew they were out of time. He pulled the chair back for a second and pulled down on the latch, then jerked the door open. In the same fluid movement, he raised his weapon and jammed it into the face of one of Bannister's guards. The barrel popped and sent a round through the center of the man's face. The round found the man directly behind him as well, dropping two enemies with one shot. Then Jordan twisted his weapon and fired four more times, striking one guard in the gut and the other in the shoulder.

The encroaching guards fell back for a moment. That was all the time Jordan needed to slam the door shut and slide the chair up against it, where he braced the top of the seat back against the underside of the latch.

"Go!" he shouted at Zeke and Philipe.

"I'm not leaving you here," Zeke said.

"That's touching, but I'm not staying here, either. You're just in my way."

"Oh right."

Zeke's face flushed with embarrassment, and then he took off at a sprint, running toward Philipe, who was already nearing the door at the other end. When Zeke was halfway down the corridor, he heard the door bumping against the chair. The noise echoed louder as the frustrated guards attempted to push through. The chair's leverage, though, was too great.

By the time the men were able to barge through it, the chair had served its secondary purpose. The chair's feet slammed into the wall, digging in and biting against the old brickwork while the seat back pressed hard against the door handle. The door only opened six or seven inches before jamming against the pesky barricade.

The guards shouted obscenities in their rage, but the words fell on deaf ears as Zeke and the others slipped through the door at the other end and disappeared into a dark corridor.

31

LONDON

Zeke switched on the light attached to his gun and cut in front of Philipe. He shined the light into the damp, unlit corridor ahead and quickly assessed the situation.

Jordan used the light of his phone to better illuminate the dark passage. He turned and looked back at the door. There was a dead-bolt just above the handle. He twisted it but knew that would only keep Bannister's men at bay for so long. It would slow them down, but it wouldn't stop them.

"Where does this go?" Philipe asked, fear lacing his voice.

"Sorry," Zeke answered over his shoulder. "First time on this ride. And I didn't bother checking for Yelp reviews or TripAdvisor about it."

Philipe looked confused, but Jordan shared a chuckle. "We need to keep moving," he said.

"And we need to get my friends out of there," Zeke added.

"How are we going to do that? Assuming they're still alive, Bannister is back there with his men, and they're all armed."

"How many did you take out just now at the door?"

Jordan rolled his shoulders. "I don't know. Three? Maybe four. I didn't stop to ask how many were down."

"At that range, though, I'd expect you at least hurt that many."

"That still leaves a lot for us to fight if we try to loop back around somehow."

"Maybe," Zeke conceded. "Come on. Let's keep moving."

The three pushed ahead, careful not to trip over the cracks in the concrete path. Dust and cobwebs adorned the walls, corners, and crevices. The interior of the corridor had looked the same as the rest of the antiquated subway. This tunnel, however, didn't look like it had been touched since the day they shut it down.

Philipe had to cover his mouth and nose with the top of his shirt to keep the dust out of his lungs. The other two were too preoccupied with making sure they weren't going to be chased down by Bannister's men, or accidentally fall into an unseen pit.

Every twenty feet, the men walked beneath dead lightbulbs. It was a haunting reminder of how far underground they were, and of the reality that they would be in total darkness if their lights went out. The thought caused Zeke to grip his pistol just a little tighter as he narrowed his eyes in search of dangers that might lurk in the shadows.

It wasn't a vision that caught their attention as they proceeded cautiously down the tunnel; it was the heavy footsteps.

The second Jordan heard boots pounding on concrete, he twisted his head around and looked back. Bending circular beams of light danced furiously on the curved wall.

"Guys?" Jordan hissed.

The other two paused and looked back at him to see what had attracted his attention.

"Great," Zeke groused.

The three took off faster this time, running almost at a sprint through the passageway. With so much in front of them to avoid, they didn't dare look back for even the briefest of moments. There were pipes to duck, debris to slip on, and cracks ready to catch a toe and send them sprawling.

Zeke and Philipe panted for air, though Jordan's breathing remained relatively calm.

Sensing his French hacker friend was as tired as he was, Zeke used Philipe to his advantage. "He's tired, man," he said to Jordan, doing his best to keep his tone quiet and his breathing as even as possible. "I don't know how much longer he can keep this up. How long is this tunnel, anyway?"

"I told you, I haven't been down here; looks like no one has for decades. And we can't exactly stop. You just want to let them shoot us all?"

"No," Zeke grumbled.

"Guys?" Philipe's voice interrupted.

The Frenchman stopped abruptly, and Zeke darted by in a blur. He barely had time to slow down before he smacked against a wall, a dark green door coated in dust to his left.

"Door," Philipe said, pointing at the portal.

"Thank you," Zeke grunted, obviously in some level of pain.

Jordan stepped to the door and twisted the latch. It didn't budge. He barged his shoulder into it and pulled down again, but it still didn't open.

The lights around the slight bend in the corridor were getting brighter, the footfalls louder.

Philipe stepped in to help and tried to grip a small part of the handle to loosen it. The two of them jiggled the latch, but the lock wouldn't come free.

"It's no use," Jordan said. He turned and pointed his weapon down the corridor. "We'll have to stand our ground here."

Zeke didn't like that idea. They backed into a corner, the worst place to be when bullets flew. They needed to get the drop on Bannister's men, but that wasn't possible from this position.

Zeke's head tilted up, and he noted a beam that was running across the center of the ceiling and over the door.

He held out his gun to Philipe. "Here, hold this."

"What?" Philipe looked confused.

"Hold my gun. I'm going to try something."

Philipe took the weapon as if it was coated in excrement and held it by the trigger guard with a thumb and forefinger.

Zeke rolled his eyes and then jumped up. He clamped his fingers on either side of the beam and held himself there for a moment. Then he pulled himself higher, held himself steady, then dropped. He kicked out his right foot as he fell. His aim was true and the heel of Zeke's boot struck the handle hard. The latch gave way under his weight. The metal handle twisted down with a screech and a loud clank. Zeke lost control of his fall and slammed into the door, his momentum bursting it open with ease.

The hinges creaked loudly in protest, but they couldn't hold back the force of Zeke's maneuver.

He tumbled through, out onto a narrow landing, and then into the opening where old rails ran along the curved dark tunnel.

Jordan shoved Philipe through and then spun back toward the oncoming gunmen. He fired one warning shot, knowing he wouldn't hit anyone but hoping that at least it would make them pause, then jumped through the door and slammed it shut.

"Good thinking," Jordan said to Zeke.

"Thanks."

"Now what?"

"We need to keep moving." Zeke reached out and plucked the gun out of Philipe's still-wary hand. "I'll take that," he said.

"Good. I don't want that thing."

Jordan motioned to an old subway train car on another set of rails. "We take them out from behind that thing," he said. "They'll come through the door, we let them all come out, then they'll be exposed."

"Like fish in a—"

"Don't say it. Come on. Get under the train. Philipe, stay behind the wheels."

The three men scurried over the tracks to the other line. The old Tube car looked like it might still run if it had power running to the electric rail.

Philipe did as told and crawled under the train. Zeke and Jordan joined him a second later and tucked behind two big rusty wheels, each taking a side to shoot from. They switched off their lights and were instantly plunged into disconcerting darkness.

They had a clear line of sight to the door, or would have if there were any kind of light in the place. Being so far underground without being able to see was unnerving. Zeke had to force himself to calm his nerves at every itch or tingle against his skin. His mind screamed that rats or other creepy, crawly creatures were swarming around him. It was all he could do to push those paranoid manifestations away and focus on the location of the door.

Two questions helped him squelch all those thoughts: Would Bannister's men fall into the trap? Or would they retreat through the tunnel and attempt to find another way to get to the fleeing men?

The answer came faster than expected. A thump came from the door, and it flew open, slamming against the wall. A man stepped out, the flashlight attached to his pistol spraying a bright beam around the tunnel. The gunman swept the barrel around in all directions, checking the shadows.

Zeke and Jordan pulled back for a moment to stay out of sight, then peeked through the narrow slit between the wheels and the chassis. More men poured into the tunnel, fanning out along the platform until there were six men standing there waving their lights around.

"Check over there behind the train," the leader ordered. It was difficult to see the face of the man who'd given the command, but it was easy to tell which one it was. He stood in the middle of the pack, nearest the door. That would be the guy Zeke took out first. Unless Jordan was planning on that. Zeke suddenly realized their plan wasn't thought out well enough.

There was no more time to think.

Two of the six men dropped from the platform and started toward the train, while the other four stayed on the ledge. The two crept toward the train, closing the short distance significantly with every step.

Their approach simplified the plan, at least in Zeke's mind. He would take out the guy on the left, and Jordan could take the one on the right. He hoped Jordan was thinking the same thing, but there was no way to communicate in the darkness.

Zeke could hear Philipe's nervous breathing next to him. He didn't attempt to console the man. Philipe was on his own with his emotions.

In the dim glow of the flashlights, Zeke cast a sidelong glance at Jordan. The mercenary gave a single nod and raised his weapon, poking it 'round the right edge of the wheel he'd taken for cover.

Zeke did the same, still presuming he was to take out the guy on the left.

He lined up his sights as best he could, trying to center them on the dark mass behind the beam of light coming from underneath the gunman's weapon.

"Now," Jordan hissed.

Zeke's finger tensed on the trigger. A wave of uncertainty swept over him.

Then Jordan's weapon discharged in a thunderous pop. His target grunted, but the man's voice was snuffed out by another shot that planted a bullet in his chest, straight through the heart.

Zeke couldn't wait any longer. His target twisted slightly to see what happened to his partner. The man's concerned, almost human, reaction only lasted a second. His training kicked in, and he spun to face the threat.

There was no more hesitation on Zeke's part as the man's gun was trained on his general location under the train. Zeke twitched his finger and sent three rounds into the man's torso, each bullet causing the man to stagger back as the force of the metal pounded into his body.

The other four gunmen opened fire on the train, shooting wildly into the windows and carriage. Their thinking was clear enough. The men they'd been chasing had taken up a position in the train car and had tried—with moderate success—to set up an ambush.

The guards emptied their magazines in a hailstorm of gunfire. The train's windows splintered, then shattered, raining broken shards down onto the ground around the wheels where the three targets were hiding. At least one or two of the shooters thought to fire at the wheels, probably because he noticed the flash of the muzzles as Zeke and Jordan took out the first two men. The bullets clanked off the rusted wheels, dangerously close to the intended targets. The rounds bounced harmlessly to the ground, though, as the trio stayed tucked in tight behind cover.

A thick haze of gun smoke filled the Tube with its bitter scent, and the flashing muzzles went dark once more.

The shooters held out their lights, pointing them through the fog. The tiny bulbs created eerie beams in the lingering smoke.

"You two, get down there and check the bodies. You and I will check the train. Move slow." It was the commander again.

This time, the men moved slower, but it wouldn't save them. Zeke nodded to Jordan again, and they leaned around the wheels, took aim, and fired.

The two men assigned to check the bodies of their dead comrades were the closest, easiest targets. Within seconds, the two were catching bullets. The hot rounds tore through flesh and dropped them helplessly to the ground. One of the men flailed wildly and fired three shots from his submachine gun. The shots were random and flew in all directions, one of which happened to be backward. The bullet struck the commander in the side of the head just as the man was hurrying to get around the line of fire and flank the enemy. He stood for a second before gravity took control and pulled his body to the ground, the hole in his right temple black from the bullet that ended his life.

The last remaining gunman tried to dive out of the way, but he tripped and fell headfirst over the platform. His head struck the nearest rail, and a sickening snap cracked from his neck. The fall was only three or four feet, but it was enough given the angle and the momentum of the man's drop. The flashlight attached to his weapon fixed its bright beam squarely on his face, making the visual that much more macabre.

Zeke and Jordan glanced at each other in the reflected lights that were haphazardly shining through the haze of smoke.

"Did that just work?" Zeke asked, beyond half-surprised.

"I think it did," Jordan said.

The two stared out from their cover and waited, expecting one of the bodies to miraculously rise from the shadows and resume the attack. Such resurrection never happened. After nearly a minute, Zeke and Jordan crept out of their hiding place and stood up.

The feeling in Zeke's legs returned, and he realized he'd been crouching like a baseball catcher for several minutes. He and Jordan checked the bodies of the dead gunmen and retrieved weapons and additional magazines.

Philipe was the last to emerge from the train's undercarriage. He reluctantly stepped over the rails and followed close behind Zeke as he finished checking the bodies.

Zeke turned to Philipe and handed him a submachine gun.

"What do you want me to do with this?" Philipe asked, holding the weapon precariously, as if it might bite him.

"Well, I don't want you to open a beer with it." He took the gun, pulled the handle on the side to make sure a round was chambered, and handed it back to the Frenchman. "Now all you have to do is point and squeeze the trigger. Just don't point it at me. Okay?"

"I've never shot a gun before," Philipe admitted, a little embarrassed and plenty scared.

"If we do this right, you won't have to," Zeke said. "But you need to be ready to do what's necessary. Just in case. Those men, these men here," he pointed at the bodies strewn around haphazardly, "they took your daughter, threatened her and your mother. They kidnapped you. They wanted you to create a new world that would have been dangerous and would have resulted in the loss of more life than we can imagine. So, if it comes down to whether or not you need to shoot, just let those facts fill your noggin. Okay?"

The words resonated with Philipe, and he nodded. "Yes. I will kill the men who took my daughter."

"Actually, that was me," Jordan said. "So, if you don't mind, maybe don't kill me now that we're on the same side. Okay?"

"I make no promises."

The dark tone in Philipe's response was the first time Zeke had seen aggression out of the man. And he liked it.

"Come on," Zeke said with a smirk. "I think I know how we can take out Bannister and the rest of his henchmen."

32

LONDON

Bannister held a radio to his ear and spoke into it. His demanding tone boomed through the control area and into the tunnels beyond.

"Come in. Johnson, come in. What's going on?"

Marilyn laughed from her seat in the middle of the room. One of the six remaining guards lingered in front of her. The weapon in his hand hung at his waist in a firm grip.

"Your men are already dead, Leo," she said amid her cackling. It was a wicked sound and made her voice come across more like an evil queen from some fairy tale.

He tried to ignore her, still talking into the radio. "Come in. Johnson, do you copy?"

The popping sounds Bannister recognized as gunfire had died off nearly as quickly as they'd began. At first, there were just a few random discharges. It was impossible to tell how far away the fight was, but it sounded like it was coming from the tunnel to his left.

"You heard the gunfire," Marilyn said. "Your men walked right into his trap."

"Shut up!" Bannister roared.

"She's not wrong," Phoenix added, sensing the man's emotions getting the best of him. "You're dealing with a highly trained GIC agent. Or maybe you didn't realize you missed one of us with your little plan."

Bannister's eyes flamed, but he ignored the barb. If his guards had exchanged gunfire with someone, it was likely the hacker had tried something stupid. Maybe Philipe had a harebrained idea to use the computers or screens as weapons. Or perhaps the keyboards. There were a few theories rattling around, but none of them involved a mysterious rogue agent that they had missed.

"Against ten of my men? I think you're overestimating your friend's abilities," Bannister sneered. "If there really is one—which I doubt. We wouldn't have missed anyone."

"How long has it been since they reported in?" Jessica pressed, joining in the harassment. "Five, ten minutes? Don't you think if they'd found Zeke and taken him out, they would have called in?"

The point drove Bannister to madness. How was this possible? His men were the best money could buy. Against one man, GIC or not, that shouldn't have been a problem for them. Still, that didn't give him the answer he sought. Why weren't his men answering? Did they get lost in the tunnels? Maybe they took a wrong turn.

His mind raced with possible explanations.

"I've seen Zeke take out a dozen men by himself," Freeman offered. "He's some kind of super agent or something. Like a real-life James Bond."

"Shut it!" Bannister snapped, whirling around and brandishing a weapon of his own. He pointed the pistol at Freeman, then turned it toward Phoenix, then Vincent, and back to Marilyn. "All of you, just shut up!"

One guard stepped close to Bannister. The man towered over Bannister, easily twice his size, and most of it pure muscle.

"Do you want us to kill the hostages, sir?"

Bannister's mind raced to the conclusion. His first thought was yes, kill them all, but that would take away the only card he had left to play—if the prisoners were telling the truth. If they were lying, they would die anyway. Johnson's radio silence, along with the rest of his team, would have some rational explanation.

"There's still time to save yourself," Phoenix said. His comment interrupted Bannister's thought. "Get out now, Leo. Or you and the rest of your men will die here."

The guy who'd been working the computer station appeared suddenly overcome with fear.

He approached his employer with a timid look, "Sir, I...um, need to check the servers to make sure the virus didn't affect the hardware."

Bannister's head spun around, and he glared at the tech. "Fine. Do whatever you have to do."

The young man hurried toward the server racks.

"You really think he's going to check those things?" Marilyn asked. "He wants to get out of here and save his own neck, Leo."

Bannister had had enough of her antagonization. "For the last time, shut your mouth, or I will kill you."

Marilyn cocked her head to the right. "I don't think you will."

"Oh no?" He raised his weapon and pointed it directly at her face.

Suddenly, a yelp echoed through the tunnel. It came from behind the server racks, close to the wall.

"What was that?" Bannister asked. Panic filled his voice.

"Hearing ghosts, are ya, Leo?" Vincent asked.

"Martin?" He shouted to the tech. "What are you doing back there?"

"Martin is taking a nap," a voice replied loudly. "He'll be fine later."

Phoenix's eyes lit up, and he shared a glance with Jessica, who also looked pleasantly surprised at the sound of Zeke's voice.

Four of the guards shifted, positioning themselves between the closest server rack and the control area.

Phoenix noted Bannister taking a step back. The man was clearly a coward. Unfortunately, there was nothing Phoenix could do...yet. He wanted to leap into action, take out the nearest guard, and then shoot the others in the back, but he knew that was a long shot. The guard closest to him appeared to be keeping a close eye on him.

Meanwhile, Bannister's paranoia got the better of him. He stared at the server rack, wondering what he should do. Should he order the four closest guards to go check it out? That would leave him with two guards and the rest of the intruders.

"You three," he pointed at the man on the far right and the two nearest him. "Take care of him."

The three guards nodded and started forward.

"I wouldn't do that if I were you!" the mysterious voice shouted. "If you send your gunmen, I can't promise you I'll be as lenient as I was with your computer...geek...guy."

Phoenix rolled his eyes at the way Zeke made the threat. It didn't help he was using the deepest voice he could muster in an attempt to sound ominous. Still, he had to give his partner credit. It seemed to be having the desired effect. The three guards even hesitated.

"Don't listen to him!" Bannister barked. "Kill him!"

The men gave acknowledging nods. One went to the right, one to the left, and the other approached the server head-on. They neared the first rack and were about to spread out when Bannister stopped them.

"Wait." He looked at one of the other guards. "Go with him on the left."

"Yes, sir," the gunman said as he trotted over to join the other guard. Bannister felt better about the maneuver now that there were two on each side. The men branched out and then stopped at the corners of the rack. One man peeked around the corner to the right. Another did the same on the left. Then they glanced at each other, made a few hand signals, and prepared to loop around into the next row.

It was clear to Jessica and Phoenix what their plan was. They would work their way toward the wall, checking each row before advancing to the next until they flushed out the troublemaker.

"I tried to warn you!" the voice thundered again.

The four gunmen hesitated. That was their first mistake.

A loud bang echoed through the tunnel. The floor shook as if a minor earthquake had struck London. The guards glanced at each other, perplexed. Another crash followed and another shortly after that. Each grew louder and closer. By the time the guards realized what was happening, it was too late.

The next-to-last server rack tipped over and smashed into the one nearest the guards. Instead of diving out of the way, their instincts told them to retreat, which was their second and final mistake. They were mere feet from safety had they just thought to roll clear to the side. Instead, they went backward and were caught under the rack as it collapsed on top of them, crushing all four.

Dust and debris billowed up from the destruction. For a moment, it was difficult to see what had happened, or rather, what caused the racks to fall like dominos.

The remaining two guards stepped forward, peering into the clouds of dust to investigate.

They didn't notice Bannister slowly retreating to the rear wall where the digital map of the world still glowed on the screen. In fact, no one noticed. Their attention was on the pile of servers and shelves.

The two guards gave each other a couple of quick signals and then fanned out wide. They weren't about to be surprised like their fallen comrades.

They approached the destruction with caution and slowed when they reached the edge of the last rack. A hand protruded from under the shelf. It wasn't moving.

"To be fair, I warned them," the voice returned.

The guards whipped their weapons up and aimed into the settling dust. They fired blindly into the shadows, emptying their magazines within seconds. The smoke from their barrels trickled out of the muzzles and mingled with the dust in the air. A pall filled the room, and the men believed they had killed the intruder.

Their thoughts of victory were soon quashed as a barrage of gunfire erupted behind them.

Bullets tore through them, cutting the two men down instantly. They collapsed before they even knew who'd ended their lives.

The captives in the control area watched the entire scene with rapt attention. Even Jessica, who was usually as stoic as a statue, sat wide-eyed at what had just happened.

From the open door, a shadowy figure emerged from the dust. He walked deliberately, moving around the destroyed server equipment to the right.

A head popped up from behind the platform about fifteen feet from the corner of the first server rack. It was Philipe. The Frenchman looked around at the destruction, then at the dead man lying nearby. The man he'd just killed.

On the other side of the platform, Jordan rose from the gap next to the platform and eyed his handiwork. He knew he'd be able to take out his guy, but he was pleasantly surprised at the efficient way Philipe had taken care of his end.

Zeke put a hand down, and Philipe grasped it. The American hoisted his new friend up from the rails and onto the platform, then turned around to where Jordan was climbing up.

"You good?" Zeke asked.

"Yeah," Jordan said, slapping dust off his pants. "I'm good."

They turned to the prisoners, who were still staring with unbelieving eyes at the men approaching them.

"How did you..." Jessica's voice trailed off.

"Leverage," Zeke said with a grin. He picked up his pace and hurried over to get everyone out of their bindings. He went to Jessica first and cut through the bonds with a knife he kept on his belt.

"Leverage?" Jessica asked as she stood and stepped away to help the others.

"Your boy here had the idea to kick the bloody server racks over," Jordan explained. "I thought he was daft, but when he showed me he could reach them by pressing his hands against the wall, I figured it was worth a go. At the very least, I'd get to see him fall flat on his face trying."

Phoenix chuckled as he stood, his hands finally free. He wrung his wrists to get the circulation going through his fingers again.

"It was obviously a good plan," Philipe said, though his mind was clearly distant.

Zeke stepped over to him and put his hand on the Frenchman's shoulder. "You okay?"

Philipe cradled the weapon in his hands. He looked down at it and then back up to meet Zeke's gaze. "I'm like an American cowboy now. Oui?"

Zeke let out a laugh that caused his shoulders to rock back and forth. "Yeah, my friend. I guess you are."

Philipe grinned sheepishly.

"Hey, guys?" Jordan said. "I don't mean to interrupt this little love fest, but you don't happen to know where Bannister went, do you?"

Everyone twisted around. Bannister was nowhere to be seen.

"Great," Jordan said. "We let him get away."

"Living will be harder than dying for him," Zeke said. "He just lost everything. He has nowhere to go. No one will help him. He'll turn up eventually, probably in a homeless shelter or on the street."

Jordan's eyes flashed, but he said nothing. He was clearly disappointed he didn't get his revenge, but deep down he was already formulating a plan to find the man. They would search the tunnels, and if they didn't locate Bannister, Jordan had ways to find people, especially desperate people. Bannister would most certainly be desperate.

"I need to get to the surface and call in backup," Jessica said, cutting into the conversation.

"Sure," Zeke said. "Use my phone."

He handed her the device and then motioned to the door behind the pile of servers.

Some of the wires sparked, and smoke puffed out of one section of the wreckage.

"We should probably get moving before that stuff catches fire." Zeke turned to Freeman. "Can it do that?"

"Probably."

"If it gets hot enough," Marilyn said. "Come on."

The group hurried past the collapsed racks and into the passage leading up to the surface. Once everyone was through, Zeke gave one last look into the Tube. "I did it," he whispered.

Then the center of the racks burst into flames, and his moment of pride ended.

Zeke turned and hurried after the others, leaving the evidence of his victory behind. *Still,* he thought, *not bad for an idiot.*

33

"I said I'm sorry," Jessica blathered. Her voice slurred, and her body tilted slightly to the left as she spoke. The beer in her hand nearly spilled out of the glass. Luckily, it was nearly empty. "I shouldn't have called you an idiot." Her face flushed. "All those times."

The group stood around a high-top table in the dark confines of the Golden Lion pub.

Zeke laughed uneasily and put his hand on her shoulder to keep her steady. "Yes, I know. And I already said it's okay. We're cool."

She looked down at his hand, and there was an awkward moment shared between them.

The rest of the people at the table appeared to be oblivious. Freeman was busy watching one of the televisions behind the bar. Marilyn and Vincent were arguing over which of the new processors on the market were the fastest, Vincent contending that the latest line of AMD was better than Intel and Marilyn countering it with her own evidence and opinions.

Phoenix wasn't paying attention to any of them, choosing to spend his time on his phone. Doing what, no one knew, but he'd been glued to the screen for the last half hour.

Zeke snatched his hand away from Jessica the second he realized she noticed it. "Sorry," he said. "Just, didn't want you to spill beer on me."

"Don't be," she said. "You didn't do anything wrong. Besides, it was nice."

"My...hand on your shoulder was nice?"

It was the first time she'd indicated anything like that. He couldn't call it interest. Was it flirting? He wasn't sure, but he definitely wasn't going to press the issue. She was clearly inebriated and not thinking straight. Or was she? He, on the other hand, was stone-cold sober and had barely touched the ale in front of him while the others had been through multiple pints.

Jessica leaned closer. Her eyelids blinked slowly, and it almost looked like they weren't in sync. "Maybe," she said.

"Yeah, okay. You're definitely drunk."

"No, I'm not," she defended with more slurred words. Her head retreated, and she blew air through her lips, flapping them for a second. "You're the one who's drunk."

"Um, right. So, anyway, what's the next assignment?"

Her face contorted into a strange looking frown. She looked at him as if he was speaking a foreign dialect. "What assignment? You just finished this one. You want an assignment? Here's an assignment." She leaned close to him and grazed her lips against his ear. "I'm in room two zero three."

"Okay...I think you need some water, and I think I need to get some fresh air."

"It's raining outside," Jessica said. "And I'm drinking water." She raised her glass and tilted back her head, dumping the contents into her mouth.

"Yeah, I see that." He turned to Phoenix. "You gonna help me out here or keep swiping left and right with your online dating app?"

Phoenix looked up, startled by the sudden attention. "What?"

"Online dating?" Marilyn asked. "Is that what you're doing?"

"What? No," Phoenix insisted. "He's just joking."

"Am I?"

"Why would you do that?" Marilyn pressed. "You could have me all to yourself if you wanted."

Phoenix blushed and bit his lower lip, angry that his friend had made him the focus of attention. "I'm not on an online dating app. He's just being an—"

"Idiot?" Zeke finished the thought for him.

"I was going to say moron, but yes."

Zeke grinned. "Fair enough." He shifted away from the high-top and glided toward the bar. He listened to the discussion, or argument, going on behind him and ordered a glass of water from the bartender. He took a few sips and then returned to the table, set the glass in front of Jessica, and nodded. "Drink this," he said. "You'll regret it if you don't."

"You'll regret it if you don't," she countered nonsensically.

"All righty then." He gave a curt nod and started to wander off.

"Where do you think you're going?" she demanded.

"I don't know. I'll figure it out when I get there."

"What does that even mean, Zeke?"

He pushed the door open amid a slurred barrage of something about throwing herself at him, but he didn't care. He'd always thought she was attractive, even wanted to see what could happen between the two of them. Now, though, he felt a little like the dog that caught the car.

Zeke looked down the sidewalk one way and then the other. The door closed behind him, and the sounds from inside faded away. Now all he could hear were the sounds of the city: cars rolling by, horns honking, a siren screaming somewhere in the distance, pedestrians chatting with each other or on their phones.

Zeke pondered how much his life had changed over the last couple of months. He'd gone from being a low-level functionary, a minor cog in the big machine that was GIC, to becoming a world-saving super agent. Funny. He didn't feel like a super agent. In fact, he wondered if he was just really lucky to get out of the situations he'd been in on his first two missions.

"Nah," he said to himself with a grin, shrugging off the notion.

The door opened, and the hinges groaned in protest. Zeke twisted his head and saw Phoenix emerge from the dark interior of the pub.

"You okay?" Phoenix asked, an eyebrow arched.

"Yeah, why?"

Phoenix's shoulders lifted and then dropped. "Just asking."

"You want to know if I'm okay because you think I've wanted Jessica since I met her and now that she's throwing herself at me I'm having some kind of existential crisis. That sound about right?"

Phoenix pinched his eyebrows together and smirked. "Actually, no. I just thought you looked tired, but we can delve into that other issue if you want."

"Oh." Zeke blushed, feeling suddenly stupid for outing himself. "No, I'm good. I mean, yes...I did want her, but it's not just that she's drunk and throwing herself at me. She's our boss, Phoenix. And honestly, I didn't like the idea of her being killed by that maniac. You know? It bothered me. It really bothered me. From now on, I don't think she needs to be in the field when we do this stuff."

"That's not our call, and you know it. Besides, Jess can handle herself, maybe better than you or me."

"What's that supposed to mean?" Zeke wondered.

"Nothing. Nothing. I'm just saying she's good at what she does."

"And we aren't?"

"No, we are, too, I guess. I wouldn't have thought it a few months ago, but now we're two for two. Not too shabby." Phoenix grinned proudly. He put his arm around his friend's shoulder and shook him. "Come on back inside, man. It looks like it's going to rain."

"You go on ahead," Zeke insisted. "I'm going to take a few minutes out here. Just need some air."

Phoenix nodded and clapped Zeke on the back. "Okay. I'll see you back inside."

"Sure thing."

The door creaked again, and Phoenix disappeared inside.

Zeke stood on the sidewalk watching the people go by. Thousands of people passed along the busy street, and none of them would ever know the danger they'd been in just a few short hours earlier. He wondered how many times something like that had happened, how many times the planet's citizens had been dangerously close to losing everything. Who had saved them then?

Now, it seemed, the baton had been passed to him, and the burden was overwhelming. He felt like retching at the thought, but he choked back the rising lump in his throat and steeled his nerves.

"The world needs heroes, I guess," he whispered. "May as well be us."

34

BLED, SLOVENIA

Jordan Bradley sat atop his makeshift perch in the church bell tower. His eyes remained firmly on the white lake house next to the shore.

Lake Bled rippled gently behind the old building. The orange-red clay tiles of the roof stood out against the backdrop of green hills and the towering Alps beyond. The air was cool and clean, the effects of human consumption somehow not yet touching this quiet bastion of nature.

Birds chirped in the trees. Some whistled their songs while Jordan kept his sniper rifle aimed on the front door of the home. It was a grim contrast between life and death. The thought barely occurred to him.

He'd been sitting there for hours waiting for the target to arrive. And it was the third day of his hunt. Jordan knew better than to allow his mind to get restless. He'd let go of that temptation long ago, though every now and then it nagged at him. A storm cloud lingered in the distance, and he thought it might be heading his way, but it drifted off to the north instead, carrying with it a stream of showers pouring out beneath it.

Jordan wondered if his target might not show up. It was possible the man had learned of his investigation, though that was doubtful. Jordan had honed that skill before any other. He knew that gathering intel was a vital component to his line of work, and the more of it he had, the better.

Asking questions, however, caused people to take notice. Searching for information drew its own kind of attention, attention Jordan didn't want. He'd quickly learned how to throw off people who might track him. Even with his current target's considerable connections, he knew that no one had spilled the beans. He'd made sure of that.

Jordan paid his sources well, and for this score, he doubled their usual fees. That along with the fact that the target had lost everything made the man's Slovenia safe house easy enough to find. Then it was just a matter of waiting until his prey thought his trail had vanished. Then he would fall right into Jordan's trap.

The days were long, though, and there was no way for a human being to keep eyes on the target's house around the clock. Jordan had to sleep sometime, had to eat. So he'd set up perimeter triggers around the house to make sure he didn't miss it if his quarry showed up during some downtime. Thus far, none of the alarms had sounded.

Jordan knelt down and pressed his eye to the scope, checking the suppressed sniper rifle was still aimed correctly. Not that it could have moved. It was on a tripod, sighted in on the cross in the middle of the front door to the lake house. The second his target walked up to the door to unlock it, he would die.

He held on to that thought, that driving force in his mind that would bring closure. Vengeance would be his, even if he had to wait months, even years, to find it.

Bannister would pay for his betrayal.

Jordan knew he was partly to blame. Never get too comfortable with an employer. It was one of the rules he lived by, one that had kept him out of trouble throughout his life thus far. He'd accumulated a massive amount of wealth as a result and never found himself in a position of real danger. Not until Bannister pulled the trigger and unloaded a cluster of slugs into his chest.

But Jordan always wore his vest, and if some of his men had been as careful as he, they might still be around. Having them for this stakeout would have been helpful. He would have paid any of them handsomely for this operation, though it was doubtful he'd have to. They would be in it for revenge just as Jordan was.

They were dead, though, and he was on his own.

Doubts crept into his mind again as he stared at the door. Would Bannister show? Would he dare show his face in public? Jordan had to hand it to the guy: he'd remained invisible since disappearing from the Tube station one month before.

Jordan shook the doubts loose the second he saw a car pull into the driveway. It wasn't the high-end luxury sedan or sports car that one might have expected for the affluent Bannister. The man had lost everything, and trying to travel with one of his luxury vehicles would have been a surefire way to be tracked down and killed.

Once more, Jordan gave him credit. The man was thinking, but that wasn't going to save him.

He watched as the twenty-year-old tan Honda Civic came to a stop next to the cottage. Jordan's heart ticked a little faster, but he immediately suppressed that instinct and calmed himself. He wrapped his hands around the rifle as he scooted forward on the milk crate he'd procured as a makeshift seat.

With his high-powered scope, Jordan could see the man in the car looking around, checking to make sure he was safe. The notion caused Jordan to snort of derision.

The driver's side door popped open, and Jordan readied himself to take the shot. It wasn't going to be an easy one, but he'd hit targets from farther away than this.

Bannister slammed the door shut and continued to look around as he made his way to the front door. His face was covered in a raggedy beard. The hair on his head was disheveled, and he looked like he hadn't had a shower in days. *Good*, Jordan thought. *Let him rot before he dies.*

The target walked hurriedly to the front door and fumbled a set of keys in his hands as he searched for the one that would open the home.

Jordan's finger tensed on the trigger. The crosshairs lined up squarely in the center of Bannister's upper back.

A grim smile crept onto Jordan's face. He felt the same rush he'd felt before when about to take another human's life. It was terrifying and exhilarating, and the swirl of both emotions intoxicated him in a most confusing way.

In this instance, though, it was much more satisfying. He was finally going to kill the man who tried to kill him.

The trigger finger started to squeeze, and then Jordan froze. He noticed movement out of the left side of his vision and pulled back from the scope.

A black Mercedes rolled up to the front of the house and slowed to a stop. Jordan's forehead tightened. "No. No. No. What is this?" He felt vengeance slipping through his fingers.

He looked through the scope again and saw Bannister's reaction. The man's head twisted around quickly when he realized the car was there. He was flushed and looked afraid.

The driver opened the back door, and a man in a brown tweed blazer exited the rear seat. Two more men in black suits climbed out of the other doors and accompanied Tweed to the front of the home.

Bannister was talking to the men. From the looks of it, he was doing his best to appear calm, probably talking his way out of something. These guys were clearly associates. Who they were, though, was another matter. Jordan hadn't seen them before, not that he recalled.

He wished he'd planted microphones around the house, but this job wasn't supposed to be a bug-and-listen gig. It was a reckoning, nothing else.

The man in the tweed jacket was balding, with a rim of gray hair wrapping around the back of his skull from just behind the ears. He wore dark brown pants and reddish-brown shoes that shone in the daylight.

As Tweed approached Bannister, he put out his hands as if he might embrace the man. The arms dropped as soon as they'd gone up, which told Jordan the guy was actually asking what Bannister was up to. He'd seen that expression before when someone asked the casual question "What are you doing?"

Bannister's lips moved, but it was difficult to read what he was saying. Clearly this man in tweed was above Bannister, which meant he had to be extremely important. Was he a member of the families like Bannister?

Jordan had heard rumors of such a syndicate before, but they were nothing more than urban legends to him. Now, he wasn't so sure.

Bannister opened the front door, motioning for Tweed to enter first. Instead, the two men in suits accompanying their employer shoved Bannister into his own home. Tweed followed and closed the door.

Jordan frowned as he kept his eyes locked on the front of the house. The driver remained by the car, waiting for the others to return.

His wait wasn't long. Tweed and the two suits emerged less than three minutes later, closed the door, and returned to their car.

The man in tweed gave a cursory glance around to make sure there were no witnesses and then climbed into the back. Once everyone was inside the vehicle, the driver sped away, and the car disappeared around the next curve.

They'd been in and out in under five minutes. And Jordan had a bad feeling he knew what happened.

He waited ten minutes before he left his sniper nest to approach the home. Since Tweed and his crew left, there'd been no movement in the house. The eerie stillness filled him with certainty, a macabre feeling of what he knew he would see the second he entered the lake house.

Jordan reached the door and drew the pistol from his jacket. He looked around once more, scanning the immediate area to make sure no one was still lurking, watching him the way he'd been doing a few moments before.

He pulled his sleeve over his hand and turned the doorknob. No surprise, it was unlocked. He stepped into the house, leading with his pistol. The bitter scent of gun smoke lingered in the house though the haze had already dissipated.

Jordan closed the door quietly behind him, making sure the bolt didn't click in the receiver. He didn't make a sound as he stepped through the foyer and into the sparsely decorated living room.

A white leather couch sat in front of a 40-inch flatscreen television set into the wall between two front windows. A white wooden coffee table sat in the center of the room. The floors were dark wood, stained almost black. Beyond the living room, Jordan could see the kitchen, something that looked like it was straight of the IKEA catalog. The cabinets were dark gray with glass façades so the tenant could see into the shelves.

None of that drew his attention for more than a second, though, as the real attraction was lying on the floor just behind the couch.

Bannister's body was prostrate.

Jordan stepped over to the dead man and examined the wound. Bannister had been shot in the back of the head with the round exiting through the front of his skull. It didn't take a ballistics expert to figure out what happened.

Tweed and his men had followed Bannister into the house and executed him, probably while Bannister was attempting to negotiate, perhaps by offering the men a drink first.

He'd never even made it to the kitchen.

Blood pooled around the dead man's face, the glazed eyes staring blankly toward the back of the house where the yard ran down to the lake.

Bannister was dead.

Jordan immediately sensed he was in danger and turned to leave the house. He pulled open the door, glanced around, and darted back across the yard, over the street, and disappeared in the shadows of the church where he'd been positioned.

Someone had taken his revenge. That part didn't bother Jordan. Bannister was gone, and that's what he'd wanted. But it irritated him that he hadn't been the one to pull the trigger. Still, that was a minor detail.

He stepped into the shadows as he considered the real problem. Whoever those men were might come after him at some point. He needed to run, leave the country, get to the mountains where he kept one of his three safe houses, and go completely off the grid.

It had been his plan for years, but now he was being forced into it.

Jordan ran up the stairs, ignoring the burning in his legs. He emerged back onto the landing atop the church's bell tower and quickly packed his gear. Within minutes, he was back in his vehicle and driving out of town, heading for the Croatian border.

One thing was certain as the town disappeared in his rearview mirror. The Syndicate was real, and he wanted nothing to do with it.

THANK YOU

Thank you for taking the time to read this story. We can always make more money, but time is a finite resource for all of us, so the fact you took the time to read my work means the world to me and I truly appreciate it. I hope you enjoyed it as much as I enjoyed sharing it, and I look forward to bringing you more fun adventures in the future. Also, if this story made you laugh, swing by Amazon and leave a review. I'd appreciate it and so would potential readers.

Ernest

OTHER BOOKS BY ERNEST DEMPSEY

Sean Wyatt Adventures:

The Secret of the Stones

The Cleric's Vault

The Last Chamber

The Grecian Manifesto

The Norse Directive

Game of Shadows

The Jerusalem Creed

The Samurai Cipher

The Cairo Vendetta

The Uluru Code

The Excalibur Key

The Denali Deception

The Sahara Legacy

The Fourth Prophecy

The Templar Curse

The Forbidden Temple

The Omega Project

The Napoleon Affair

Adriana Villa Adventures:

War of Thieves Box Set

When Shadows Call

Shadows Rising

Shadow Hour

The Adventure Guild:

The Caesar Secret: Books 1-3

The Carolina Caper

Beta Force:

Operation Zulu

London Calling

The Relic Runner:

Out of the Fire

For my friend Brian Parrish, one of the funniest people I know.

ACKNOWLEDGMENTS

As always, I would like to thank my terrific editors for their hard work. What they do makes my stories so much better for readers all over the world. Anne Storer and Jason Whited are the best editorial team a writer could hope for and I appreciate everything they do.

I also want to thank Elena at Lı Graphics for her tremendous work on my book covers and for always overdelivering. Elena is amazing.

Last but not least, I need to thank all my wonderful fans and especially the advance reader team. Their feedback and reviews are always so helpful and I can't say enough good things about all of them.

See you next time,
Ernest

www.ingramcontent.com/pod-product-compliance
Lightning Source LLC
Chambersburg PA
CBHW030330200626
46816CB00006BA/1993